Souljourn

Jim Burklo

[signature]

SOULJOURN
ON
2!

5/2015

BURKLO @
USC.EDU

pathos press

Souljourn

Dedicated to Bruce Urbschat

Busca el tú que nunca es tuyo.
(Seek the you that is never yours.)
~ Antonio Machado

Table of Contents

Table of Contents

1. Encounter on Cobre Mountain

If Seedless Thompson ever laughed before, I never knew about it. Maybe hearing him laugh was the point of it all.

And not what I thought it was about when it started, on a Sunday morning when I bounded out of bed and into my boots and jammed my slingshot into my pocket with a couple of ball-bearings Dad got for me from the shop at the Phelps Dodge. The screen door swatted shut behind me so loud that Dad cussed pretty loud, too. But before he could get out of bed, I was already up the trail behind our house, zig-zagging up Cobre Mountain with the dawn stretching a dark streak of myself ahead of me. People still say that today, at 24 years old, I'm all arms, but at 14 my body seemed little more than a frame to hold them up. So when I waved them to see their shadows, they looked as gangly as ocotillo stalks.

In those days I would rather hunt jackrabbits at dawn than do just about anything else. Computer games sucked back then, and the girls, with maybe a couple of exceptions, were as awkward as I was. I did kill one once with my slingshot. A jackrabbit, I mean. It hobbled under a mesquite tree and quivered and shuddered for a long time before it stopped moving. I told Dad what I had done and he ordered me to go back up the mountain and fetch the damn critter and bring it back. "You gotta eat what you kill," he used to say. But when I got back up there, the vultures were already done with it for breakfast, leaving nothing but bloody bones and patches of fur. "Just as well," Dad said when I got home. "Jackrabbit meat tastes like shoe leather."

This time, when I got most of the way up the mountain, I spied a pair of jackrabbit ears poking out of the brush near a four-foot-tall jumping cholla cactus. I pulled back the sling and shot at him but he was better legged than I was armed.

I searched all around for my ball bearing and could not find it. Did it roll down a rattlesnake hole? I spent at least half an hour poking in the brush and looking under rocks. I found some dirty socks, empty food containers, and one of those plastic water jugs the *mojados* carry with them when they walk north. I found tire tracks running through the brush. Were they from a *migra* truck?

Finally, I went back to the big cholla and there, right in front of it, laying neatly on the ground, was a crystal about two inches long. I picked it up and held it in the palm of my hand. I had seen plenty of rocks out in the desert around Portales but never one that looked anything like this. In front of the densely-spiked cholla cactus I held it up to the sun. The little crystal shimmered with pink light.

Then I looked at the cholla and I saw that the sun was shining directly behind it so that its spines glowed like a thousand splinters of green-gold glass. It seemed like time stopped and nothing else existed except that cactus. Not even myself.

Then a powerful tingle ran from my tailbone up along my spine, up my neck, and seemed to shoot out of the top of my head. I glowed all over, for a long time.

As I stared at the cactus, I saw a young woman holding her hands out toward me. Was it the Virgin of Guadalupe? She was framed by the brilliant spines of the cholla. Her face was pale, peaceful, and pretty, but she had an indentation, some kind of injury, on the upper right side of her nose as I faced her. I reached out to touch her but then she disappeared. In her place appeared an old man with a long white beard. Somehow I knew his name was Lorenzo. He wheezed a few words to me, with a grave expression on his face. "Follow her," I heard him say. I also saw the words he was saying, as if they were coming out of his mouth on a ribbon of cloth, except they were written in letters I'd never seen before. The intense tingle came back up my spine and through the top of my head. "I AM," said Lorenzo in that strange, wheezy voice. And then the glow in my body faded away, and the visions dissolved, and there I was again, holding the crystal in my hand in front of the cholla cactus.

What was that all about? I took a bunch of deep breaths and looked all around me to make sure there wasn't something else I was missing. Across the desert below I saw the green stripe of the town of Portales. And the wide expanse of the Tohono O'odham reservation to the east. Behind me was the peak of Cobre Mountain, a pile of rocks glowing in the early morning sun. It looked more real than I had ever seen it, like it was alive and powerful. I had discovered something hidden in the normal world around me.

I laid my slingshot down in front of the cactus and left it there. I put the crystal in my pocket and from then on it went with me wherever I went.

Like usual in those days, I told Dad everything when I got home. I could see I was making him nervous. His salt and pepper hair hadn't been combed yet. He was in his bathrobe, trying to make coffee, but the pilot light on the stove was out. He aimed his cigarette lighter at the burner and it lit in a puff of flame that singed his hairy fingers.

"Yow!" he yelled. The burnt hair stank up the whole house.

"Boy," he demanded of me, "have you been smoking that wacko tobacco?"

"No sir," I said. At least I wasn't high at the time I had the vision.

"So, what is this business about seeing people in a cholla cactus?" he asked as he opened the fridge and fumbled for his carton of half and half.

"I don't know, Dad, I never saw stuff like that before. But it was cool," I said.

"Well, if it ever happens again I want to know about it, you hear?" he said, frowning. "And let me look at that crystal."

He put on his glasses and held it up to the light streaming through our screen porch. "This is rose quartz. It's not native to this area. I've seen it in the field in the Black Hills of South Dakota, and I've seen it down in South America, but never anywhere here in Arizona. So are you playing some kind of game with me? I'm supposed to believe what you're telling me?"

"Why would I lie to you, Dad?" I asked him. "Yeah, it's weird that I found this rock, and it's weird that I saw that stuff in the cholla. I don't know why it happened. You're the smart guy. You explain it."

He gave the crystal back to me shook his head. "Can't explain it. But I am sure there is an explanation."

"Whoever explains it first gets a week off from washing dishes," I yelled.

Dad smiled and sighed. "Whoever figures it out first will save me a bunch of new gray hairs," he said.

For a while after that, Dad asked me a lot more questions than usual. He asked me what I was doing, what I was thinking, how I was feeling, where I was going. I wasn't used to it, and it started getting on my nerves. Dad and I were always pretty close. It was just the two of us most of the time. But he wasn't the kind of Dad who was up in my face about stuff. He was uptight about television and video games, but I still had a lot more freedom than a lot of my friends, and I liked it. I was getting irritated by so many questions all of a sudden. But at the same time, I remember feeling like it was nice that he was paying more attention. I had always told him everything before, mostly, but now he was really listening.

I rubbed that crystal a lot. People probably
thought I was playing pocket pool, but the other kids
thought I was a little weird anyway. I used to sit in
class and stare out the window at Cobre Mountain
and imagine the Indians hunting up there, with their
bows and arrows. I was sure I could see the
silhouettes of the Spanish explorers on horseback
with their lances poking into the sky, walking along
the high horizon. My math teacher kept saying,
"Earth to Josh, Earth to Josh" to get me to pay
attention to the lesson, and the other kids would
laugh at me.

I had a really hard time concentrating in Little
League. I'd be in left field, and the bases would be
loaded, and the bat would crack against the ball, but I
would be staring at the grass and imagining I was an
earthstronaut in an earthcraft that could bore its way
to the center of the planet, and then the baseball
would fly my way, and it would take the whole team
screaming at me to snap out of my daydream and try
to catch the damn ball. "Your mouth hangs open so
wide the flies moved in." That's what my so-called
friend Ronnie Morales kept saying. After a while I
stopped caring what Ronnie or anybody said about
me. I started to figure it this way: if you are going to
be a little weird, why not just go the distance and be
all the way weird?

Yeah, that crystal was like a cholla spine in my
sock. Like a zit I couldn't pop. Like a really obnoxious
cell phone ring tone. It was there in my pocket all the
time, reminding me that there was this problem that

had to be solved. I didn't tell my friends what I saw and felt that morning up on Cobre Mountain. What was the use? How could they help me?

So I went back up the mountain at dawn again, about a month later, and stood in front of the cholla. My slingshot was still lying in front of it. I stood and stared at the cholla for a long time, and then it began to dissolve and disappear. Then that electric sensation shot up my spine again and out the top of my head. I looked up and there, in the cactus, was the Virgin, or the young woman, the same one as before. She was reaching out to me with her arms open wide, full of joy. "Come with me," she cried out. Her eyes dazzled with energy.

This is the first time I will admit to what happened next. While the Virgin, or whoever she was, was reaching out to embrace me, I got a tool-steel hard-on. As soon as I noticed it, she disappeared from the cholla.

The next weekend, I went back up the mountain again and stood in front of the cactus as the sun was rising. This time, it was just another of the zillion chollas in the desert. No Virgin, no body rush, no tool-steel nothing.

I went up there pretty often after that. The idea that I was having visions made me wonder if I was going crazy or something. So, in a way, I was relieved that I didn't see anything anymore. But, in another way, I was disappointed. I'd walk back down the mountain, rolling the rose quartz crystal between my fingers. Who was that woman? What were the visions all about?

***

I didn't want to go to Mass with Grandma Greta. She was staying at our place in Portales while Dad was in Peru checking out a new mine. I didn't like the idea that she was there to babysit me. I was taller than Grandma Greta anyway. So how was she going to make me do anything, much less make me go to church? Religion was a sore subject between her and Dad, anyway. She was for it. He was against it. All these thoughts ran through my smart-ass brain.

"Remember your deal with Dad," I told her. "He made you promise never to make me go to church with you."

"And I am not going to make you go to church with me now," she said. "But your dad told me what happened with the cactus when you were out chasing jackrabbits. There is something happening at church that might help explain what you saw."

Even my pubescent self couldn't deny how much I loved Grandma Greta. Dad said she was an old hippie. She had long gray hair in a ponytail and she usually wore a peasant shirt and a skirt over a pair of old blue jeans and a pair of Mexican leather sandals on her callused feet. I always believed that she had so many wrinkles on her face because she had been smiling for so many years that it just crinkled up her skin. Dad said that when I was about four years old, I sat in her lap and poked my finger in one of the wrinkles on her round cheek and said, "We live riiiiight here."

Her adobe house up on the flanks of Mt. Lemmon was surrounded by her cactus garden. Flowers grew in the pots she threw on the wheel in her garage studio and hardened in her backyard kiln. Inside the house were paintings and photographs from her travels around the world. Each one of them—and there were a lot—was the occasion for a different story that I loved to hear, over and over, when I was younger. Whenever I stayed there, she let me tinker in her workshop, make odd stuff out of clay, and experiment with the kiln. I put an old computer keyboard in it and it stank up the whole neighborhood as it cooked. When I got it out of the kiln, it looked like a burnt waffle. She framed it and put it on the wall of her living room. "Beyond Words" was the title she gave it.

I'm grateful that memories of Grandma Greta surround me every day. Her art is still on the walls, and her flowers and cacti still grow in the front yard. If I had not inherited her house, my life today would be tough indeed, as I go to law school while supporting a family.

Grandma Greta could talk me into doing practically anything. To get me to eat vegetables, she would tell a story about a forest in Borneo where she got lost once—a forest, she said, that was as dense as a billion heads of broccoli. She would then eat her broccoli with such gusto that I could not resist doing the same.

So I agreed to go to church with her.

I stood in the courtyard of the Catholic parish where Grandma Greta attended. The Mass was over. It was the feast day of Our Lady of Guadalupe, and the priest had given a sermon about her. A big banner with her image was hanging in the sanctuary. But it wasn't until I stared at the statue of her in that niche in the outdoor adobe wall that I felt it again. It was a ceramic image of a dark-skinned young woman in a blue cloak with stars, surrounded by a spiky halo, standing on a crescent. Garlands of flowers surrounded her. I stared into her eyes. All of a sudden she came alive. She was looking at me, reaching toward me, and I felt her love pouring all over and into me. "Follow me," she said eagerly. I got that rush up my spine and through my whole body and out the crown of my head.

I had seen her image before my visions, even though I was clueless about who she was or what she was about. There were old tinplate pictures of her in Grandma Greta's house. Ronnie Morales' mom had a couple of statues of her in their house. *La Virgen de Guadalupe* was on tee shirts and car windows and she dangled from the rear-view mirrors of cars in Portales. I saw her a lot in Mexico when Dad and I made trips down there.

But it was one thing to see *La Virgen*, and something else to be seen by her.

Was she the same as the young woman I had seen in the cholla cactus a few months earlier? In the church courtyard, *La Virgen* was darker and more perfect. The woman in the cactus was pale and had an injury on her face. But the love was the same. Love that took over my body completely and left me with tingling heat all over.

"Josh, do you want to talk about it?" Grandma Greta asked.

She had been talking with other parishioners at the other end of the courtyard when I wandered over to look at *La Virgen*. I turned around. Coffee hour was over. Grandma was sitting on a stone bench, watching me. She was sitting with another older woman named Magdalena Gonzales.

I could feel the glow fading from me, but there was still enough of it in my face to amaze my grandmother and Magdalena.

"She's alive," I said. "She saw me."

"Milagro," whispered Magdalena. Miracle.

In his sermon earlier that morning, the priest had told the story of how an Indian campesino, Juan Diego, saw *La Virgen* on a hilltop in Mexico in 1531. The mother of Jesus appeared in the form of a young Indian woman, in the same place where the Indians had worshipped a goddess before the Spaniards arrived. After three encounters with *La Virgen*, Juan Diego was finally able to convince the bishop that he was telling the truth about what he saw.

I told Grandma and Magdalena that this was my third encounter with the Virgin, or whoever she was. They wanted to know every detail of where and how I saw the Virgin. I gave them all but one of those details.

"I believe you," Grandma Greta said, holding me by the shoulder. "What you saw is very, very important to you and to me."

"If Dad hears that I'm still seeing this stuff, he'll take me to the doctor or something," I said. "Do you think I'm going nuts?"

"No, Josh. I don't think you're crazy at all," she said. "I think you have a gift."

Back at her house, Grandma and I sat in the patio on Mexican leather chairs and drank sodas. Her parrot cackled in its cage, and the late afternoon sun glowed gold off the top of the adobe wall.

"I am so mixed up. How did the Virgin get to Mexico? Wasn't she in Israel? Why is she dark in some pictures and light skinned in others?" I asked.

She said that for white people in Europe, the Virgin Mary was white. But because of Juan Diego, brown people saw her as brown. "That is what made the Indians willing to be baptized," she said.

"But how does she change color?" I asked. The more I learned, the more confusing it was getting.

"It's a mystery," said Grandma Greta.

"Yeah, right, 'mystery'—but that doesn't help. Why does she change color? When I saw her in the cactus, she was white, and then today at church she's brown. If you speak English, she's the Virgin Mary. If you speak Spanish, she's *La Virgen de Guadalupe*. Help me out here."

"It's a mystery," she said, her smile creating entire mountain ranges on her face.

"Dad said he used to ask you hard questions about religion and you'd always say, 'It's a mystery.' That wasn't good enough for Dad and that is why he hates religion."

"I don't think that is the real reason he hates the church," Grandma said.

"Okay, what's the real reason?"

"You have to ask?" she sighed.

"Well, you brought it up," I said.

"Okay, okay. I think your dad hates religion because of what happened to your mom. She started going to Mass a lot just before she died. He thought the Catholic Church had something to do with her troubles."

***

Yesenia Hernandez de Morán Stoneburner, my mother, died when I was four years old. I don't remember much about her. I just remember her soft body. I know she loved me and that I loved her and that's about it. I don't remember what she looked like, except for what I see in the pictures and videos: she was a *morenita,* dark and very pretty. I remember being confused when she died. I didn't understand what it meant to be dead. I still don't understand what it means to be dead.

Dad told me that she died accidentally. She was taking different medications for health problems, and the mixture killed her. I believed that until I was about ten years old. I was getting nosy, going through all of Dad's stuff to find out secrets. I found academic journals in Spanish that included articles by Mom in a drawer in his old steel desk. Then I discovered the death certificate. It said the cause of death was suicide. I told him what I had found.

He told me she had a disease called bipolar disorder. She would get very energetic for a while and say crazy stuff and act wild. Then that would go away, and she'd be so depressed she couldn't get out of bed for months. She went to doctors, went to psychiatric hospitals, took different medicines, but she never got completely better. In a period when she was starting to go from being depressed to being manic, one morning she took a bunch of pain pills she had been saving and died while Dad was at work and I was at preschool.

Dad said he met Mom in Mexico when he was surveying a copper mine in Michoacan. He stayed in a hotel in the tourist town of Pátzcuaro. Dad took me there once. It's a small town near a big lake in the caldera of an exploded volcano. Mom was a professor of history at the university not far away in Morelia. She was there for a meeting of scholars who were studying the culture of the Purepecha Indians who lived around Lake Pátzcuaro.

They met at breakfast in the hotel restaurant. He liked her looks. In Spanish, he asked her for directions to the dock where he could catch the boat to the island of Janítzio in the lake. "I already knew how to get there, but it was all I could think of to get a conversation going." In British English, she told him where to go.

"Her English was better than my Spanish, and her Spanish was *castellano*," Dad said. "That really intrigued me. So I asked her to come with me to Janítzio. She got mad. 'What kind of woman do you take me for, sir?' I said, 'One smart enough not to trust me.' That broke the ice, and we sat down and talked for two hours straight. The rest is history."

Mom had studied at Oxford in England as well as at UNAM, the university in Mexico City. I guess she was the source of my bug for books. She was a *chilanga*, born and raised in the capital. My Mexican grandparents were Communists and part of the social circle that included the artists Frida Kahlo and Diego Rivera. Dad always said I had Frida Kahlo's eyebrow. My grandfather had come to Mexico as a refugee from the Spanish Civil War. My maternal grandmother was a full-blooded Purépecha Indian who had made a name for herself as a folk artist. My aunt, Teresita, lives in their house in Mexico City, and Dad and I visited it once. It is a lot like Grandma Greta's house. Full of paintings and photos and interesting old books. And now that I think of it, there is a statue of *La Virgen de Guadalupe* in the house, too. Except she has a bandolier of bullets over her chest, and a rifle in her hand. Next time I go to Mexico City, I need to ask Teresita what that is about.

Dad and Mom got married and lived in the old colonial city of Morelia for a few years. He said she had manic episodes there a few times. That was why they moved to Tucson. Dad thought she could get better medical care in the U.S. She did get better here in Arizona, going to a psychiatrist and taking medicine. But she didn't want to be on the pills when she got pregnant. So shortly after I was born, she went into a deep depression. Grandma Greta had to take care of me most of the time.

A few years later, Mom went into a manic phase, and that is when she joined the Catholic Church. She went to Mass every day, repeated the Hail Mary with the rosary all the time, and talked a lot about ecstatic visions of God. Dad didn't understand why his wife, who had been raised by godless Communists, could be telling him that she was the "bride of Christ." She wanted to have me baptized, but Dad refused to allow it.

Not long after that, she overdosed on the pills. Dad found her dead on the bed clutching rosary beads to her chest.

I was really worried that maybe I was going nuts, too, with my visions of the Virgin. If Mom was the bride of Christ, who did that make me? I wanted to be Karl Stoneburner's son, not Jesus'.

So it was very reassuring that Grandma Greta told me that I was okay, especially since she died not long after that.

***

I had no idea that things like this could happen. Grandma Greta died in her sleep of an aneurism in her brain. A time bomb in her head that went off without her even knowing it was there. Makes me think about the fact that I don't know much of anything about what is going on in my own head, where my ideas and visions happen. I experience what happens in my brain, but I don't really experience my brain itself.

Grandma Greta's funeral mass was the only time I ever saw my dad do something religious. It was held at her Catholic parish in Tucson. Dad was trying to act like he didn't belong there. But he stood up and sat down at all the right times, and he knew what to say and when to say it. "I haven't been here since I was a choir boy," he whispered to me. "Haven't missed a thing, I must say."

But as the priest gave the final prayer, Dad started crying so hard he was choking on his tears.

After the Mass, I went to the patio again by myself and stared at the ceramic statue of *La Virgen de Guadalupe.* Nothing happened. I kept staring, hoping she'd come alive and tell me something or maybe help me feel better about losing my grandmother. Nothing.

But I did get gripped with a conviction as I stood there. Grandma Greta would have wanted me to take those visions seriously and try to understand them. It would be the best thing I could do to honor her memory.

2. Smells, Bells, and Hell

I devoted my weekly trips to the library with Dad to learning as much about religion as I could. But reading wasn't enough. It was time for my "souljourn" to begin.

On a hot Sunday morning I walked down the hill for the early Mass at the Church of the Immaculate Conception, just a block off the plaza of Portales. Its bells clanged the hour. The church was a white dome that blinded the eyes in the brilliance of the sun. One little wisp of brilliant white cloud hovered over it, high in the sky. I wondered if that was some kind of sign.

It turned out to be the Mass in Spanish. Every move I made was out of sync with the rest of the congregation. I watched the woman next to me in order to figure out how to cross myself. I gave up trying to recite the litanies, since my Spanish wasn't so good. The sound of Spanish being spoken in the church stirred a deep memory of my mother. At one point I turned my head quickly to look to be sure she wasn't sitting in one of the old wooden pews.

I watched the parishioners to learn how to hold my hands and move my head when receiving the wafer from the priest, an old guy wearing thick black glasses above his wide smile. He must have been from Mexico to have a head full of gold teeth like that.

Children wandered placidly between the rows of pews, sucking fingers, looking at people, staring at the ceramic Stations of the Cross on the walls of the sanctuary. Adults whispered to each other, lowering their heads, smiling at each other and at the kids. This place was full of love, the one thing in it that made perfect sense to me.

The church had several images of the Virgin. One of them, a statue in a cove in the wall, was a Virgin of Guadalupe. I stared at the crescent upon which she floated with the golden rays around her, not unlike the glow of a cholla in morning sunlight. Her face was dark and beautiful. Then I remembered my vision of the pale young woman with a round face and dark hair; there was a scar on the right side of her nose. She wasn't perfect like the Virgin of Guadalupe, but there was an arresting beauty about her. As I sat there, I meditated that she was beautiful partly because of her blemish.

It took me another week to work up the nerve to make an appointment to see the priest, Father Crespi. After school one day, after going down the dusty alley behind the church instead of using the sidewalk where any of my friends might see me, I knocked on the rectory door.

An older woman holding a spatula greeted me in Spanglish and welcomed me in to have a seat in a big, strange-looking stuffed chair. The place smelled stale and dusty. Father Crespi came down the hall, flashed his big gold teeth at me, and welcomed me into his study, which was encrusted with crucifixes and lined with bookshelves. My immediate impression was that behind the "mystery" of the Catholic Church that

Grandma Greta always talked about, there was an infinity of religious trivia that lay out of reach to anybody but old guys like Father Crespi who spent all their time reading about it in musty rooms. It was appalling and fascinating.

"What can I do for you, young man?" asked Father Crespi, leaning back in his huge desk chair. "I saw you in Mass a few weeks ago. How's your Spanish?"

"Well, not very good. Sorry, but I didn't know …"

Father Crespi laughed. "The Mass is still the Mass, English or Spanish or Latin—it's the same rite."

"I have a lot to learn about the Mass and about Spanish."

"So are you Catholic?" he asked me.

"I guess not. I mean, my grandma was Catholic. My mom was Catholic. Does that make me Catholic?"

"Well, you have to be baptized in the Catholic Church, or confirmed, in order to be a Catholic Christian," explained Father Crespi.

"I guess I'm not Catholic, then. Am I allowed to go to Mass if I'm not Catholic?"

"Sure, you are always welcome at Mass. But you cannot eat the host unless you are Catholic," said Father Crespi.

"Is the cracker the host?" I asked.

"Yes, I'm sorry. Should have explained. The wafer is the host, the body of Christ."

"I'm sorry I ate it, then. I didn't really know the rules," I said.

"That is perfectly okay. Happens a lot. Don't worry, lightning will not strike you dead because of it," laughed Father Crespi. "So what brings you here today? What can I do for you?"

"Well, there is one thing I want to know. Why is the Virgin of Guadalupe standing on a crescent?" I asked. It seemed like a safer question than the ones I really wanted to ask.

Father Crespi smiled. "That's the only reason you came to see me?"

"Well … yeah," I lied.

"Okay, then. She's standing on the crescent of the moon because the Aztecs believed that there were battles in heaven between the sun god and the moon god and the other gods. She came to the Aztecs to show them that those battles were over. There was peace in heaven and would be peace on earth because of Jesus Christ whom she was bearing in her womb."

This jogged my mind out of a daydream about battles between celestial gods. What a cool computer game that would be … The sun blowing the moon away into gray chunks hurtling end-over-end into space. "Yes. Yeah. I saw a painting of the Virgin of Guadalupe in my grandma's church in Tucson, and she explained part of the story to me, but she didn't know about the moon part."

"You see your grandma pretty often?" asked Father Crespi. "Tucson's not that far away."

"Not any more. She died," I said.

"Sorry to hear that. How long ago?"

"A couple of months."

"You loved her?"

"Very much," I said, and started to cry.

Father Crespi leaned forward over his glass-topped desk and reached his knobby hands for a box of Kleenex, which he handed me. "I'm really sorry to hear that." Then he just sat and said nothing for a while as I blew my nose and wiped up my tears. He seemed to have all the time in the world for me, and that felt good.

"What kind of family do you have? Brothers, sisters?" he finally asked.

"Just Dad. Mom died when I was four years old."

"Sorry to hear that. Does your dad go to church somewhere?"

"No. He doesn't believe in God. He's a geologist for Phelps Dodge."

Father Crespi laughed. "Well then, he is almost God himself, here in Portales."

"What do you mean?"

"If he finds a way to open the mine again, this town will have a resurrection," Father Crespi chuckled. "What will you do when you get out of high school? Where do you want to go for college?"

"Haven't thought much about it. My grades aren't so good," I said. It was worse than that.

"Well, it's time you did think about it. Sooner the better. I don't want to see you just pushing a broom somewhere at the plaza. You need to get out of this town and make something of yourself. I can see already that you are a very bright young man, curious about things. That's good."

"Thanks. I'll try to do better at school. I have a hard time concentrating, I guess. That's what everybody else says, anyway."

"So why do you think you are so interested in the Virgin of Guadalupe?" asked Father Crespi.

With my hand in my pocket, I rubbed the rose quartz crystal. "Well, you know, it's just kind of weird—this picture of a lady with sun rays all around her, standing on a moon that is held up by a little angel. I just got curious, that's all." I said.

I walked out the rectory door and there, of all people, was Ronnie Morales walking by.

"What were you doing in there? Confession? You got some pussy, huh, Josh? Come on, man, you can confess to me, too." Ronnie slapped me on the back and laughed.

"None of your business, Ronnie."

Now it would be all over town, I thought. Joshua T. Stoneburner, religious fanatic. Just another title to add to my long-standing reputation as "space cadet." I turned at Malachite Street and walked home. I was pissed. But then I thought to myself, my cred with the boys is shot anyway. I might as well go all the way with this religion stuff.

***

That crescent of taut belly flesh, occasionally revealed between her glittery tank top and her tight pants, was a crack in the outer shell of my universe. All else was but a platonic shadow of the luminous delicacy that lay on the other side.

"What's your name, by the way?" Tekla asked. A new kid in class, she had been assigned to the stool next to mine at the lab table in chemistry class.

"Joshua T. Stoneburner," I answered.

"That's a funny name for a Mexican," she said.

"Tekla is a funny name for a *güera*," I answered.

"What's a *güera*?" she asked.

"Good question. First you answer me this question. What's a Mexican?" I asked. "Somebody who looks like what you think a Mexican looks like? What if I told you I was born on this side of the border? What if you noticed that I have no accent? What if I told you my dad's grandparents all came from Germany? What if I told you that I don't feel Mexican at all? I mean, I get bad grades in Spanish class. What kind of Mexican can't speak Spanish? So now, tell me, do I still look Mexican?"

"I don't know. Excuse me," said Tekla. "I didn't mean to offend you."

"No worries. Happens to me all the time," I said. "The people who look white think I'm Mexican, and the people who look Mexican think I act too white. I'm used to it."

"I guess that must be kind of awkward for you," said Tekla with a face expressing sympathy. "But what is a *güera*?" she asked.

"Somebody who thinks that Mexican is a skin color," I answered.

"Okay, I'm sorry. I'm new here, okay? From Missouri. And I don't know much about Mexicans. So I hope you'll forgive me."

"Forgiven. Really." I put out my hand and we shook on it. "What brought you to our God-forsaken part of the world?" I asked.

"My dad is a pastor," she answered. "He got a call to a new church, down in Cuprite."

"Does he believe in hell?" I asked her.

"Sure, he believes hell exists."

"It doesn't get any hotter there than it does here. You'll find out soon. Do you drink coffee?" I asked her.

"No."

"Good. Because it gets so hot here that the water evaporates before you can boil it."

***

Tekla invited me to come to her church youth group. I accepted, mostly because Tekla was hot, and partly because it was a different religion that might help me on my quest. There were a few kids from Portales whom I knew in the group already, and some others I didn't know, from Cuprite. The church had a mission to the Tohono O'odham Nation. But the mission church had no youth group of its own, so a few teenagers came to the Cuprite church from the rez.

The worship service was completely different than Catholic Mass. There I was again, not knowing what to say or do, not being able to sing the hymns, which had words that I didn't understand. Pastor Bob, Tekla's dad, was a pudgy guy with pasty skin who wore an American flag necktie. One sermon was about how one time he lost his keys and couldn't open the door of his house. "Jesus is the door to heaven. Believing in him is the key. If you don't put the key in the door you'll miss out on heaven." Phrases like "washed in the blood of the lamb" and "to Jesus I repair" and "accept Jesus as your personal Lord and Savior" were used as if everyone ought to understand exactly what they meant. I certainly didn't. So I asked a lot of questions. Mostly, I got answers that just took me in circles.

But compared to playing video games for hours with Ronnie Morales, or smoking weed with Jed and Mike and Eddie in Mike's back yard, going to the youth group at the Cuprite Baptist Church was refreshing. A lot of what happened at the church seemed strange and even ridiculous, but some of what we were talking about was serious. Like how to live. What is right and what is wrong. What matters in life and what doesn't. At least we were talking about how we felt about things. I'd never been with a group of people like that.

And oh, that fleeting view of Tekla's belly flesh, shaped like the moon that held up *La Virgen de Guadalupe* …

***

One hot day in May, after school, I worked up the guts to ask her if we could go downtown for a milkshake together. "I have a lot of questions about religion that maybe you could answer," I said.

The plaza of our town was a square with a crabgrass lawn and tall palm trees and a derelict fountain in the center. The square was surrounded on three sides by stucco buildings shaded by a covered walkway with a tile roof held up by graceful *portales*, or arches, after which the town was named. Portales was a company town created by the huge Phelps Dodge mining company in the 1930's. After the mine closed, many of the storefronts went empty.

Tekla and I leaned against one of the arches, sucking marble fudge milkshakes from our straws as we talked. She didn't show as much of her cleavage as a lot of girls. I guess it was because she was religious. But then there was that little crescent between her shirt and her pants, which was hard for me not to stare at. I was thrilled with the prospect that at some point she would giggle enough so that her shirt would come up and I'd get a flash of her belly button. It made me meditate later on the function and purpose of clothes. Being covered up just made the possible revelation of what was under it all the more exciting. A lot like religion, I guess.

"So tell me, Tekla. How do you know if you are saved or not?" I asked.

"It's so simple. All you have to do is accept Jesus as your personal savior."

"What if said I accepted Jesus as my savior and didn't know what it meant? Would I be saved?"

"Of course not," said Tekla.

"But what if I accepted Jesus as my personal savior, but wasn't smart enough to know what that really meant? Would I be saved?"

"Of course you would," she said.

"Why?"

"Because Jesus didn't come to condemn mentally retarded people," she said.

"Did he come to condemn smart people, then?"

"Well, no—" she hesitated.

"Okay, let's say I'm not a retarded person. Let's say I accepted Jesus as my personal savior, but for some reason I got it all wrong in my mind, and didn't understand it the right way, and thought that accepting Jesus as my personal savior meant something completely different to me than it did to you. Then what? Would I be saved or not?"

"You wear me out."

"Would God make me burn in hell forever because of the way he made my brain?" I demanded to know.

"Josh, I think that the Lord is going to help you stop being so mixed up and bring you to Him real soon," she said, putting her hand on my shoulder.

"So all this time you have been thinking, knowing, that if died right now I'd be going to hell."

"I don't want that to happen to you. I want you to get saved, get right with God, so you can go to heaven when you die." She looked me in the eyes, pursing her mouth, her crimson lipstick with its tiny speckles of Mylar glittering in the reflected light. Suddenly, I thought of a way to get those lips closer to mine.

I gazed into her face, then rolled my eyes, then gagged, coughed, clutched my neck, fell against the archway stucco and slid to the sidewalk, splattering my milkshake on the concrete, with my arms and legs going into spasms and my face contorting in anguish.

"My God! What's wrong?" she screamed. She leaned down and held my head.

I gasped out the words as she held me in her lap. She leaned close to me and stroked my face. "I'm ... going ... to ... die," I wheezed and rolled my eyes and thrashed my limbs. "I'll send you ... an email ... from HELL ..." I whispered in a hoarse voice. And then I started laughing.

"That was mean. I thought something awful was happening to you ..." She tossed me aside like I was a wet pool towel.

"I'm sorry," I said as I stood upright. I was smeared with spilled milkshake. "I just couldn't believe that after all this time, you have been thinking I am going to hell because I haven't accepted Jesus as my personal Lord and Savior. I mean, it just seems funny to me. Think about it this way, Tekla. How would you feel if I thought you were going to hell if you died right now? What kind of friend thinks that about his friend? What kind of friendship is that?"

"If you were a believer, you'd understand," she answered, smiling.

"Look," I said, poking my finger at her. "I'm a believer, because I saw God—or something like God. I saw an old man who was whispering something to me from a cholla. And I saw the Virgin Mary, I think."

"What?" Tekla's nose crinkled.

"Okay. I know it sounds weird. So don't go telling everybody or they'll think I'm even weirder than they already say I am."

I told. She listened.

"Have you ever talked to a psychiatrist?" she asked.

***

"Dad, do you think I'm nuts?" I asked from the kitchen. I was doing my geometry homework. Sort of.

"No." Dad was in the living room reading one of his desperately boring geology journals.

"Dad?"

"Yes?"

"Do you think I need a psychiatrist?"

"No."

"Dad?" I raised my voice and put pencils up my nostrils. "Dad?"

Finally, he turned around and chuckled. "Son, you don't need a shrink. You need a job as a hod carrier for a while. Then you'll get it about how you need to do your homework." He turned back to his geology journal.

"Dad?" I put on my dad's sunglasses, upside down.

"Dad?"

He turned around again, and grinned. "Yes, I see you. What is it now?"

"Dad, what's a hod carrier?"

"A guy who carries a hod."

"What's a hod?"

"That doesn't matter. All you need to know is that whatever a hod is, you would not want to spend your life carrying one every day, all day long. Schoolwork is bad, but hods are much worse. Just remember that. Repeat it to yourself all day long at school: hods are bad, hods are bad."

"Hods are bad, hods are bad."

"Good boy," said Dad, his face still aimed at the geology journal. "Now, back at it."

***

Tekla pulled up to my house at the top of Malachite Street. We were still in the middle of our conversation, so she turned off the engine. Heat shimmered off the hood of her mom's red Ford.

"But what about a guy from Egypt who believes in Mohammed, or whatever. He wears a funny hat and bows down toward a rock somewhere in Arabia, but he is a good guy. He loves his family and works hard. Is he going to hell? I don't think so. It doesn't make any sense," I declaimed.

"You are completely missing the point. Christianity is not about punishment; it's about salvation. The question isn't who is going to hell, the question is how to reach out to everyone with the gospel and bring them all to Christ." The sweat on her face was streaking her makeup foundation. I wanted to get under all this stuff.

"And how do you expect to bring them to Christ if you teach a religion that says that people who don't belong to it are going to hell?" I asked. "It's insulting."

"That's not the most important part of the message. It's—it's like this. You don't tell people how awful life without ice cream is. You tell them how wonderful life is *with* ice cream."

"Good point. I agree completely," I said.

"Finally, you agree with me about something," groaned Tekla.

"I agree. Life *is* wonderful with ice cream. Let's go inside now and have some. There's a gallon in the freezer waiting for us." She followed me into the house, where we found Dad soldering some wires together on the kitchen table. He was rebuilding an old scintillation counter to see if he could get it to work again.

"Dad, this is Tekla, Tekla, this is Dad."

"Nice to meet you," muttered Dad. The solder hissed as it melted onto the circuit board. The whole house stank of hot soldering flux.

We filled two bowls with peach ice cream, went through the living room with its cases of minerals, fossils, and dusty books, opened the sliding glass door, and went out on the screen porch with its view of the town below.

Portales was but a small patch of human habitation in a vast desert landscape. As Dad liked to say, we were centrally located in the middle of nowhere. Flat-roofed houses with swamp-coolers on top, chain-link fences between the yards, and the occasional pepper tree or green lawn. Near the plaza in the center of town, the white stucco dome of the Catholic church, like the distant range of mountains on the horizon, glowed watermelon pink in the sunset light. Beyond the plaza, the rim of the Phelps Dodge open-pit copper mine was visible, and beyond it was a long, flat-topped mountain of mine tailings. Near the tailings were the smokestacks of the long-abandoned smelter.

"So I get it that the main message is positive. But the negative is still there. Like you said before, you think you are being a good friend by trying to save me from terrible danger. It's still a big problem, this thing about going to hell if you don't accept Jesus," I said.

"Oh Josh," she said. If you'd just accept the Lord, it would all become so clear," she sighed as she stirred her rapidly melting peach ice cream.

"I don't know if I accept Christianity, I don't really understand what it means to accept Jesus as my Savior, but I do accept God. At least I think I do, ever since I saw what I saw in the cholla cactus. I decided I'm not crazy, by the way. I'm not going to the psychiatrist. I just think I need to learn more and figure it out on my own. I want to meet God again, if that was God that I met in the cactus. I want to meet him or her and ask it some questions. Like, what really happened to Mom. Why did she have to get sick and die so young, before I could even get to know her?" I was shocked to feel tears streaming down my face, surprised to feel more welling up from where those had come.

Tekla hugged me. "I didn't know—"

I was lost somewhere between missing Mom and being excited by the press of Tekla's body against mine.

***

"Josh."

"Yeah."

"Josh."

"Yeah."

"Josh!"

I finally turned around, away from the computer, where I was blasting away at dinosaurs in the jungle on the screen. There was Dad, with pencils hanging out of his nostrils and his sunglasses on, upside down.

"Let's go blow up stuff," he said. "How about it?"

I leaped into my boots and ran out of the house with him faster than a jackrabbit.

It was a cool day with still air. The only sound was that of the truck rumbling down the road. Every boulder on the cliffs and hills seemed to stand out with stunning clarity in the long shadows of winter. We rode in Dad's ancient Power Wagon truck a long way on a dirt track till we got to a gate marked "Do Not Enter" and entered. We drove some more until we got to a big hole in the ground.

"Let's get to work," said Dad.

We found some boreholes in the side of the pit in an area streaked with green. Down the holes, Dad placed the charges.

"Keep your mouth open and cover your ears!" yelled Dad. I tried to keep my mouth open as wide as

I could, despite my urge to smile as the blast shook the ground under us violently. Rocks shot out of the pit away from us, and a cloud of dust mushroomed up and over and then down and around us.

"Cool!"

When the dust settled, we went down into the pit to see what was broken loose. Dad picked up a mass of green crystals. "Very nice. Dioptase—see the green? That's good."

"Copper, right? But why is copper ore green, when copper is, well, copper-colored?" I asked.

"When oxygen binds with it, copper turns green. Ever seen a green penny? That's how they get when you leave them outside long enough, exposed to the oxygen in water and in the atmosphere," explained Dad.

"Yeah. Okay."

On the way back, I asked what he was doing with the explosives.

"I've been doing seismic testing to see if the ore is good enough for leaching. We blow charges underground that shake the earth, then use sensors in different places to triangulate and measure the shock waves that come back to the surface. From the wave patterns we can tell a lot about what is down there. Does this beat playing computer games?"

"Yeah!" I was still smiling. "So what is leaching?" I asked as we bounced along the washboarded road, stirring up clouds of dust behind the truck.

"That's where we spray nasty chemicals onto the ore to dissolve the copper out of the rock, then use electrodes to get the copper out of the solution."

"So you can dissolve copper?" I asked.

"You can dissolve just about anything, except maybe a bad memory," replied Dad.

"Got any that you wish could be dissolved?" I asked.

He went silent for a minute.

"Yeah," he said, finally.

"Such as?"

"What happened to your mom," muttered Dad.

"Do you worry that it will happen to me, too?" I asked.

Dad swallowed hard. "I am not sure, to tell the truth. But I think you'll be okay." he said. "One thing I am sure about. Today, you are a normal, fun, funny, interesting, cool kid. There is nothing wrong with you, Joshua T. Stoneburner. Maybe the rest of the world is screwed up, but you—you are good. Don't let anybody, including yourself, convince you otherwise." Our eyes met in a sober stare. "You hear me?"

"I hear you. I love you, Dad. I'm sorry it was so hard for you."

"I'm so sorry you lost your mom. She was a beautiful woman, a wonderful person, and I wish you had known her better. I wish I'd known her better myself."

As we drove between the gate to the test hole and the main road, we saw a helicopter racing low above us. It made a tight left turn just as we came to the top of a rise. "I bet they're dusting a bunch of illegals," said Dad. He stopped the truck and we got out and watched. Down below, about a mile out, the helicopter descended and hovered right over the mesquites. A cloud of pale sand swirled out in every direction from below the blades of the copter. We could see people scattering, running out of the cover of the mesquites to get away from the dust. But they were surrounded by *migra* trucks.

3. The Letters of Seedless Thompson

I leaned back on my skateboard to cut turns as I rolled down Malachite Street and down to the plaza. A few people were clustered in front of the Chavez Market. One of the ladies from the Dar al-Islam Mosque outside of town, a blue-eyed woman wearing a white scarf over her head, was pushing a shopping cart full of groceries down the walkway. The sound of my skateboard echoed under the *portales* till I stopped in front of a bicycle, the old three-speed that Seedless rode, locked in front of the library.

I spent a lot of time at the Portales Library, a branch of the Pima County Library System. We had no television at our house. Dad believed that TV was "junk food for the mind." Sometimes he let me play computer games, and watch the occasional movie, but he got grumpy if I spent too much time in front of the screen. So he and I made plenty of trips to the library. We read books almost every evening, back at home. Each of us had our own favorite chair with stuffing leaking out of the worn upholstery. Books were about the only thing that could focus my mind and get me to stay still. I loved old Western novels about cowboys and Indians. I loved to read history. I loved to read about conquistadors and explorers and adventurers. Even though I did poorly at school because I was constantly distracted, my reading gave me a big vocabulary for a young kid. In those days, however, my gift with words got me in more trouble than it did me much good.

C.D. "Seedless" Thompson spent a lot of time at the library, too, reading books and writing letters. He was a church janitor who lived in a trailer. Dad and I first met him when I was about 11 years old. Seedless told us that he had adopted 25 children from all over the world. They were his kids, and he needed to stay in touch with them. Seedless had offered to teach me how to play chess, and I was eager to learn. At first, Seedless beat me almost every time, and on those few occasions when I won, I wondered if Seedless had just let me prevail to keep me hooked on the game. But I was getting better with every match, and I could tell that Seedless was making more and more of an effort to win the games.

Seedless gave me a lot of advice about what to read, and I trusted him because the books he suggested were really good. I guess Dad let me be friends with Seedless because he figured it was good for me. I didn't pay attention at school, but at least I paid attention to Seedless.

He was a big man, balding, with an asymmetrical face. He almost always wore the same kind of rumpled but clean khaki clothes: a baggy shirt and a floppy pair of pants, and a pair of black military boots. He would sit at the oak table in the library, writing. His huge right hand smothered the ballpoint pen. His lumpy face was twisted in ever-changing expressions. The neon light cast a glow on his shiny head.

There was no mistaking Seedless for anyone else in the town of Portales. He was a little scary to look at, very odd, but people knew he wouldn't hurt anybody. I knew him as well as anyone did, and that wasn't very well, even after a few years of playing chess with him now and again. Seedless was a veteran of the first Iraq war. I asked him what it was like for him. He was in the military police, working alongside Kuwaiti prison guards who summarily shot and killed Iraqi prisoners when they complained or broke any jail rules. Seedless was badly traumatized by these experiences, I could see. He got so loud and agitated that I was frightened. I was relieved when the librarian told him to leave.

Years later we were able to get copies of the letters Seedless sent to his "kids." Here's one of them, addressed to an African child named Evans Banda:

Dear Evans:

I was glad to get your letter and to hear that things are going better for you at home. I am very happy that your mother is feeling better and able to work again. I can see how that was scary for her and for you, when she was so sick.

I have learned that when times are hard, you have a choice. You can give up, and be unhappy. Or you can decide to have a good attitude. Sometimes it is hard to choose, because you think you don't have a choice about whether or not to be happy. But you have to choose, anyway. And you always have a choice.

41

Maybe you can't control the world, and make your mom's sickness go away completely, and have enough money for all the things you need. But you can decide to have a good attitude. And that might be the most important thing of all—more important than health or money.

I don't always have a good attitude myself, I have to admit. But sooner or later I remember that I have a choice about my attitude, and then I think about it, and choose to be happy. And even though everything else is still a problem, my attitude is fixed, and that makes everything else easier.

Because what you do isn't the most important thing. You can work hard, and try hard, and still fail. What is more important is having faith that life is good and that life is worth living and that you can be happy now, even when things are not perfect, even when you fail. I'm trying to have faith, and it is hard sometimes for me. But it is the most important thing.

You are very welcome for the shoes. I'm very glad I can help in this small way. If I had more to give, I'd give it. You are a wonderful kid and I hope to meet you someday. Let me know how it goes with your football team. I hope the shoes will help you get the ball past the goalie!

Your friend,
C.D. Thompson

Ronnie Morales, who made everybody's business in Portales his own, told me that Seedless got his nickname because his initials were C.D., and because he said he had adopted kids all over the world when in fact his own "seed" came to nothing. He never married and had no children of his own. I thought that was a pretty cruel name, but everybody in town called him that, and Seedless didn't seem to mind.

One evening I went into the library, refreshed by its air conditioning, and found Seedless hunched over a table. He wasn't ready for a chess game. "I got a bunch of letters this week. Gotta write back," he said in a voice too loud. I put my finger to my lips. "Shhhh, Seedless! The librarians already hate us."

Seedless had "adopted" the children through the World Christian Children's Fund, an organization in Chicago that matched third-world children with Americans who sent money to them for necessities like food, clothes, and school expenses. In return, the children wrote the donors letters describing their lives and the ways they used the money. Seedless had been doing this for many years, and I was amazed that he would spend so much of his church janitor's salary on the children.

"Hey Seedless. Why is it that they always write on the same kind of paper?" I pointed to the stack of letters, all written in different childish scripts in bad English, but on the same wide-lined, grainy paper.

"Oh yeah. The World Christian Children's Fund sends the paper to them, because in most places they can't afford to buy it."

"Seedless … too loud," I whispered.

"Okay, okay," Seedless tried to whisper back. "Gimme a minute. I'm almost done with my letter."

Here's another of his letters, this one to a girl in India:

Dear Sarla:

Thank you so much for the wonderful birthday card! You sent LOVE in big letters to me, and now I send LOVE in big letters to you! Maybe you remember that I work in a church. People there talk about how they love everybody and how they want to help them. I think they talk too much. It's just a bunch of words, a lot of noise. But I can tell that you have real love in your heart. Your birthday card was more than just a word. I felt the love from your heart, and I hope you feel mine.

I am sorry that your father lost his job again. That must be pretty scary. I lost my job a few times, too, and it scared me. How would I make enough money to live? But then I found another job, just in time, and life started fresh for me again. I hope that happens for your dad.

Your friend,
C.D. Thompson.

While he wrote, I pulled a book off the shelf in the religion section. I had read a lot of the books already in my search for God, who or whatever he/she/it was. This was a new one from the central county library, about something called Kabbalah. *The Jewish*

Mystical Tradition was the subtitle. I leafed through it, trying and failing to find any handle in it with which to pull myself up into an understanding of its contents. But it fascinated me with its complex scheme of interacting spiritual forces. It made me wonder if there was any bottom to the open-pit mine of religion, or if I just would keep digging spiritual ore out of it forever.

As the library was closing, Seedless walked out under the *portales* with me so we could talk about religion without having to pretend we were whispering. Seedless saw the kinds of books that I was reading. "I've read a lot of the books in the church library," he said. "Mostly insipid crap. But the pastor has given me some good ones. Smart lady, Pastor Kate. Well-educated, knows the books. God, she's a boring preacher, though. I can't stand going to worship there. I'd rather memorize the telephone book. Sometimes I show up for coffee hour; that's as much as I can handle. I'd rather read something, or write to my kids. If you want God, you don't need to read books or go to worship. People get all worked up about theology and the Bible when it all comes down to something really simple. Kindness. That's it!" Seedless was bellowing so loud that I could see heads turning at the opposite side of the plaza. People were backing away from the two of us, away from the door of the library. But I stayed and braved Seedless' voice as if I was leaning into a windstorm.

"Okay, so what does Pastor Kate say that *does* make sense to you?" I asked.

"She and I talk a lot about Kierkegaard lately," thundered Seedless.

"Keerka what?"

"Kierkegaard. A Danish philosopher. Really more of a theologian, but he had a big influence on philosophy. Doesn't make good bedtime reading. But God, the guy was brilliant. With his mind, his insight, his writing, he sliced through the human condition and laid it bare." I darted aside as Seedless swung his heavy arm down with a chopping motion.

"That must have hurt," I joked.

"What?" hollered Seedless.

"Slicing through the human condition."

"Yes, as a matter of fact, it did hurt. Kierkegaard died young and unhappy. Pastor Kate and I went through his book *Fear and Trembling* together. We engaged the questions Kierkegaard raised about faith. Is faith about something you can explain? Or is real faith a faith in something you cannot see or explain, something that may even be absurd? Pastor Kate says faith must be existential, it must be a conscious leap into the unknown and unknowable, an embrace with seeming nonsense. Me, I don't think so. I get embraced by the absurd all the time."

His voice was quivering as he clutched his own ribcage with his arms and enormous hands, holding on too tight, too long. "I don't need to embrace it. I get more absurdity than I can handle. I just want it to go away," he blurted, still clutching himself tightly. "Abraham was crazy, agreeing to sacrifice his only son Isaac because he thought God wanted him to do

it. That's not faith. That's child abuse!" he roared.
"Same thing with Christianity. God sacrificing his son
on a cross of torture, to save us from our sin. Terrible.
That's not salvation. That's murdering your child. If
that is what God wants, he's the sinner. He's the one
who needs salvation."

I watched Seedless pedal back to the little
trailer he called home. It was a Field and Stream,
17 feet long, made in 1963. It was parked in back
of the Federated Church of Portales. The people of
the church were kind to Seedless Thompson. They
tolerated his unusual demeanor, his disturbing
utterances, his peculiar clothes and habits. He kept
the floors clean and nicely buffed. But he got
frightfully upset when people inevitably made
messes on the floors after he cleaned them. He
always kept a few extra rolls of toilet paper
available in each stall, to make sure there was
enough. But he had also been to the church
council meetings more than once to complain
about the waste of toilet paper.

"People use way too much," he would loudly
declare in the meetings. "That wasted money could
go for missions to help needy people abroad." The
church paid him rather generously compared to the
wages of other janitors in town. But Seedless never
seemed to have any money. He had no car, he
wouldn't move out of the trailer into better housing
even though the church thought he should be able to
afford an apartment. The pastor, Reverend Kate
Walker-Thorwaldsen, told me she kept inquiring

about his well-being. And Seedless would say, "Don't worry about me, pastor. I'm fine. Worry about the children in Brazil. Worry about the kids on the streets of Mexico City. Thousands of street urchins sniffing glue and stealing to survive. Worry about them, pastor. I've got a tight roof over my hooch, three hot meals and a cot; a job. I got no excuse to complain, pastor," and so on, for forty-five minutes if she would let him carry on that long. She kept asking him to call her "Kate," but he persisted in calling her "pastor."

From Seedless, to a girl in Guatemala:

Dear Lupe:

You are an amazing kid. One minute you are sick in bed with a terrible fever, and the next minute you are dancing for your town fiesta! One minute you are homeless because your family runs out of money, and the next minute you are back in a nice house living with your aunt and uncle. I would really like to meet you someday so I can find out how you do it.

Me, I'm not that tough. I went through some hard times years ago and I'm still getting over it. I don't know what keeps me going sometimes. But hearing about your life makes me want to keep going. If you can do it, I ought to be able to do it.

Your friend,
C.D. Thompson.

***

For the next few days, instead of paying attention during English class, I meditated about faith and absurdity. Is faith about having faith in something concrete, or is faith just about faith itself, a way of being rather than a system of beliefs? I went back to the library and got a copy of *Fear and Trembling*. It was slow going, but finally I began to catch on to what Kierkegaard was saying. There was something about the book that staked a claim on my mind. It seemed as if Kierkegaard had discovered the inner workings of the human soul. The book took me right up to the edge of the bottomless pit of emptiness at the center of my heart, and forced me to look down into it. Kierkegaard had revealed the paradox contained in the particular biblical story of Abraham's near-sacrifice of his son Isaac. Abraham was asked to do the impossible. For the first time in my life I experienced the chill of existential, rather than just situational, despair. But then the book led me to sublime heights of hope of a quality reachable only after a confrontation with despair. Was faith possible only through a full recognition of its impossibility?

I called Tekla and told her I'd go to youth group with her that night, but not to her church for worship. I walked down the hill to town on Sunday morning for worship at the Federated Church on the other side of the plaza. If Pastor Kate liked Kierkegaard, maybe I would like her.

Seedless was right. People were friendly enough. The first part of the worship was chatty:

announcements, an introduction to some new "inclusive language" hymns, whatever that meant; reminders about committee meetings, something about advocacy for undocumented immigrants. I recognized four of my former teachers, as well as the junior high school principal, sitting in the congregation. I read a flyer in the pew rack in front of me that explained that the church was a "federation" of people from the Methodist, Presbyterian, United Church of Christ, and American Baptist denominations, all of them Protestant churches. The flyer said that Pastor Kate was an ordained United Church of Christ minister who had a Masters of Divinity from Yale Divinity School. The idea of anyone mastering divinity amazed me. I certainly was far from it.

The litanies and the hymns seemed dull and odd. Pastor Kate moved and spoke stiffly. She used certain words a lot. She said "folk" or "persons" instead of the word "people," and I found that especially peculiar. It was as if she belonged to a special ethnic group that I'd never heard of before, with its own dialect. Her sermon was about the responsibility of Christians to create a just society, to influence the government so that it would do the right things for the poor and the immigrants and the disabled. She talked about God, but I didn't feel any tingle up my spine in that worship service.

But clearly, Pastor Kate was smart, and that intrigued me. So during the coffee hour I went up to her. She was standing near the cookie table, wearing her stiff white robe, and I asked her if I could talk to her sometime. "Seedless Thompson told me that you and he read Kierkegaard together. I read it, too, and I want to talk to you about it." She said she'd be delighted to have a conversation right after coffee hour.

We met in her office. "By the way, how old are you?" she asked as she ushered me in.

"Fifteen."

"Wow. So you and Seedless are friends?"

"Yeah. We play chess together. He's always at the library. He's a little weird but I like him."

"I like him, too. And he does a great job of keeping this place clean," reported Pastor Kate. "We're lucky to have him," she said with a formal tone of voice that made me question her sincerity.

"So when did you get interested in matters spiritual?" she asked me.

"Last year I met God. I guess it was God. In a cholla cactus. Maybe it sounds weird, but that's what happened." I proceeded to tell her the details. All but one.

Pastor Kate reached for two Bibles in her bookcase and gave me one of them. "Have you read the passage from Exodus about the burning bush?"

"No, but I heard about it."

"Well, let's read it together, if you don't mind."

I read it out loud, and I got gooseflesh when I got to a part I hadn't heard before: the part where Moses asked God, who was in the burning bush, for his name. God said, "I AM THAT I AM. Tell them I AM

51

has sent you." A rush of energy went up my spine. Maybe God was in this church after all.

Then Pastor Kate reached for her Hebrew Bible, and opened it so I could see it. I noticed that she seemed to be reading it the wrong direction. "What are you doing?" I asked.

"Hebrew writing goes from right to left."

So God wrote backwards. More evidence for how long and complicated this search was going to be.

"Here. Look at this. Do these letters look familiar?"

She showed me the words "I AM THAT I AM" in Hebrew. "I don't know if those were the exact letters. I can't remember. But I do remember that the letters were squiggly, a lot like the squiggliness of these letters. Maybe it was the same."

"Have you heard of the Virgin of Guadalupe?" she asked. "Because in the vision of Juan Diego, the Indian, she was standing on a crescent moon like the girl in your vision."

"Yes. I talked to Father Crespi about the crescent moon."

"So he knows about your vision?"

"No, I just asked him about the crescent."

"Well, he is my good friend. We work on the Immigrant Justice Covenant together. I think he'd be a very good person to talk to about it," she said.

"So what is this immigrant thing?" I asked.

"People of faith working together to advocate for the human rights of undocumented people."

"*Mojados*?"

"Yes. We're setting up water stations along the border, so they don't die of thirst so often when they come across the border."

"Oh yeah. I heard about that."

"And we give them legal help with their rights if they get detained. And we work on lobbying the government for immigration reform."

"Because that is the duty of a Christian," I said. "Like in your sermon today."

"Yes, I think so. Jesus says, 'Whoever gives to one of these little ones even a cup of cold water, he shall not lose his reward,'" she answered formally.

"So back to Father Crespi. How can you be friends with a Catholic? My Baptist friend thinks that Catholics aren't Christians," I reported.

"Well, Catholics are definitely Christians, every bit as much as Baptists."

"So what do you think about hell?" I asked.

"I'm against it," she laughed.

"So am I. But do you think there is a hell? Who goes to it and why?"

"I think hell is a state of the soul, a state of being right here and now, in our world today. If you are despairing, or lonely, or angry, you are in hell. It's not in the afterlife; it is in real life right now. The Christ has come to save us all from this kind of hell by giving us faith and hope."

"So non-Christians don't go to hell?"

"I think all of us go to hell sometimes, but all of us can get out through taking the leap of faith, whether we are Christians or not."

"I think my Baptist friend would say that isn't true Christian teaching."

"Lots of people think my teaching isn't true Christian teaching," answered Pastor Kate. "You be the judge, Josh. What do you think?"

"I think I have no idea what true Christian teaching is. I haven't even read the Bible. So what kind of Christian are you?" I asked.

"I'd call myself a progressive Christian. One who doesn't think my religion is necessarily superior to other ones. One who takes social justice as seriously as private morality. One who takes the Bible seriously because she doesn't have to take it literally," she answered.

"Pastor Bob thinks people like you are false teachers sent by the devil to lead people astray during the end-times," I said.

"I think the devil would be better at leading people astray than I am," she laughed. "Joshua, I hope we talk some more. Your vision: I don't know what it all means, but something tells me it is very important. At the very least, it is important for you to cherish it and discover as much as you can about it. Any way I can help, I want to help. You are a very special person, Josh, I'm quite sure about that. Call me any time if you want to talk more."

"One more question, if you don't mind," I said as I stood to leave.

"Sure, go for it."

"Have you ever met God?" I asked.

She paused before answering, taking longer than she did after any of my other questions. "Yes. I meet God every time I feel my heart opening to somebody. Like to you, right now."

***

Genesis was okay, and so was Exodus, but after that, it was hard to concentrate. The Bible seemed to drift off into trivia. Maybe that trivia mattered in the Bronze Age, but I could find no allure in Leviticus, Numbers, and Deuteronomy.

I skimmed my way to Joshua and Judges. It was a lot more interesting, but halfway through Judges I stopped. I'd had enough Old Testament for a while. It was too long, too dry. I felt like I needed one of those watering stations in the desert that Pastor Kate was talking about if I was going to make it to God through the Scriptures.

I started reading the New Testament gospels and was captivated by the character of Jesus, especially by his gift for storytelling. For some reason I really liked the one about yeast. "The kingdom of heaven is like leaven which a woman took and hid in three measures of flour, till it was all leavened." One little thing can change everything. I go up Cobre Mountain one day and happen to look at a certain cactus, of all the chollas on the mountain, and I see something in that particular cactus, and my life is never the same. One little thing gets inside me and turns all of me in a direction I never would have imagined.

4. How God Rocks the Brain

One scorching afternoon, I went swimming at the Portales Recreation Center. I saw Eddie Contreras there. After a while, talking by the side of the pool, Eddie asked if I wanted to go to church camp with him.

"It's great. It's up in the mountains near Globe, up in the trees. And the girls are hot. Lots of them from Phoenix, even a few from L.A."

"What kind of camp is it? What church?"

"Seventh-day Adventist. It's our conference's campground."

"Why do you call it Seventh-day Adventist? What does that mean?" I asked. Again, I felt like the more I learned, the more there was to know.

"Seventh-day means we have church on Saturday. That's about all I know. My family doesn't go to church that often. But camp is cool, man. You gotta go. They have a big pool there, too. Beats Portales in July, man. It's up in the mountains."

***

The allure of being up in the woods with a bunch of girls from Phoenix stayed with me that week. Besides, this was a religion I hadn't tried yet. So I asked Dad if I could go.

"Why do you want to do this?" Dad asked as he stirred an iron skillet full of *chile verde*, my favorite dinner.

"You know, I'm into religion."

"Do you know anything at all about Seventh-day Adventists?" he asked.

"Not much. Do you?"

"Not much. But I do know that they are some kind of fundamentalists. They believe that all the nonsense in the Bible is literally true," said Dad.

"So?"

"You're 15 years old, and I think it's time we talked about this religion business."

"Okay. We're talking."

"I'm just concerned that you are getting in over your head," he said, putting the lid back on the skillet.

"You're still afraid I'm going to turn out like Mom, aren't you?"

He frowned. "That is not what I said, and not what I mean. You don't have that problem. But still, people get carried away with religion. It's easy for people, particularly young folks, to get sucked up into cults, get brainwashed, lose their perspective and their priorities. I guess I worry about you because you aren't doing as well in school as you could be doing. You're a really smart kid, but here you are, bringing home C's and sometimes D's. You're reading Kierkegaard but pulling a C in English. What sense does that make? 99.99 percent of the kids at Portales High School have never even heard of Kierkegaard, and here you are, reading the kind of thing you read in a senior seminar in philosophy at the university. I'm all for intellectual curiosity, mind you. All for it. But we need to keep our priorities straight. Let's get a decent grade in English before we study existentialism and theology, okay?"

"You're saying this because you're an atheist," I complained. "You don't like religion."

"Well, it is true that I have no use whatsoever for organized religion, or much use for disorganized religion, for that matter. It isn't just because I'm a hardheaded scientist, either. It's because religion has a way of dividing people from each other, turning them against each other in the name of God. And it is true that I don't believe in God, because I see no evidence of an intelligent creator of the universe. God is a useful hypothesis neither in science nor in my personal life."

"That all depends on what you mean by 'creator,'" I said. "Maybe God isn't sitting on a throne on the other side of the universe, telling everything when and how to happen. Maybe God is the process of creation itself." I was pleased with my newly acquired ideas, and eager to nail my dad to the Wittenberg door with them.

"Well, if that is all God is, why bother talking about God at all? Why not just talk about the process? Which is what we do in geology. The universe is awesome enough, without having to bring God into it," answered Dad.

"Maybe God is awe," I suggested. "Awe is God's name. Budd-awe, Krishn-awe, Y-awe-weh, All-awe ..."

And so on we bantered until the *chile verde* was cold.

***

I rode with Eddie Contreras and his dad to the Seventh-day Adventist camp. The air was noticeably cooler as we went up the winding, narrowing roads. "So where do you work, Mr. Contreras?" I asked.

"*La migra.* That's us."

"You catch illegals?" I asked.

"Yup. I patrol the Tohono reservation. Business is picking up, as we say!"

"I was talking to Pastor Kate at the Federated Church, who says there is a group that is trying to get water out in the desert for the illegals to drink so they don't dry up and die coming across. What do you think of that?"

"Shut up, Josh, don't get him started on that," moaned Eddie.

"No, I'm curious. I really want to know what your dad thinks about it," I insisted.

"He thinks too much about it, that's the problem," groaned Eddie.

"Hey, he asked me the question, not you. Let me answer," said Mr. Contreras. "I think they have good intentions. They're nice people, the church folks with the water stations. But they are a bunch of mushy-headed liberals who think that problems will just go away if you are nice to everybody. Too bad reality isn't like that. They care, but so do we.

"We carry water in our trucks, so that when we catch the *mojados* we can get them hydrated right away. We save lives every day. Believe me, I've seen some grim stuff on my patrol. One illegal, lying under a *saguaro* with his eyes pecked out by a *buitre.* He probably died of thirst, which is not a good way to die. Your bladder dries up and your urine crystallizes. Terrible pain. So the best thing that can happen to these poor souls is for us to come along and rescue them before it is too late. You know, you put a water station out there, but they are still stuck in the middle of the desert. Sure, we send them back over the border, but those are the rules. Our job really is to save lives."

"But aren't they coming over because things are so bad for them in Mexico? Wouldn't you have to be really desperate to risk your life like that?" I asked.

"Those people down there, they're ignorant. It isn't their fault. Their government ought to do a better job of warning them how dangerous it is to try to cross the border. Usually, they are trying to get ahead by coming over here, not because they're oppressed or starving or anything like that. Hey, my father came over when he was 16 years old. He came over because he had an uncle here who could get him a job. My dad could have stayed in Aguascalientes and carried on the family business. His family was well-to-do, for being in a small town down there. He had it a lot better off than a lot of other people in his town. He wouldn't have starved. He wouldn't be rich, he wouldn't have had the nice house in Mesa that he has now. But he would have been okay. I respect him a lot for having the *huevos* to come over, but if he had got caught, that would have been fair and square, and he would have had a good life on the other side."

"The trouble with illegals is that they make it chaotic on this side. Look at how many cars get stolen in Portales. It's crazy. They come over the border and get desperate. Remember the time there was a truck full of them and it blew a tire and crashed into a rock and half of the migrants died, a few years back? They were packed into that truck like tamales steaming in a *tamalera*. I'm glad I wasn't on the job that night. That's why we have immigration laws, to regulate people coming here so that crazy, dangerous stuff like that doesn't happen."

"I wouldn't want to be poor down there," I said. "I've been all over Mexico with Dad, and it looks pretty bad for the poor people. If I was them, I would take the chance of having my eyeballs pecked out."

"Stop it, you'll just get Dad going," begged Eddie.

"Now Eddie, this young man needs me to straighten him out. We gotta keep out the terrorists. We can't just let them walk across the border with bombs and chemical and germ weapons. And the narcos. It's terrible what they do! And even though most of these migrants are just coming up to go to work, just because something seems like the right choice for one person, that doesn't make it good for society. If everybody in Mexico who wanted to be here could be here, if everybody in Asia who wanted to be here was allowed to come, it would be a disaster. We'd be overrun with poor people who couldn't speak the language, had no skills, needed health care and education, needed housing. We couldn't absorb them fast enough, and our way of life would be ruined. The very reason that people want to come here would be gone."

"Then maybe they'd stop coming," I suggested. "When things got equal with how it was for them back home, the people back home would stay home. The problem would fix itself."

"You are really ready to see America turn into another Mexico? If you like Mexico that much, move down there yourself," laughed Mr. Contreras. "It's a nice place to visit, but who wants to live there?"

"So do you think Pastor Kate is doing the wrong thing?" I asked. "Should we help these *mojados* while they are trying to cross the desert? Or should we let them die if they want to stay away from *la migra*?"

"I think that church people should stick to church stuff and let us take care of the illegals. We are better equipped to save lives than the church people ever will be. They are just in the way, trying to set up their water stations, while we are trying to do our job."

"Is your church part of the group that is doing the water stations?" I asked him.

"No, thank God. Our church stays out of politics. In fact, I'm one of the few government cop-type of guys in our church," said Mr. Contreras.

"Why is that?" I asked.

"Because Seventh-day Adventists don't believe in killing or wars. We don't put our trust in governments, but only in God. Seventh-day Adventists will serve as medics in the army, but not as soldiers carrying guns. I carry a gun but us Border Patrol guys almost never use them. Our job is to protect people, not to kill them. We aren't soldiers, and we aren't really cops, either. We're public servants. We're saving *mojados'* lives every day. That's how I see it, so I don't think I am going against my religion. I think I am practicing my religion by doing my job."

***

The Seventh-day Adventist camp was a sprawl of big tents, cabins, recreational vehicles, and a large dining hall in a big clearing among the pines. The pool was immense, and I of course noted that, indeed, there were some fine-looking young ladies in it. One in particular.

A whistle blew and it was time to get out of the pool and go to a meeting in the youth tent. It was a lot cooler at the camp than in Portales, but the tent was still plenty hot inside. I didn't bother to change out of my swim trunks, so I was the only guy in the whole tent, with 100 other kids, who didn't wear a shirt and shoes.

A band played. "It's crap," I said to Eddie, who nodded. But it gave me time to take stock of the girls. Oh yeah, there she was again, and this time she was checking me out. A wave of extra heat spread through me.

A guy stood on the stage with a mic wrapped around his cheek, walking back and forth. He was a young man talking about the end-times. Jesus was coming back soon, he said. "We need to get ready, to live pure and holy lives worthy of the sacrifice that

Jesus made for us on the cross. Jesus has entered the inner apartment of the heavenly sanctuary." (God lives in an apartment? Couldn't he afford better? I thought.) "He is going through the records to establish who will have eternal life. Jesus is getting ready. How about you? And you? And you? Are you ready?"

The meeting went on and on. It was a lot like the worship at the Baptist church, but with its own flavor. This group had its own culture, language, and ways of doing and being.

That became more obvious at dinner. I thought I had put a hot dog on my paper plate, but I spit it out when I bit into it. Eddie laughed at me. "Hah! A Loma Linda Linkett. Made out of soybeans. Pretty fucked up, huh?" he said.

"Terrible. I'll stick with the lasagna," I decided. "It doesn't even pretend to have meat in it. What is it with the food here?"

"There's a Seventh-day food company that makes the hot dogs. Lots of Seventh-day Adventists are vegetarians. Especially when they come to Conference camp, where they have no other choice."

"Why?"

"I don't really know. I just know that Ellen White taught that people shouldn't eat meat."

"Who is Ellen White?" I naturally needed to know.

"She started the church."

***

One of the tents had a bookstore in it, and I wandered through in a spare moment. There I found a book about Ellen White. The pictures in it, from the 1800s, showed a pale, broad-faced, unsmiling woman with dark hair. Then I got to the part of the book that talked about her childhood. She had been hit in the face with a rock by a schoolmate when she was nine years old, and from then on, she had visions of Jesus and the angels. From those visions, the Seventh-day Adventist Church was born. I flashed to my memory of the girl or Virgin in the cactus, who also had a pale, broad face. That tingle went up my spine again. And the rock: did it have anything to do with the one I found in front of the cactus?

I bought the book, even though it cost most of the spending money Dad had given me to take to the camp.

***

"You don't want to go there," complained Eddie. "That's for adults. And boring. You can't be serious. I know the youth tent meeting isn't so great either ..."

"It's a long story, but I gotta go." I told Eddie I'd meet him at the pool afterwards. I asked my camp counselor if it was okay to go to a seminar about the teachings of Ellen White instead of going to the youth tent. The counselor was surprised, but told me it was fine.

It looked like Ellen White wasn't too popular with anybody under the age of about 60, judging by the crowd in the tent. I sat in the back and listened to a

lively older fellow, pacing across the stage with a
cordless mike, doing a Power Point presentation
about the life and works of Ellen White. It seemed
odd that a church with a female founder did not
appear to have any female preachers. Ellen White had
a lot of visions and revelations. Some of them had to
do with diet, and that explained the vegetarianism.

After an hour, it was time for questions. I waited
for a while, then shot up my hand: "Excuse me, but
could you tell me … what kind of rock did she get hit
with when she was nine years old?"

***

She met me as I came out of the seminar tent.
"What did you think of it?" she asked.

We'd been checking each other out that first
afternoon. I swallowed hard before speaking.

"It was interesting," I finally managed to say.

"Why are you interested in Ellen White?" she
asked. She was a strawberry blonde, with freckles just
barely showing through her buttery tan that was
melting in my mind. "It's kind of unusual for
teenagers to be into that stuff," she said.

"I was trying to figure out dinner. Somebody said
that Ellen White is the reason that Seventh-day
Adventists are vegetarians. I figured I'd find out more
about the food here if I went to the seminar. I mean, I
had the weirdest hot dog I ever tasted in my life last
night. I figured I'd better learn about the food, or
maybe I'd starve."

I stared at her breasts, which rolled as she laughed, moving wonderfully slower than the rest of her body. "You're crazy," she cackled.

"You wouldn't be the first to say that."

"What's your name?" she asked me.

"Josh. Yours?"

"Rhea."

"Never heard that name before."

She grinned some more. "Lots of Seventh-day Adventists have funny names," she said. "Old-fashioned names. Farmy names. Josh … that's more modern."

"Modern is good. But hods are bad," I said. "Very bad."

"What was that?" she laughed. More lovely rolling.

"Hods are bad. My dad taught me to remember that. You should remember it, too. Repeat after me: hods are bad, hods are bad."

"Hods are bad!" she giggled, and as she tried to repeat it again, she bent over with spasms of laughter.

I never made it to the pool to meet Eddie. Rhea and I laughed our way into the crafts tent. Everything in it was sold to support the Adventist Development and Relief Agency. I learned that the Church had its own elaborate welfare system. Ladies were selling quilts and handmade baby clothes, men were selling homemade painted stools, mailboxes that looked like barns, and wind chimes. We came upon a booth that had a display of goat cheese from a ranch near Flagstaff. Nobody was tending the booth, so I took

Rhea's hand and pulled her behind the counter with me. She failed to contain her laughter as I yelled out, "Get your goat cheese here, get your goat cheese here. Fresh squeezed from ripe goats. Step right up. My wife, Rhea here, squeezes the goats herself every morning at dawn." People turned their heads and smiled as they passed by, and a couple of them even bought some cheese from us. Rhea was gasping for air, she was laughing so hard.

"Why is your wife laughing?" asked one old man who passed by.

"Because goat farming is *fun*," I declared.

***

"I guess you are not a Seventh-day Adventist," she said when she caught her breath as we left the crafts tent.

"I guess you don't really care," I answered. "Do you?"

"No. I don't really care at all. In fact, I'm glad you are not a Seventh-day Adventist. You are the most fun person here."

"No, I am not," I said. "You are the funnest person here. I never saw anybody laugh like that before. I thought you were going to gag. So what is the deal? You think Seventh-day Adventists aren't fun?"

"No, we aren't that bad. It's just … you are different. I can tell," she said, slipping her arm around mine as we drifted off the path to the dining hall and headed for the woods.

We went up a trail that led to a rocky promontory, and sat on it, looking out to the west over the camp and the folds of the mountains draped in forest. The sunset light glowed red against the trunks of the scrubby pines. I felt the feeling that still comes to me so often at sunset and at dawn, standing outside facing the desert. It was a delicious sense of longing, of anticipation. A feeling as if something, or someone, was trying to get through to me. Was it God? Whatever it was, I savored that feeling. This beauty came out of something even more beautiful. There was a source behind all of it that I wanted to reach.

"So how did you wind up here at camp?" she asked, breaking the exquisite silence.

"Eddie Contreras asked me. My friend. But now I think God sent me here," I said.

"Yeah, right," she laughed.

"No, really. I mean … maybe. I don't know for sure. But if there is a God, maybe he or she or it sent me here."

"So you are religious after all," Rhea quizzed me.

"Am I? I think about it a lot, but does that make me religious? I don't belong to any religion yet. I just look out at this …" I waved my arms toward the mountains, "… and at you … and it feels like there is something inside all this beauty, and I am trying to find it. So I'm reading books and checking out different religions."

"What are you reading?"

"The last one was called *The Way of a Pilgrim*. There is an old guy I play chess with sometimes at the library. He's nuts, but he's really smart, and he told me about this book. It's cool. It's about a guy in Russia a long time ago who prayed all the time. Day and night, repeating the same prayer: 'Lord Jesus Christ have mercy upon me.' Then he wandered all over Russia, and amazing things happened wherever he went, all because the prayer was so deep inside him that his whole life became a sort of prayer. He helped all sorts of people along the way, changing their lives, just by doing this prayer over and over in his mind all the time. I tried to do it, but it was too hard. I could do it for a while, but it got too boring and I gave up.

"So what do you think about religion? I see you whispering to your friends during the Bible studies in the youth tent. Doesn't look like that big of a deal for you," I said.

"Like, I believe in Jesus and the Bible and all that," she said. "But I don't know. I love my church and all, but a lot of what happens in it is, like, so boring and strange."

"Tell me about it. I visit all these churches, and so far all of them are really dull. All these people in them, listening to boring crap. And the music sucks. Then I ask myself: why am I going to these places and listening to this stuff? I must want to figure it out really bad."

"I think it is really cool that you are so serious about it. It's cool that you are interested in something unusual and you're doing something about it," she said as she stroked my thigh with her hand.

***

71

Back home, I read the book about Ellen White. Most of it was pretty boring until I got to the part about the connection between her physical problems and her visions and revelations. The Seventh-day Adventist Church denied that its religion was the result of brain damage. But it seemed obvious to me that the church would not have come into existence if Ellen White's schoolmate hadn't thrown a rock into her face when she was nine years old. This made me wonder: is religion just for people with rocks in their heads? What was wrong with my brain when I had those visions? Was it something I ate? Did I have a virus in my brain, and didn't know it? And how could I have had such a vision, including things that came from so many different religions? Was it Ellen White I saw standing on the Virgin of Guadalupe's crescent moon? What did she have to do with the Aztecs? How could my mind have put it all together? Where did the parts of my vision come from, since I had so little exposure to any of these religious traditions up to that point?

It might have disturbed me more if I did not have other things on my mind as well. The memory of the tantalizing taste and texture of Rhea Larson's full lips. The feeling of her soft body against my chest. The delicate patterns in the green irises of her eyes. The graceful curves of her strawberry blonde eyebrows. If I was crazy at all, I was crazy for Rhea Larson.

5. *La Virgen de San Lorenzo*

Seedless Thompson sat across from me, silently muttering something as he wrote a letter in the library. I read a book called *Prayer* by Abhishiktananda, a European Christian monk who lived in India and followed Jesus in the way that a Hindu would follow a guru. I had special-ordered it from the Tucson library system. Seedless told me about the book. I was fascinated with the idea that somebody following one religion would do it according to the traditions of another religion. Reading the book, I felt surrounded by God. It felt warm and comforting. Hard to explain, like so much I was discovering.

Another of Seedless' letters, this one to a kid in India:

Dear Surinder:

That was awful, that your house got burned down by a bunch of radical Hindus, just because your family has a Muslim last name. I hope you find a place to be safe from them, so I'm sending along some extra money to help you and your family find a new home.

Sometimes I think religion just gets in the way of what really matters. I work at a church, you know. Sometimes people say one thing there and do the opposite. They'll sing songs in church about love, but then they gossip about each other during coffee hour. I hear them doing it, while I'm cleaning up in the kitchen. Sometimes I wish they'd give up going to church and just DO faith instead of talking about it or arguing about which faith is best. It looks like religious arguing gets pretty out of hand there in India sometimes. Maybe if people just stopped being proud and defensive about being Muslim or Christian or Hindu, and just DID what their faiths are really all about, then houses wouldn't get burned down and people wouldn't need fancy church buildings and boring church services.

I care a lot about you and hope things go better for you and your neighbors.

Yours,
C.D. Thompson

*** *

"You owe me sixty dollars, young man," Dad said, waving the cell phone bill in my face.

"Sixty dollars!" I howled. "Sorry about that, Dad."

"So what's her name?" asked Dad.

"None of your business," I snapped.

"I wish it wasn't, but I got sixty bucks worth of business here. No allowance for you this month." Dad stomped back into his study, its walls covered with maps and cases of rocks. "And if you keep this up, it's no cell phone for you, either."

I followed him. "Dad, I got a question. It's personal, and I hope you don't mind. I've been wondering for a long time. Are you lonely?"

"Why do you ask?" Dad busied himself with paying bills.

"I'm curious. It just seems like after all these years since Mom died, you would be lonely. I know you have your geologist friends all over the world that you talk to, but I don't know. That wouldn't be enough for me. Have you ever gone out on a date?"

"You do have girls on your mind, don't you?" he muttered.

"Yeah, as a matter of fact, I do. A real hottie, up in Phoenix."

"What happened with that Tekla kid?" he asked. "Not your type?"

"She thinks I'm going to hell because I'm not saved. I guess that makes me way too hot for her," I said.

"Some problems solve themselves. That's a good example," he chuckled.

"So back to you, old man. Don't you ever wish you had a girlfriend?"

Dad turned around in his old oak swivel chair and leaned back, his folded hands over his belly.

"Yeah. I think about it. I've been on a few dates over the years."

"I never knew that. Why didn't you tell me?"

"None of them were very serious," replied Dad. "Why get my son attached to some woman who wasn't going to be sticking around?"

"So why didn't any of them stick around?" I asked. "If you don't mind me asking."

"Because I didn't want them to stick around. Look, it's like this. Your mother was the only real love of my life. I had plenty of girlfriends before that, but once I met her, she was it. She was the only one for me. After she was gone, I'd look at other women, but they just didn't interest me. I'd remember how Yessie talked, how she moved, how she smelled. I know that sounds strange. But I didn't like the smell of other women. A woman is supposed to smell like Yessie."

"I'd meet women, nice enough, pretty, but not like Yesenia. I went out on dates, but I couldn't pay attention to them, really. I upset a few women that way, and I got sick of the routine. I just gave up. When you meet the love of your life, you'll understand. After that, other women seem like they are made out of plastic. I exaggerate, but it is sort of like that. They are fine, of course; they are all wonderful in their own way, I'm sure. Each one of them is perfect for somebody else. Just not for me," said Dad. "I hope that helps explain. I probably should have talked to you about it a long time ago. I'm sorry."

"You have your reasons, Dad."

"So I talked to you, now you talk to me. What's this girl's name, in Phoenix?"

"Rhea."

"How does she smell?"

"Great."

"Okay. I'll raise your cell phone plan so you can talk more. But no extra past that. Deal?"

"Deal. But Dad?"

"Yes?"

"I think you should date again, Dad. I really do. I think it isn't healthy for you to be all alone. I'm not going to be around here forever. I don't want to think of you all by yourself up here, with just your rock collection to keep you company. Maybe nobody else smells like Mom, but I think it would be okay for you to find a woman who smelled almost as good."

***

Seedless wrote this one to a boy in India:

Dear Kumar:

From your letter, I'm not sure if I should be happy that your older sister got married. I didn't know how expensive weddings can be in your country! I'll bet her wedding cost less in American money than it would cost here just to send the invitations. I know what American weddings cost, because I clean up after them at the church where I work. But your family has so much less money than people have here, so it must have been a terrible burden for your parents.

I don't know much about marriage, since I never did it. So don't ask me for advice about stuff like that. I guess I'm married to my job instead. I work pretty hard keeping the church clean. And weddings are the hardest part of the job! People toss drinks on the social hall floor. They try to flush food down the toilets. There's wrapping paper thrown everywhere. I find pins all over the floors, from people putting flowers on their suits. It's dangerous! I'm the wrong guy to ask for an opinion about weddings.

*But I know it must be an important thing for your
family, and I hope it all works out really well for
your sister, with her new husband. And I hope
your family doesn't go completely broke because of
it. I have a lot of doubts about marriage, but where
would we be without it?*

*Your friend,
C.D. Thompson*

***

School started on a scorching late August day.
After my last class, I ran into Ronnie Morales by the
parking lot. Clouds were boiling above Cobre
Mountain, piling up into a thunderhead. Ronnie and
I hadn't seen much of each other that summer.
Ronnie had spent a lot of time water skiing with his
uncle at Bullhead City on the Colorado. I told him
about Rhea Larson, and Ronnie reported on the girls
he met along the river.

"Hey, let's go over to Mike's," said Ronnie. "His
cousin got him some great weed."

Ronnie, Mike, and I smoked some of the weed and
got a good buzz together in Mike's big backyard at the
edge of town. It was a dusty acre of car parts and rusty
motorcycles. The sky was going black with the
looming thunderhead. "Hey, let's take turns on the go-
kart," suggested Mike after crumpling and tossing the
second bag of tortilla chips we had just consumed.

It was a beat-up buggy that Mike's dad had built
when he was a kid. It had a lawnmower engine and

wide, slick little tires. It had a padded seat from an old VW bug. The steering wheel was a chromed loop of chain. It took some jerking on the rope, but just as the downpour hit us, the go-kart noisily started, spitting out smoke. I went first. Ronnie and Mike watched as I drove up the dirt alley next to Mike's place.

The rain started in sheets, then became one continuous flood, then the lightning struck Cobre Mountain and tremendous thunder followed. By the time I got to the top of the alley, where it ended at the edge of town, the dirt had turned into slick mud. I went down a few side alleys, then turned around and went back to the top of the first alley. I turned and roared down the hill, howling in the joy of disequilibrium, hair and clothes soaking wet, legs covered with mud. The go-kart slipped and spun in crazy loops down the alley, which had become a river in just a few minutes. The wheels spattered gobs of muck all over my face. I was shrieking with laughter by the time I got down to Mike and Ronnie again.

***

When we ran the go-kart out of gas, I left for home. It was two hours after the storm had passed. There were a few scattered puddles in the gutters of Utah Street, and curved ghosts of dust marked where the water had flowed across the streets, but otherwise the sky was baked enamel blue and the town was as moisture-free as it had been that morning. The bank sign at the corner of the plaza registered 110 degrees at 5:35 p.m. I got a few funny looks from people who could not help noticing me. Could they tell I was high, or was it because I was spattered with pale dry dirt from head to foot? I went past the plaza and made a right turn up Malachite Street, past the old hotel that was now an antique store, past the big, mostly-empty Phelps Dodge office building, and up toward our house at the end of the pavement.

On the way up the hill, I saw a couple of pickup trucks full of furniture in front of the Andrews' place. Les Andrews was a couple of years younger than I, and we had gone jackrabbit hunting with our slingshots many times when we were in elementary school. I remember that Les' parents were always struggling. His dad got laid off from the mine and later got a much lower paying job as a mechanic at the tractor dealership. Then Phoebe, Les' mom, got cancer and nearly died, but now was in remission. She worked part-time at the antique store in the Plaza.

"What's up?" I asked as Les tossed a plastic bag full of clothes into one of the pickups.

"Moving," said Les. "We lost the house. So we're going to rent a place down in Cuprite."

"Moving? I didn't know you guys were moving," I said.

"Well, we're bankrupt, Dad says. Whatever that means. Broke, I guess," said Les.

"Need a hand?" I asked.

"Need a bath?" asked Lew, Les' dad, coming out of the garage with a chair over his head. "You are a mess, young man," he laughed as he put the chair into the pickup.

***

"Dad, what's with the Andrews' having to move out?" I asked when I got home.

"They're moving?" wondered Dad. He lowered his newspaper and shook his head. "That's too damn bad."

"Les said they went bankrupt," I reported.

"Yeah, well, that's no surprise," said Dad. "You see, when Lew got laid off and had no job for a while, he couldn't pay the insurance premiums. Right then, Phoebe got cancer and racked up huge medical bills they couldn't pay. Later, Lew got a job with L. D. Young's heavy equipment shop, but like most of what few jobs there are in Portales these days, the health benefits don't amount to a hill of mesquite beans. And it was too late to help with Phoebe's bills, anyway. So I'm not surprised they went bankrupt. Makes me mad, to tell you the truth. It's not right, what happened to them. Hard working, nice people, and here they are, losing their house."

"How did they lose their house?" I wondered.

"That's what happens when you can't pay your mortgage and the bank forecloses. And then they have all that debt from the medical bills. I've been all over Europe. Over there, health insurance is guaranteed for everybody. Lew and Phoebe would never have gone bankrupt over there. But here in America, if you support universal health insurance, they call you a communist. You just have to hope Phoebe doesn't get sick again, and hope neither one of them loses their lousy jobs."

"So this is why I should study hard, so I can be like you and have a job with good health insurance?" I wondered.

"Yeah. And remember to be really lucky, too. In America, hard work isn't enough, I'm afraid. Meanwhile, remember: hods are bad, hods are bad," said Dad with a grin.

"Hods are bad, hods are bad," I repeated.

"Why are you completely covered with mud, by the way?" asked Dad.

"Thought you'd never ask," I said as I headed for the shower.

***

The day after my 16th birthday, I took my driver's test and got my license. Dad gave me the old pickup. "But you have to pay for everything," he told me. I already had a plan. Seedless told me that I could make money washing motor homes for all the "snowbirds," the thousands of elderly people from places like Minnesota and Ohio who came out of the cold every winter and descended on towns in southern Arizona. They were fastidious about the appearance of their "coaches." Dad helped me get the gear I needed: an electric power washer unit, water tank, hoses, buckets, poles, brushes, ladders. Some of it we got out of the mine warehouse. In a few days a week after school and on weekends, I earned enough to keep the truck on the road. I had plenty of spending money and even some to put in the bank.

***

La Virgen de San Lorenzo

My first solo trip in the truck was a visit to Rhea in Phoenix.

When I got there, she didn't seem sufficiently glad to see me, despite all the phone calls and emails we'd traded in the previous months. We went to the mall and walked around, and finally she sat me down in front of a frozen yogurt shop and told me the truth. She cried, admitting she'd been dishonest, but that she really liked me and if she didn't have a boyfriend already, she'd …

I drove back down the long empty road across the Gila River, through the Air Force bombing range, and through the *saguaro*-studded mountains toward Portales. The setting sun illuminated the lightly dusted air behind the mountain ahead, casting a long, distinct ray of light above the desert. A tingle of awe went up my back. And then I was no longer there. Just the ray of sun, the shadowed stony mountain, the perfect azure sky. The textures of dust and rust and leather in the cab of the old pickup. Hands gripping the wheel. I was gone, and what I saw and felt and smelled was all there was.

As I rounded the bend into Portales, I returned to myself. Something wonderful had happened along that stretch of road, but I lost it the minute I got to town. And I wanted it back. As I drove, I chanted, "Lord Jesus Christ, have mercy upon me, Lord Jesus Christ, have mercy upon me," over and over.

***

One fine Saturday morning in December, I washed a big motor home in the Snowbird Roost RV Park north of town. The couple that owned it pulled up in their "dinghy"—the little pickup they towed behind their coach—just as I finished the job. They told me they were "full-timers," traveling from place to place in their motor home all year round. As she wrote out the check to pay me, she asked me about myself. "Are you in school?"

"Junior in high school, ma'am," I replied.

"You go to church?" her husband asked.

"Yeah, a lot. Lots of different ones, actually."

"Really? Ever been to the Church of Jesus Christ of Latter Day Saints?" he asked.

"The Mormon church," his wife added.

"No, I haven't tried that one yet."

"Well, it is time you did. Are you interested?" asked the wife.

"Why not? Sure," I said. I certainly had heard of the Mormons—there were a lot of them in Arizona. I knew they tried to convert the Indians, just like the Baptists and the Seventh-day Adventists were doing. I wondered if maybe the Tohono O'odham nation would prefer to be left alone. I knew they must have had their own faith once. That was another religion I wanted to check out.

I spent the next two hours inside Jack and Wanda Horton's motor home, looking at illustrated Mormon literature and listening to them talk. I wondered what it would be like to look at these pictures after smoking some of Mike's weed. Until this encounter,

La Virgen de San Lorenzo

I thought that Mormonism must not be very interesting, because their church building looked really boring, and because I heard they were really conservative. On the contrary, their religion amazed me. Their stories were full of adventure. It seemed far-fetched that they believed that Jesus came to America and that the Indians were related to the Jews. But then, I thought maybe it was another way for religion to bring both sides of the border together. It was kind of similar to the idea of the Virgin Mary appearing as an Indian to the Indians. The Mormons believed that the Indians heard about Jesus in America before white people arrived. From what I learned in history class, this made no sense at all. But millions of Mormons were sure that it was true. Or at least acted like they were sure.

I really liked the Mormon idea that people can become gods. That they can become more and more spiritually perfected, in this life and in the afterlife. I knew for sure that I had a long way to go.

But most of all I was excited that Mormonism was yet another religion started by a young person who had visions. I was captivated by the vivid paintings of Joseph Smith's encounters with the angel Moroni on a hill in the woods of upstate New York. It made me wonder again. Was I going to start a new religion? Will people start a church based on my vision in the cholla cactus? Will there someday be a temple on the side of Cobre Mountain, dedicated to the angel Lorenzo?

***

For a while I had noticed that there seemed to be more people than usual parking their cars along our street and hiking up Cobre Mountain. Then one lunch hour at school, Ronnie Morales told me what was up. "Dude, there are all these people who think Portales is a holy place. Some old lady is leading people up there to see the Virgin Mary. Crazy, dude! We should go up there with them sometime and see what is going on.

"Dude, your mouth is hanging open so wide the flies are gonna move in," he said.

I should not have been so shocked. I had wondered if it would happen. That old lady friend of my grandmother's, Magdalena, had spread the word all over Tucson that there was a kid in Portales who had seen an apparition of *La Virgen de Guadalupe* in a cholla cactus.

But I was not ready for this at all. I wanted to know God, but religions seemed plenty weird without my own weirdness being at the center of one of them.

"Hello. Does Joshua Stoneburner live here?" Magdalena asked my dad when he opened the door. I could hear from where I was eating a bowl of cereal on the screen porch.

"Why do you ask?" asked Dad.

"Could I speak with him?"

"About what?"

"About a vision he had up on the mountain behind your house," she said. Dad slammed the door in her face.

"Fuck," I yelled.

La Virgen de San Lorenzo

There was another knock on the door. We ran upstairs and looked down from Dad's bedroom window. There was a group of about 20 people in front of our house. A couple of them were fingering rosary beads as they stood and waited. One odd-looking man was muttering the Hail Mary.

"Dad, this wasn't my idea. That old lady was a friend of Grandma Greta's and when I was visiting in Tucson she heard me tell Grandma about my visions. I don't want to be the Juan Diego of Portales, Arizona. Honest, I just want to get girls and hang out with my pals and smoke weed and do normal stupid stuff. I'm into religion but this is ridiculous, Dad. This is not what I had in mind at all."

"What are they doing here?" asked Dad.

"They're making a pilgrimage up the mountain to where I saw the Virgin of Guadalupe, or who or whatever it was, in the cactus. A while back, Ronnie told me this was happening. I knew they'd find me eventually. What do we do now?"

"I don't know. Wait till they go away?"

"They'll just keep coming back. They're like me. They want God and they won't stop till they get her or it or whatever he is. I have to go talk to them and convince them I'm not holy."

He and I argued for a while about whether or not I should talk to them, but in the end he relented. "You're a good kid, but you're definitely not that good," said Dad. "So go ahead and convince them, and make it quick."

I had no idea what I was going to say when I walked out the door. But I said it.

"Okay, folks. Yeah, it's me. Joshua T. Stoneburner." They gathered around me but kept a respectful distance. Is this what it is like to be worshipped, I wondered? If so, I didn't like it.

"Yeah, it is true what Magdalena says. About a year ago I was looking at a cholla cactus up the mountain behind you. In it I saw a woman who looked a lot like *La Virgen de Guadalupe.* I also saw an old man whose name was Lorenzo, who told me to follow her. Later I was in Tucson and I was looking at a statue of *La Virgen* and she came alive and talked to me, too. So I don't think *La Virgen* is just up there on this mountain. I think she is everywhere. You could see her for yourself in your own house, if you want to see her. Or at the grocery store. It doesn't matter where. Save yourselves the trip out here to Portales— it isn't worth it to burn up all that gas. Or risk one of those speeding tickets they give you out on the rez even if you aren't speeding at all.

"Do you know how many chollas there are out here in southern Arizona?" I continued. "Just go look at the one in the nearest vacant lot and you're as likely to see *La Virgen* in it as you are to see it in one here."

"And about me. Here's the deal. I'm just a stupid teenager. I don't know anything more about God than you do. Honest. If I had any kind of special thing going with God, I wouldn't be nearly as confused as I am about almost everything."

La Virgen de San Lorenzo

"Beautiful," said Magdalena to the crowd. "The Holy Mother shows herself to an ordinary teenager."

"*La Virgen de San Lorenzo*," muttered a dentally challenged old man, waving his arms skyward in supplication.

"Take us to the cactus where you saw the Holy Mother," yelled one of the people. "Please," called out another.

Humility is a sure sign of deep spirituality, and I just had hyped my humbleness. So that tactic didn't work.

"Okay," I said. "Let's go up the mountain."

It took a while to get them up the hill, since some of them were leaning on canes for the whole hike. But finally, we got to the cholla. My slingshot was still there.

As I talked to the crowd I put no energy into my story at all. I told it with a sense of clinical distance. I hoped they'd pick up on that and leave me alone.

It seemed to be working until I showed them the rose quartz crystal I had found in front of the cactus. At that moment, a young Hispanic woman rushed up to me and showed me a rose quartz crystal that looked just like the one in my hand.

Every hair follicle on my body stood straight up at attention. Even my unibrow must have been sticking straight out of my face. We didn't say a word. We put our crystals together and found that they fit. They were two parts of one mass.

The woman's name was Rosa María Beltrán Contreras. With Magdalena translating, Rosa and I sorted out what happened to the crystal. It had been a gift to her from her boyfriend, Ángel Luis Escamilla Hernandez. Before he crossed the border as a *mojado*, she gave back half of the crystal to him as a keepsake and reminder that the two of them were halves of one whole. He had lost his half of the crystal when he was caught by *la migra*, apparently right in front of the cholla where I had the vision. He was deported back to Mexico. There, he and Rosa got together again, sad that half of their treasured keepsake had been lost.

"Where is Ángel now?" I asked.

"*No sé*," she said, her eyes brimming with tears. They made another border crossing, together, just before she gave birth to their daughter, Ana. But he was apprehended and deported again. She stayed in touch with him regularly. He had called her to tell her he was making another border crossing. But since then, she had heard nothing. She prayed constantly to see him again. She was afraid he had died in the desert. She was looking for a miracle, and that is why she came to Portales to see if *La Virgen* could help her find her beloved Ángel.

I held her hands around the reunited crystal and closed my eyes and prayed. I had never prayed my own prayer before. I prayed my guts out.

"God, whatever, whoever you are, I have no idea, are you there? Help us, right now. Get this woman's boyfriend back, and hurry up about it. This is terrible, what happened. These people love each other and they have a baby together and it is not acceptable for them not to be together. You hear me? She can't handle it, I'm sure her boyfriend can't handle it, and I can't handle it. If you made this terrible thing happen, shame on you! Fix it, and fix it now. If you had nothing to do with it, then get something to do with it, quick. Amen."

I gave Rosa a hug and told her, with Magdalena translating, that I would do anything I possibly could do to help her find her boyfriend. "I'm glad I could give you back the other half of the crystal, but that's not enough. Not even close." We exchanged phone numbers and promised to stay in contact.

I turned to the people in the crowd. "Forget about visions of *La Virgen*. This woman needs to find her boyfriend, and we have got to help her. That's what matters. God better get busy and help, too. Or I'm gonna be pissed."

I stomped down the hill, every cell of my body oxygenated by an overwhelming conviction: this woman's situation was unacceptable, and I wasn't going to accept it.

The crowd followed. "Where are you going?" they asked.

"I'm going to deal with this. Right now." I stomped down the mountain to town. I stomped all the way to Pastor Kate's church office. I pounded on the door, and, to my great relief, she opened it.

"What is going on?"

There I stood, with the pilgrims standing behind me. "We have a problem, Pastor Kate. There's a man missing in the desert and we've got to go find him.

Can you find all those faith people you were talking about and get them together to go look for this guy?"

Kate gently dismissed the crowd. I gave Rosa one more hug and once more I held my hands around her hands, holding the precious crystal. Kate ushered me into her office and closed and locked the door. "What on earth is going on here?"

I told her what had happened. "So we have to go find him. Why else would I have found that crystal?" I said.

"Josh, Ángel is probably dead, you know. Why else did Rosa lose contact with him? It's been months since she heard from him, and she was in contact with him until right before he crossed the border. It doesn't sound like he would have abandoned Rosa and her baby, but that is possible, too. Do you know how big the desert is? Thousands of square miles out here. A thousand ways to die, a million places for it to happen. She doesn't even know where he crossed the border. The coyotes wait till the last minute to pick the spot. And you can be sure the coyotes aren't talking about what happened. It's very sad. It is a terrible, terrible thing. But all the volunteers in the state of Arizona wouldn't be enough to find Ángel, dead or alive."

"Fuck!" I yelled. "Fuck fuck fuck …" I pounded on her office coffee table and fell to my knees and cried.

6. Urim and Thummim

Dad picked me up at the church. I told him what happened with Rosa and the crystal. "This one wasn't a vision, Dad. This was as real as you and me talking right now, okay? There were witnesses, too."

"Told you there was an explanation about that crystal," he said. "Told you it wasn't a native rock."

"You so don't get it," I moaned. "But I'll take a week off from washing dishes, just the same."

My fury lasted for days. It was hard to sleep at night. I was certain that something had to be done right away, but I had no idea what to do. It was like my brain had been dusted by a *migra* helicopter.

***

The news kept spreading, in various garbled forms, that I had seen "the Virgin of San Lorenzo" in a cactus and that pilgrims were going up to the place where my vision had happened. The editor and only writer for *The Pit*, our town newspaper, called our home phone number and asked Dad if she could interview me. "No," said Dad, and hung up. "Thank you," I said to Dad. On this, we were a united front. The Tucson paper called, too, and I refused to be interviewed. Then a radio station, then the television news from Tucson, and then somebody from the Associated Press. "Leave me alone," I kept saying.

But that didn't make the media leave the story alone. It just meant that they didn't get what really happened. In a way, that frustrated me. But in another way, it liberated me from feeling like I was the center of it all. A new version of the vision, different than the one I had experienced, was now the focus of the attention. There were reports of pilgrims seeing *La Virgen de San Lorenzo* in the cactus on Cobre Mountain, and other places, too, and that she was the patroness of *mojados*. She would reunite couples who were separated by the U.S.-Mexico border. Praying to her would ensure safe passage into Arizona. Perfect, I thought. Let them harass the Virgin Mary, and leave me out of it. I was pretty sure that following her meant something different for me, though I wasn't sure what it was.

The focus on the Virgin didn't spare me merciless harassment at school. "Saint Josh," they called me. Kids would pass me in the hallway and cross themselves and giggle. Mr. Lopez, my math teacher, was cruel, too. He told the class that I wouldn't need to study for the test because the Virgin Mary would whisper all the right answers in my ear. I know Jesus said to turn the other cheek, but I just got cheeky: "The Virgin just whispered another math fact in my ear, Mr. Lopez. Your pecker is shorter than the square root of pi." That won me back some cred with my buddies.

It also won me a trip down the hall.

"We're going to let this one go, just this time," said Mr. Hawkins, the principal. "I get it that you are under a lot of pressure. Do we agree that you can't talk that way to your teachers?"

"I agree. Sorry about that," I muttered.

"Look, Joshua, you need to get serious about school. I'm looking at your grades here. Not so good. What's the problem? All your teachers think you have a lot of potential."

"Potential for what?" I asked. 'I'm dying to know. Mr. Hawkins, my mind is all over the place. I guess I am one of those people who needs a reason to do well in school, besides just getting good grades. I haven't found the reason yet, but believe me, I'm out there looking."

***

Within a month, the number of people assembling in front of our house on the weekends had swollen to over a hundred. They were singing hymns in Spanish and English, they were praying, they were fingering their rosary beads and whispering prayers and crossing themselves before going up the hill. They'd knock on our door and we'd tell them to beat it, but they just came back. The *paleta* vendors pushed their jingling carts up our street to sell frozen fruit and ice cream bars. The old lady who sold tamales out of a cart under the *portales* downtown moved her business across the street from our house on Saturday and Sunday mornings.

Looking out Dad's bedroom window one morning I saw someone holding up a banner with an image of The Virgin of San Lorenzo on it, leading a line of pilgrims up the mountain. The Virgin had a blemish on her dark face near her nose, but on the wrong side. Instead of a cherub holding up the crescent upon which she stood, it was an old man with a beard, something like the Lorenzo I had seen in the vision. A similar image was erected in a makeshift stone grotto at the end of our street by the start of the trail up Cobre Mountain. Next to it, pilgrims put plastic flowers, prayer cards, and other offerings.

***

One evening, when nobody was on the trail, I hiked up Cobre Mountain to search for clues about Ángel. As the sun hung low, I felt foreboding that I might find his body in gruesome condition. I peeked with trepidation around each pile of rocks and thicket of cacti. As it was getting dark I went down to the place where it all started, to the cholla, which was heavily decorated with strings of rosary beads, crosses, and plastic flowers. A little sign with a simple painting of the Virgin of San Lorenzo was placed near the cactus. I apologized to the cactus. "I am so sorry I made your life so complicated. I don't know what to do about it. They won't leave us alone."

"Neither will I," boomed a voice behind me, scaring me out of my remaining wits. I spun around and there was *migra* himself. A laughing Border Patrol officer. I could see his ATV in the distance behind him, higher up the mountain. "Are you the kid who saw the vision?" he asked. I caught my breath. "Yup. I'm afraid that's me."

"Seeing any visions now?" he snorted.

"Nope, just a bunch of beads and plastic flowers. This thing is getting way out of control," I said.

"Well, it was your idea," he laughed.

"No, sir, actually, none of this was my idea at all."

"Well, this isn't the best place for you to be after dark. You're near a popular campsite for *mojados* and *mulas.*"

"Big deal," I said. "This whole town is a *mojado* campground. They walk right into our yard in the middle of the day and take showers with our garden hose. But tell me something, please, officer. I know a woman whose boyfriend is lost out here someplace. A *mojado.* She was in touch with him right up till he crossed the border, but then she hasn't heard from him for months. What can anybody do to help her find her boyfriend?"

"It's a big desert out here, son. He's probably dead, and it's anybody's guess where. The *buitres* have probably picked him down to a skeleton by now. If he walked and camped along one of the usual routes, we'd have found his bones by now. There might be some kind of ID on him. The girlfriend can report him missing to us and we'd look for any link to his remains or possessions. But she's probably too scared to talk to *migra*—that's the way it usually goes."

"Can I talk to *migra* for her?" I asked.

"Sure you can, but why would you get mixed up in this?"

"It came to me in a vision," my smart-ass self answered.

***

Father Crespi's face was serious. "It's miraculous that you found the other half of that crystal. I have no other way to describe it. No wonder you feel compelled to do something about this situation."

I sat across from him in his office. His hands were folded as if to pray.

"I'm going to find him," I declared.

"But you can't find him. Maybe his body will be discovered along some trail in the desert someday, but there is no way to search for him. You'd have to walk every square foot of southern Arizona."

"Well, can we call Rosa and get some information to pass along to *la migra*? Won't that help?" I asked.

I gave him Rosa's phone number. He talked with her in Spanish and got a page full of information about Ángel that might be useful in identifying him.

"She says *muchissimas gracias* to you. She says that finding the other half of the crystal gave her hope. I hope a miracle for her, too, but I don't think we can expect it."

Father Crespi then called his friend, who worked for *la migra*, and gave him the details.

"My *migra* friend says what I say, Josh. You have to prepare for the worst. It would be a double miracle if he is found alive."

"Father Crespi, what do you think about miracles? Are they really miracles, or just coincidences?" I asked.

"Years ago I read the *I Ching*, a Taoist book of aphorisms," he said.

"What's that?"

"The *I Ching* is ancient wisdom from China. You could call it both religion and philosophy. The introduction to this edition was written by Carl Jung, the famous psychoanalyst. He described what he called synchronicity. These are things that happen together that are not caused by each other, but still have very meaningful connections. I think it is a way of describing what some people call miracles, but in a way that does not conflict with science. There may well be processes of nature that we do not understand yet, resulting in what looks like the miraculous to us. I certainly cannot explain what happened to you. It is amazing. The shimmer of hummingbird wings is just as miraculous as what happened to you, even though science can explain that shimmer." He pointed out his window to a hummingbird hovering by a flower outside in the church courtyard. "But just because you can explain something doesn't mean you really know what it is."

I did feel better when I left Father Crespi's office. But I kept having nightmares that I was lying on the ground in the desert, trying to drag myself to civilization, begging for water, with *buitres* whirling around above me. When one of them dived down to peck out my eye, I would wake up in a sweat.

***

A few weeks after my first encounter with Mormons, I saw a poster in the plaza advertising a dance for teenagers at the Mormon ward in town. It was the sort of thing I would have ignored before, but now I was curious. And I needed a break from sainthood. The price was right: free. Time to check out the Mormon girls.

No Christian rock at this church. The DJ played stuff right off the radio. And people were really dancing. The place was a big, blank, empty room with basketball hoops on either end. I danced with a few girls, hung out with some people I knew, and afterward got into a conversation with one of them, Tyler Crenshaw. He was a couple of years older than I was. We sat outside in the cool air under a clear sky studded with stars.

"Didn't know you were a Mormon," I said.

"Didn't know you were one, either," laughed Tyler.

"I'm not. I'm totally cool with it, so don't worry about me, but you came out gay, didn't you?" I asked.

"Yeah. So?" said Tyler.

"I mean, isn't it a problem being gay and Mormon?" I asked. "Isn't that tough for you? I don't know much about the Mormon Church, but I'll bet it says being gay is bad."

"Yeah, my parents aren't happy about me being gay, and the bishop, Mr. Young, talked with me about it. He said that the church has compassion for gay people as long as they don't have gay sex. So yeah, it's a problem, but I think I can find a way to be a good Mormon and still be who I am."

"How? By not having sex? That would be weird," I said. "I mean, I can't imagine how a guy would want to be with a guy, but I can imagine how intense it would be if a guy wanted to be with a guy as bad as I want to be with a girl."

Tyler laughed. "The Church doesn't have to know everything a person does. I figure that part of my life is my business. I think I can work this out just fine. I respect Mr. Young and I respect the Church and I want to be a good Mormon, and I'll find a way to do it."

"Okay then. Good luck," I said. "Anyway, I sure don't know much about the Mormon Church."

"Want to know more?" asked Tyler.

"Yeah, I do. I want to know about the underwear," I said.

"Everybody gets worked up about the underwear. Yeah, it's true. When people go to the temples, they are given specially blessed undergarments. It's part of the ritual. Some people wear them all the time."

"There's nothing sacred about my underpants, that's for sure," I said. "So what's it like, being Mormon?"

"It's a family thing. My parents are Mormons, all my grandparents, aunts, uncles. I have 30 cousins, almost all of them Mormons. I'll tell you this. I look around at people who aren't Mormons. Some of them are nice, but you know, the truth is, Mormons really are the nicest people I know. We are into family in a big way. There's less divorce, less drinking and drugging. Mormons are happier and more secure than most other people. I look around and it seems to me this is a pretty good way to live. Why would I change?" asked Tyler.

"Well, if you can figure out the gay thing," I said, "then, yeah, why change, if it makes you happy to be Mormon?"

"I bet our church looks pretty weird to non-Mormons, doesn't it?" asked Tyler.

"Well, what I learned is pretty strange, I'd say. This thing about Indians being Jews, about Jesus coming to America. How did you guys come up with these ideas?"

"Here's how I look at it. I'm just Tyler Crenshaw. What do I know? Am I God?" Tyler waved his arms at the sky. "Am I even supposed to know it all? All I know is that the people I love and trust the most say that the Mormon Church is true. That's good enough for me. I wouldn't argue with you if you said otherwise, but that's how it is for me."

"Sounds good," I nodded. "But for me, it's different. The people I love and trust say all sorts of different things, for and against religion. None of it adds up."

***

"Josh, where were you last night?" Tekla asked me in the hall as I made my way to math class. "We missed you at youth group."

"Well, I went to the Mormon dance."

"First you start your own cult. Now you are into the Mormons? When are you going to stop?" she complained.

"Hey, I'm just checking it out. Besides, it was a good dance. They don't play that weak Christian rock music there. They had a real DJ."

"That's just a trick to lure you in. The Mormons are a cult, you know."

"Sure they are. So are the Southern Baptists," I said.

"Oh come on. Baptists are Christians. Mormons aren't."

"That's not what the Mormons say," I said.

"Of course they don't say that. They want you to think they are Christians. Look, you better talk to my dad about the Mormons. He knows a lot about them. They are bad news," declared Tekla.

"Okay. I'll do that," I said. I had a lot of questions for Pastor Bob, anyway.

***

After youth group the next Sunday night, Pastor Bob asked me to come into the mobile home that was the office of the Cuprite Southern Baptist Church. The office walls were lined with bulging fake wood paneling. On one wall was a framed picture of Ronald Reagan grinning under a cowboy hat. On Pastor Bob's desk was a bronze bust of John Wayne. Another frame on the wall held a yellowed picture of Jesus looking up while praying with his hands folded.

"So you want to learn more about the Mormons?" he asked me.

"I want to learn more about religion, period," I said. "As you know, I'm into it pretty deep now."

"Yes, I know, and I'm worried about you. These visions you had—they were hallucinations. God does not speak to people that way in this dispensation."

"Maybe they were hallucinations. But guess what, Pastor Bob? I would never have gone to your church if I had not had the visions. They are what got me interested in religion," I said.

"So what got you interested in the Mormons?" he asked.

"Well there are a lot of Mormons around, and I didn't know anything about their religion, so I started checking it out."

"Josh," he said, leaning over his table, "you need to understand that the Mormon Church is a cult."

"All churches are cults," I said. "What's the big deal about that?"

"There is a difference. A big difference. The Mormon Church teaches a false doctrine. They believe that God has a wife, for instance. They believe that God used to be a man," said Pastor Bob, his voice working down to a whisper. "That isn't right. There is nothing in the Bible that would ever suggest that God was ever a human, or that God ever had a wife. And not only that, they think the Book of Mormon is Scripture, when it is not. Look at the last chapter of the last book of the Bible, Revelation 22 and verse 18." He opened up his Bible with its flimsy gold-edged pages and read from it: "'I warn every one who hears the words of the prophecy of this book: if any one adds to them, God will add to him the plagues described in this book.'"

"I read that the Bible was assembled by the Catholic Church in the fourth century from a bunch of different books in circulation at the time, so how could the writer of Revelation know that his was the last book?" I asked.

"God inspired him to put those words there," declared Pastor Bob.

"Okay, Pastor Bob, I see how strongly you feel about this. But please help me understand why it bothers you so much. What is so special about the Mormons? Lots of other churches teach things that are different from what you teach. You don't seem nearly as excited about them."

"It's because the Mormons are a powerful and insidious cult. If their church were a corporation, it would be one of the biggest on earth. If it were a nation, it would be one of the richest. It has its tentacles in government, the military, industry, everything. It is a huge conspiracy to lead America and the world astray from the true Christian religion."

"Okay, but they sure seem like nice people. Family-oriented. Clean, well-behaved, hard-working. Just as nice as people in this church," In a rare display of self-restraint, I left out the part about how the Mormons knew how to dance a lot better than the Baptists.

"But as Scripture teaches us, we must look deeper than the appearances of things," argued Pastor Bob.

He went on to explain that Joseph Smith, the founder of the Mormon Church, had been arrested as a young man for using "peep stones" to dig for buried treasure. He would look at special rocks and get information from them that would supposedly reveal the location of treasures underground. In the early 1800s this was considered a disreputable occupation and was grounds for prosecution. Pastor Bob said that later, Joseph Smith claimed to use special crystal glasses: glorified "peep stones" called the Urim and Thummim, to interpret the gold plates he said he had discovered.

A tingle went up my spine. "Peep stones." Rocks that give revelations, like the rose quartz at the cholla.

"Here, read this. Tell me what you think. I really would like to hear your opinion about it," he said. It was a book called *Behind the Zion Curtain*.

***

I went home, said goodnight to Dad, and went to bed. The moonlight bathed my bedroom. The silence seemed to beg to be filled.

I opened the bedroom window and leaned out and looked up at Cobre Mountain, faintly glowing in the white light. I felt like I could reach out and touch it, it seemed so close. The weight, the mass of the mountain overwhelmed me. There really was something holy about it.

I thought about the rose quartz and the "peep stones". I thought about my visions. I questioned everything. Maybe Joseph Smith made it all up, lied about the "peep stones" and the Urim and Thummim and the golden plates that recorded the Book of Mormon. Maybe he was just a con artist, a flim-flam man. Maybe Ellen White's visions and revelations were indeed the result of a rock thrown at her head. Maybe the Bible was mostly a bunch of myths made up by people who bumped their heads, too. Maybe the Bible stories lacked any historical accuracy. Maybe the visions I had were just the jumbled result of my imagination, and it was only accidental that any of it related to the stories of several religious traditions. So what? Maybe that didn't matter.

Maybe what mattered was that my visions were meaningful to me, no matter how they happened. The visions of Ellen White were meaningful for Seventh-day Adventists, whether or not she had temporal lobe epilepsy. Whatever the real story behind it might have been, the Book of Mormon was meaningful for Mormons. Whether the imprint of the image of the Virgin of Guadalupe on Juan Diego's tunic was put there by God, or was just the first silk-screened Hispanic tee-shirt art in the Americas, that image of the Virgin meant a great deal to Catholic Mexicans.

Behind all the claims made by religion, many of them fantastic, I was finding another level of truth. These stories and scriptures and beliefs pointed to a reality beyond factual explanation. Maybe it didn't matter how a rose quartz crystal could open my heart to a hurting woman who had lost her boyfriend in the desert. Maybe it was enough that my heart had been opened at all.

I gazed at the moon and chanted, over and over: "Lord Jesus Christ, have mercy upon me" until I fell asleep.

***

I found Pastor Kate pushing a cart full of groceries at the Chavez Market one afternoon. I was buying an ice cream bar.

"So, what are you reading these days?" she asked.

"A book about Mormons," I answered.

"Where did you get it?" she asked. "At the Mormon ward?"

"No, I got it from the minister at the Cuprite Baptist Church. He thinks the Mormons are a cult. The book says Mormonism is a hoax, really. What do you think?"

She smiled and said, "I don't think I'd fit into the Mormon Church very well, but I don't think it's very helpful to call them a cult. Any more than to say my church is a cult. It's not really fair for one church or religion to be judging another, I think. On the other hand, it's a good idea to be informed. If you want to read something about the Mormons that is a lot less biased, I have a suggestion for you. I'm interested in the LDS church, too, because there are so many Mormons in this town. I can suggest a book I read recently, written by serious journalists. I think it is accurate while being sensitive toward the Mormons."

She told me the title of the book, and since I was only a few doors from the library, I looked for it after

I finished my ice cream bar. I read a lot of it in the library before checking it out.

This book seemed a lot less opinionated than the one Pastor Bob had given me. This one had a big appendix with references at the end; obviously it had been researched carefully. It read a lot more like a history book. But like Pastor Bob's book, this one said that Joseph Smith had been arrested for digging for treasure with "peep stones." Without saying outright that the Book of Mormon was a hoax, the book described its background in a way that made it obvious that it was a product only of Joseph Smith's mind. And the book also made it clear that Joseph Smith was no angel; he did more than his share of lying and cheating. And his polygamy seemed like nothing more than a clever theological excuse to have all the women he wanted.

But the question remained: who or what had created Joseph Smith's mind? Who or what planted such an elaborate set of stories and ideas in his head? Why would Joseph Smith go to all the trouble of writing it down, if it hadn't really meant something to him? And if you have to be a perfect person to get a vision from God, then I wouldn't have qualified for what I saw in the cholla cactus, either.

Seedless came in as I was leaving. "Got some letters to write," he muttered.

Dear Sammy:

Thanks for the great picture of you and your family! I could see the mountains of your island in the background—what a beautiful place you call home!

I hope the extra money I sent for your schoolbooks will get you through the year. It costs your family a lot for you to get educated, but it is worth it. I ought to know, because I never went very far in school, and as a result I don't make a lot of money. At least by American standards. By world standards, I'm a very rich person. Which is why I can send you money and still have a roof over my head and plenty to eat. If I had got a better education, maybe I'd have more money to give away. That would be good. But I'd hate to have to play all the games that rich people have to play to get their money. I think I'm just too honest to act smiley all the time and try to sell things I don't really believe in. I think the most important thing is to be true to yourself. To be real. To be straight. There's nothing worse than being all proud and puffed-up. These rich guys, usually they try to act like they are God or something. I guess that is what it takes to get rich. You can have it. I'll just push a broom, thank you. I'd rather be empty and real than full and fake.

But maybe with more schooling you can find a way to be true to yourself and make more money than your parents. Good luck figuring it out! I'm probably the wrong guy to tell you how to do it.

Your friend,
C.D. Thompson

7. Dying for a Drink

The next time I saw Pastor Kate was at the high school. Her husband Jeff was one of the social studies teachers, and she was there to pick him up after school. We met in the hallway in front of the school office.

"I've been thinking about you. I wonder if you'd be interested in going out to set up the water stations in the desert, with the Immigrant Justice Covenant?"

"Yeah, sure," I said, without hesitating. "I'm curious about it. And I've got a pickup with a water tank. Would that help?"

"I'll bet it would. I've never done this before, either, so let's find out," she said.

***

I went to a meeting of the Covenant at the Catholic Church. At the meeting, another new volunteer, Rachel Parmenter, invited the group to set up a water station on her land. I volunteered to go with her to map the spot where the station would be placed later.

She picked me up the next morning and we drove down to her place near Organ Pipe National Monument. The desert was dotted with brilliant red clusters of blooms on the tops of the tall, spiny ocotillos.

She was a middle-aged woman with wrinkles fanning back from the corners of her eyes, and a warm, bright, and easy smile.

I rode with her in her pickup to pick out a place to put the water tank. The spot would be marked by a long pole with a blue flag on top, so the *mojados* could see it over the mesquites from a distance. They wanted the sites to be far away from roads, so that the *mojados* would feel like it was harder for *migra* to find them. Rachel knew the routes that the *mojados* used to walk across the desert around her property, so she had a spot in mind.

"So, you are all alone out here?" I asked.

"Well, I live by myself in the house, but I've got a few trailers on the land where some of my hired help lives."

"You have kids?" I asked.

"Yes. Grown up and gone. Ever since my husband died, they have wanted me to give up the ranch and move to town. I want them to move back and run the ranch with me, but I can see why they aren't interested. It's a hard life, and with the illegals and *la migra* all over the land, it isn't as peaceful as it used to be. So tell me, how did you get interested in this project?" she asked.

"Pastor Kate invited me to be a volunteer. It sounded like a cool thing," I said. "And what got you interested?"

"Something happened out on my land one day," she said. We stopped at the site she'd picked out for a water station, and she told me the story.

Rachel had been driving out in the desert in her old truck when the radiator boiled over. Her other truck, the newer one, was in the shop getting repaired, so she had taken the old one out to check the level on the horse troughs on the east side of the ranch.

It wasn't that big of a deal. She knew what to do. It was probably a bad thermostat. The truck engine was so old that it could run just fine without a thermostat at all, unless the air was freezing. It was a cool December day in the desert, but certainly not frosty. All she had to do was wait about half an hour for the engine to cool down enough for her to get out a wrench, take off the housing, pull out the bad thermostat and put the housing back on. Might be a problem if the gasket fell apart, though... she'd need to be careful removing the housing. She'd need to take a hike out to a trough to get some water for the radiator, too; she didn't have any on the truck. Might as well take the hike now; that would give the engine time to cool off.

From the ground, she picked up a couple of empty plastic water jugs, probably left by *mojados*, and started walking. The desert looked and smelled wonderful under a turquoise sky on that late afternoon. A roadrunner strutted across the road; jackrabbits darted through the brush.

Cholla cactus, mesquite trees, and ocotillo spines lined the side of the powdery dirt road that led to the clearing around the tank. Suddenly she heard someone moaning, and she froze. She panicked for a moment, then gathered her wits and yelled, "*No temas, no temas*"—telling whoever was there not to be afraid of her. "*No soy la migra.*"

The moaning sound stopped. Only the sound of Rachel's heart pounding inside her chest. She hadn't even thought about the danger, hadn't taken the pistol with her, the one she kept in the other truck.

There were some ranchers further east along the border who had recruited others from around the country to become vigilante border agents. The Border Bouncers, they called themselves. Cattlemen and other adventure-seekers chasing *mojados* with ATVs and big guns and delivering them to the Border Patrol. Looking for trouble, and causing more of it, Rachel thought. And the coyotes, the Mexicans who smuggled people across the border, were sometimes known to have a violent streak. What had once been a game of harmless cat and mouse along the border had now become a game for keeps. As the border was more tightly controlled by the U.S., the mojados were more desperate to get across. An endless march of the poor confronted the armed might of the United States government and a motley crew of self-anointed guardians of the border. It was a deadly drama playing itself out, sometimes on her ranch property. She was angry at everyone, *mojados*, *migra*, and the vigilantes, for ruining her once-sacred solitude. Since her husband Hank died, her friends kept telling her to sell the place and move to town. "It isn't safe anymore, especially for a woman all alone," they told her.

"No temas." Fine for her to say, but she was scared half to death herself. The silence itself was frightening.

Then she heard a high-pitched cry. She'd uttered that cry a few times herself. She followed the sound into a thicket of mesquites. And there, before her on the ground, was a young woman writhing in pain, her belly swollen with child, her man cradling her head in his lap.

All anger at *mojados* evaporated as she faced the woman in labor on the ground. Rachel motioned with her water containers at the man. *"Camioneta,"* she said, using her very limited Spanish and some arm waving to indicate that her truck needed water. The man nodded, grabbed a jug and forced it under the water of the trough. When it was full, he handed it back to Rachel and then ran to his woman and picked her up in his arms and trotted, panting, behind Rachel as they went back to the truck.

The man knew what to do, just as Rachel did, but he was even more motivated than Rachel was to get that truck back on the road. He almost grabbed the wrench out of Rachel's hand once he saw what she was about to do, and in no time the rusty thermostat was out and flung into the brush. Rachel was in awe as he ripped the tongue out of his boot and fashioned a gasket out of it with his buck-knife, soaking the leather in water for a moment before cinching it down between the halves of the housing with the wrench. This truck was not going to overheat on the way to the hospital; he made sure of that. Rachel concluded that this baby was going to have a very resourceful father.

***

I interrupted at this point. I was getting very nervous. I did not want to ask, but my curiosity boiled over. "What were their names? The man and the woman?"

"Enrique, Marta, and they named the baby Monica," she said.

"Thank God," I said. I could not deal with any more miraculous coincidences.

***

Rachel continued her story.

Enrique slammed the hood down on the old Chevy. Rachel gave Enrique the key and then held Marta in her lap on the passenger side. Enrique spun the truck around on the wash-boarded dirt road and headed for the clinic. Marta winced and moaned as they went into ruts and over rocks on the road. Finally, after 15 minutes of listening to her agony, Enrique stood on the gas pedal as the truck drove off the dirt road and onto the paved highway, into the pink and purple sunset. Border Patrol vans and other vehicles passed; the truck was so old and the gearing was so low that it couldn't top 55 at full throttle.

Marta's labor pains were coming at shorter and shorter intervals. Rachel knew that time was running out, and while she was a good horse midwife, she was not ready to help deliver a human baby, especially in a pickup truck. Finally, the little line of lights that marked the town of Portales was visible in the distance as they drove over a rise.

They went further over the rise and the *migra* checkpoint came into view. Rachel filled with dread. At least there were no cars waiting in line to be searched by the officers.

Enrique said something excitedly to Rachel that she did not understand. She said something excitedly back to him which he did not understand. Marta was moaning in pain. By then they were bearing down on the checkpoint. An agent stood in the path of the truck, wearing body armor and holding a rifle. Enrique honked the horn. Rachel screamed out the window – "Get out of the way. Follow us. Woman in labor!"

She had no idea if they heard a word she yelled as the old pickup sailed through the checkpoint. The *migra* agents scrambled into their trucks and gave hot pursuit. Horns, lights, sirens followed the truck all the way to the edge of town.

They made it. About half an hour after leaving the tank in the desert, the truck pulled into the driveway of the little private medical clinic on the outskirts of Portales. The locals called it the "Doc in the Box". It wasn't much of a clinic; just a way station between a hurt and a real cure, a place for curing earaches and skin rashes and getting a few stitches.

As the truck pulled into the driveway, it was surrounded immediately with a swarm of Border Patrol vehicles and armed men. As soon as Marta and

Rachel got out of the truck, they stood down and helped Marta get into the clinic. Meanwhile, others of them handcuffed Enrique and were leading him off to one of the *migra* trucks.

"Wait a damn minute," Rachel protested before she even had a chance to form a conscious opinion about what was happening. "Stop right there."

The *migra* officers stopped.

Rachel walked toward them and put her face in theirs. "You just stop right now, turn around, and march that fellow into the clinic and let him be with his woman till the baby comes."

The agents, speechless, embarrassed, did as they were told. One of them came back out and spoke to Rachel.

"So, lady, what makes this any of your business?" he asked.

"I found them out by a tank on our ranch, on the edge of the Tohono reservation. Now you tell me, what is a decent human being to do?"

After a pause he answered: "Another U.S. citizen, thanks to you."

"Another human being on this earth, thanks to God," she said.

The officer's mouth tried to form words that would not come.

After being questioned, Rachel went into the clinic and sat in a plastic chair in the waiting area. After a while the clerk at the admitting desk spoke. "So you brought us a new citizen tonight, eh? These people will do anything for a U.S. birth certificate, won't they? Wait till the last minute, then try to get across. If you had left her out there, you know there'd be no proof that the kid was born on this side, no *acto de nacimiento*, no U.S. birth certificate. It's all because of you that this kid will be a citizen. Are you proud? Oh well." The nurse shook her head in disgusted resignation.

Rachel didn't know what to say. How many times had she said the same thing, in so many words? How many times had she cursed these people who had no respect for the laws of the United States, no respect for the sanctity of the nation's borders, these people who sometimes stole cars and trucks from local people in their desperate rush to get deep enough into the country to escape the watchful eye of immigration officials? And now, here she was, facilitating an act of illegal immigration. The child would be a U.S. citizen, and this would make it easier for the parents to someday claim residence. She had just opened the immigration floodgate a bit wider.

The moans of Marta in labor could be heard in the front waiting room.

"Have any kids?" Rachel asked the clerk.

"No."

"Well, let me tell you something," said Rachel. "Motherhood is its own country. All mothers are citizens of it, and that is why I gave her the ride."

Silence.

"Know how the Mexicans say 'give birth'?" asked the clerk.

"No, I only know a few words of Spanish," answered Rachel.

"*'Dar la luz'*," said the clerk. "It means 'to give light.' Kind of a neat way of saying it, huh?" They sat in silence. Twinkly lights flashed in the lobby, over a plastic Christmas tree decorated with Mylar tinsel.

An hour later, when the door to the treatment area opened, they could hear the cry of the baby. The doctor invited both of them in. The mother lay on the bed with a wan smile, a perfect baby girl, Monica, curled on her breasts. Enrique grinned. He smelled strongly of sweat, not surprising after his ordeal. He had walked about 30 miles over very rough country just to get to the tank, to say nothing of running with his pregnant wife in his arms. Marta lifted the swaddled baby up and handed her to Enrique, who wept as soon as he held the child against his body. He kissed her, kissed the mother, and said "*Nos vemos*"— we'll see each other later. "*Me voy a regresar, de veras*"—I'll be back, for sure—he whispered.

The agent who had been in the waiting room with Rachel pulled a camera out of his pocket. He told Rachel to stand next to the young family, and then took some pictures which he promised to send to Rachel. Then the agent handcuffed Enrique, marched him out of the "Doc in the Box" and into a waiting *migra* van, and drove off into the dark.

For reasons Rachel never understood, *la migra* took no interest in detaining Marta and the baby. Rachel picked them up outside the clinic after the nurse phoned her, and she drove them to the barrio in Tucson. Rachel watched them merge into a sea of humanity whose possession of green cards or citizenship papers, or lack thereof, could never be determined just by looking at them walking or driving on the streets of the city. The futility of the U.S. border policy impressed itself on Rachel as she drove west toward home.

"I never heard from the family again," Rachel told me. "For a while I worried about them. And I was mad at the way the father was treated. Then I decided I should take my feelings and channel them into action that was worthwhile."

***

I finally found motivation to do well in at least one subject. The Spanish teacher was shocked that I went from C's to A's almost overnight. I spent extra time in the language lab at Portales High and practiced conversation often with the old lady who sold tamales downtown. She and I called it *intercambio*—exchange—where she would help me with a little Spanish, and I would help her with a little English. It made a big difference in my pronunciation. Except that my teacher wondered why I was speaking Castellano instead of Mexican Spanish. Finally, we figured it out. I was lisping because my *intercambio* partner had no front teeth.

In a few months I felt confident enough to make my own phone call to Rosa in Tuscon. It took several attempts before I reached her, because it was somebody else's cell phone. With some difficulty I learned from her that *migra* had contacted her for more information about Ángel.

***

"Your fake ID won't work here, Mike," I said, as we pulled up near the all-night market. "This is a small town."

"No problem. Watch," said Mike as he got out of the car. Mike approached Emily Luis. He flipped her a few bills and she went inside the liquor store and returned with a 12-pack of cheap beer and a little paper bag. She gave Mike the twelve-pack, and she stumbled away toward the plaza with her wrapped reward.

When she wasn't in jail, or in rehab, or in the hospital, Emily Luis was leaning against the *portales* in the plaza, sprawled on the cool pavement, sleeping off a drunk. It didn't take much imagination to see that at one time she had been a beauty: a small woman with high cheekbones, now swollen and bruised.

"Hey, it's Papago tradition," she told me when I met her for the first time outside the Rinconada Cafe on the plaza. Her hand was quivering, spilling the coffee out of the paper cup she was holding. "Our people used to drink *saguaro* wine till they barfed it all up, as part of the rain ceremony. If I don't drink, the rain won't fall in the summer, then the wells will run dry and my people will die of thirst," she chuckled.

"But your people didn't do that every day, did they? Wasn't that only for ceremonies?" I asked.

"Yeah, but that's because the *saguaros* put out fruit only once a year, and they made the wine out of the fruit. But hey, now you can get vodka every day. That's good. More rain for my people," she laughed hoarsely.

***

"Mike, that was wrong, giving her money to buy booze. Look at her; she's going to die from drinking," I complained, holding the 12-pack in my lap. We drove by her as she stepped sloppily toward the plaza, her tongue flicking out of her toothless mouth every few seconds.

"Give it up, Saint Josh. We're all gonna die, man. She'll just die sooner than us. Now chill, don't worry about it. It's not my fault she's an alkie." Mike's primer-gray Camaro, its glass-pack mufflers rumbling, bounced up the dirt alley behind his house.

A cold wind blew down Cobre Mountain into town and around us as we got out of the car. Mike's dad had gone to visit his girlfriend in Phoenix, so all was clear for a party that night.

After a few beers and bong hits, after listening to increasingly banal conversations about the latest cars and the loosest girls in town, I pretended to go to the bathroom and instead slipped down the hall and out to the back yard. The air was perfectly clear; a thin slice of moon hung above the mountain. The shadows of the rocks and the *saguaros* were outlined in the vague light from the town of Portales. The stars shivered in the cold wind. I didn't intend to whisper

"Lord Jesus Christ have mercy upon me" over and over. But I did. And when I caught myself doing it, my heart ached for Emily Luis. Vividly, I imagined her lying on the pavement, shaking in the cold. "Lord Jesus Christ, have mercy upon her," I prayed. I thought, what am I doing at this dumb party, when right now Emily Luis is passed out someplace downtown, shivering to death? I slipped out the back gate of the yard and closed it behind me, and headed down the alley toward town.

I walked through the *portales* from one end to the other, but Emily was nowhere to be seen. I walked behind the buildings that faced the plaza, looking behind the dumpsters. Just as I was about to give up on my search, I was blinded by the searchlight of a police car.

It was Tommy Keady, one of our town's five cops.

"What's up, young man?" Tommy asked me in his baritone voice.

"Uhhh, nothing, really."

"Mind if I see your ID?" asked Tommy.

I obliged. I hoped the aromas of beer and weed had worn off.

"Karl Stoneburner's son? Your dad works for the Phelps Dodge? Aren't you the kid who had the visions?"

"Yes," I groaned, wishing there was some way to redefine myself.

"You know it's just a bit unusual for somebody to be walking behind all the stores at 10:30 at night on a Friday when all the stores are closed. You can understand my curiosity, I hope," rumbled Tommy, a big guy with an impassive, jowly face. Ronnie Morales called Tommy a "wanna-be," one that put on a show of being tough. "Tommy must have seen too many cop shows on TV," said Ronnie. "Like this place is L.A. or something."

"I was looking for Emily Luis," I said. "I saw her earlier this evening and she looked drunk. I was worried about her, because it is pretty cold tonight. I went looking for her to see if she was okay."

"You are a friend of Emily Luis?" asked Tommy.

"No. I just know who she is, that's all. I got worried about her," I said.

"You care about what happens to her? Or are you going to get her to buy you some more beer?"

"Really, Mr. Keady—I, uh, yeah, I was with some guys who got her to buy beer, okay? And yeah, I'll admit it to you, I had some of those beers tonight. But I got really upset about her, because she looked so sick. I'm not out to get any more beer. I just couldn't handle it, thinking about how bad off she looked. It was bugging me all evening, and I couldn't stand it anymore, so I left the party to find her."

"You really want to see her?" asked Tommy.

"Yeah."

"Well then, hop in the car and I'll show you," said Tommy.

I paused, surprised.

"Come around the other side, and get in. I'll take you to her," insisted Tommy.

I got in the passenger seat and Tommy drove too fast down the alley a few blocks to the rec center. Behind the swimming pool bathrooms there was a lump under a blanket.

"She's sleeping it off," said Tommy. "I gave her the blanket. I always carry a few in the trunk. She'll be okay; she won't freeze."

"Isn't there something else we can do to help her?" I asked.

"She's been an alcoholic for a very long time," explained Tommy. "I've put her in jail, I've helped her get into detox, I worked with the tribe to get her into a long term alcohol recovery program. She even did the Indian sweat lodge thing to get the booze out of her system. But when she gets out of jail or a program, she always comes back here and drinks again, every time. She and I have a deal now. As long as she is willing to go sleep it off someplace, I won't give her a ticket for being drunk in public."

"Is that all we can do?"

"I don't know. It's all I can think to do," replied Tommy. "I really feel sorry for her. One of these days we're going to check up on her in the morning and she'll be dead."

Tommy drove me to my house.

"You keep it under control, Josh. Don't wind up like Emily; alcoholism is a bad business," lectured Tommy.

"Yes, sir."

As I walked up the gravel driveway, I repeated the Jesus Prayer, focusing on Emily.

8. I Am That I Am

They were black. That alone was unusual in Portales. I listened to their pitch.

"Come on in!" I said, swinging wide the screen door.

Dad sputtered in exasperation. He tossed the *Arizona Republic* weekend edition onto his stuffed chair and went to the garage, to work on things he actually could fix.

"Have a seat," I said, ushering them into the living room.

"Interesting things you have here," said the woman.

"Yeah, my dad's a geologist. He loves rocks and fossils. Dad? Dad? Where are you?" There was no answer. "Funny, he was here a minute ago."

The man and woman, a married couple, explained that they wanted to see if I was interested in studying the Bible with them. I asked if they were ministers.

"All Jehovah's Witnesses do ministry. For my day job, I'm the operations manager of an electronics company. My wife's day job is being a title company officer. We work in Phoenix."

"And you live all the way down here in Portales?"

"No, we live in Phoenix, too. We come down here on weekends."

"To knock on doors? Whoa, you must be dedicated," I said.

They asked me a bit about myself, and I in turn asked them some questions.

"Why are you Jehovah's Witnesses and not something else?"

"Because through the Witnesses, God's word was opened up to us more completely than anywhere else," said the woman. The man and the woman were dressed professionally, much fancier than the usual Levis and flannel shirts that people wore in Portales in the wintertime.

They explained that all the answers to life's hardest questions were to be found in the Bible, and that through Bible study and a faithful life, all life's hardest problems would be solved.

"I go to a Baptist church a lot," I said. "They are really serious about the Bible there. Is anything different between what you teach and what the Baptists say?"

"Oh, we have had many Baptists take our course of Bible study and profit greatly from it," said the man. He went on to explain that about 300,000 people from all denominations and backgrounds all over the world are baptized as Jehovah's Witnesses every year.

"What's Jehovah?" I asked.

"That's God's name in the Bible," replied the man.

"I thought it was just God, or the Lord."

"No, those are just words used by the Hebrews in place of the name of God, which was Jehovah."

"I thought that when Moses asked God who God was, God said 'I AM'. So wouldn't God's name be I AM?" I asked.

"No, no. I AM is not God's name. Jehovah is his name. But Jehovah exists—he *is*—and that is what God said to Moses. He told Moses that he existed."

"So what about heaven and hell? Who do you think is going to heaven, and who do you think is going to hell?"

The couple explained that there is no hell. Instead, those who don't go to heaven just cease to exist. "It is as if they had never been," said the woman. "Christian faith is not about punishment. It is about gaining eternal life."

"Those who are not saved will return to dust: ashes to ashes, dust to dust," continued the man.

"So who gets into heaven?"

"The Bible tells us that 144,000 people will be sealed into the new heaven and will rule the earth from above. All others who are saved will have life everlasting in a wonderful, regenerated earth. It will be a perfect world: no sickness, no war, no hunger, no crime, no drugs. Peace and plenty for all," smiled the man. He showed me a brochure depicting happy people of all races walking through orchards and fields in the sunshine. I was fascinated with the tract, noticing that it had its own distinctive graphic style, clearly out of the cultural mainstream, just as was the case with Mormon and Seventh-day Adventist literature.

"So only 144,000 will actually get to heaven. But you baptize 300,000 every year. Don't we have a math problem here? Doesn't sound like too many of your people are going to make it to heaven," I observed.

They had a ready answer for that. "Jehovah God will solve all the math problems. We don't have to worry about that. That is not our place. We don't have to be afraid. God wants us to be happy, he wants us to join him in the perfect world he is preparing for us. Our job is to study his Word, follow it faithfully, and trust in God to fulfill his promises."

Over the next two hours, I grilled them about what their worship was like, how they were organized. Then I asked them what they were they doing about the people coming across the border.

"We are reaching out to them with Bible study in the jails," said the woman. "You know some of them get locked up for a while, so we visit them and offer them encouragement and Bible teaching."

"But what about the people drying up and dying of thirst in the desert trying to come across? What are you doing about that? Anything?" I asked.

"Well, no, we aren't really doing anything about that. It's a touchy subject, immigration policy and illegals," said the man. "We don't get involved in political issues like that. The Bible tells us to render unto Caesar that which is Caesar's, and to render unto God that which is God's." They went on to explain that Jehovah's Witnesses have gone to jail many times over the years for refusing to obey laws that were contrary to Bible teaching. The couple told me several stories of imprisonment and martyrdom of Jehovah's Witnesses around the world. They have gone to jail for refusing induction into the military, and in some countries even for refusing to salute the flag.

"So you don't get involved in any kind of politics?" I asked.

"No, that is of the world, and we don't take sides on such things," the woman answered. "Our first priority is salvation, to make sure that all people have a chance to hear the Bible truth. That takes up all our free time, doesn't it, honey?"

"Yes, it does," the man smiled back to his wife.

"I guess you people are pretty serious about your religion, then," I said.

"Very serious indeed," replied the woman.

"We'd risk our lives gladly for the Bible truth," said the man.

And I wondered: For what, and for whom, was I willing to risk my life?

***

On the way home from the youth group meeting at the Baptist Church at about ten that next Sunday night, I approached the Plaza from the south and had the sudden urge to turn right and drive behind the Chavez Market to see if Emily Luis was okay. The thought of her sleeping outside on these cold and windy nights overwhelmed me with sadness. And there she was, propped up against the back wall of the market, sitting on a pile of cardboard, wrapped in a dirty blanket, her high cheekbones shadowed by the moonlight beaming down on her. A bottle of cheap wine was by her side. I pulled a wool blanket from behind the seat of my truck and took it over to Emily.

"Are you all right? " I asked her, approaching her cautiously.

"Who's that there?" she yelled, groping around on the ground for something.

"It's me, Josh Stoneburner. Remember me?"

"Oh yeah. The kid who saw *La Virgen*. You're a nice kid. I remember you," she said. "What do you want? Too late to buy you beer, isn't it?"

"No, no, Emily. I don't want you to buy any beer for me," I said. "I just came to see if you are okay."

"I'm okay. I'm always okay." The odor of metabolized alcohol surrounded her like a force-field.

"I brought you a blanket. I don't want you to be cold out here," I said.

"I'm okay, really. But that's nice. Thanks." She took the blanket and wrapped it around the other one, over her shoulders.

"Is there anything I can do for you now?" I asked, frustrated that I couldn't think of anything else to do.

"You wanna fuck me?" she said, loudly, laughing.

"No, no, Emily, I don't want to fuck you."

"What? I'm not good enough for a handsome young stud like you?" she laughed, suddenly grabbing my hand.

"No, no, that's not it. I mean, Emily, I just want to help you somehow if I can. It's cold out here and I hate to think of you out here like this."

She gripped my hand with both of hers, pulling me toward her, as I tried to pull away. "Good boy, good boy, Josh. Nice boy." Finally, she let go. "I'm okay. I'm gonna be all right. It's very nice of you to come by and see me. It's like this. I'm gonna die someday, probably pretty soon. I drink too much, see? It is gonna kill me. Elder Brother comes around here and teases me. He talks crazy at me and tries to trick me into following him. But someday I'll probably follow him. Any time now. But hey, it's not bad. I'll die right here with the moon shining down on me. And nobody will care. Just another dead drunk Indian, that's all they will say. It doesn't matter."

"Oh yes it does matter," I said. "It does matter if you live or die. It matters to me."

Emily laughed loud. "You're a nice boy. Go home. Take care of yourself." And she took another swig of the wine.

***

"Dad."

"Josh?"

Dad was in the garage, tinkering with his antique electronic equipment.

"I want you to come along tomorrow to help with the water stations. I think it is a cool thing. I want you to see what's going on," I said.

"What good would I do anybody?" Dad asked.

"I just want to show you what I'm up to. You know, a father-son communication thing."

He laughed. "Yeah. I'm not so great in that department, am I? Well sure, if you want me to come, I'll come."

***

"You go with her," I said, aiming him at Rachel's truck. "I gotta go pick up Pastor Kate. I'll meet you at Rachel's ranch."

"Okay …" grumbled Dad, not quite understanding why he had to ride with somebody else. I drove the truck down to the Federated Church.

We worked all day. Dad and Rachel were on one team, Father Crespi and I were on another, refilling tanks, cleaning up trash around them, and placing new ones. Five new blue flags, marking the new tanks, waved defiantly against the demon of thirst, and fluttered in the breeze over the desert at sundown that evening. The crew enjoyed a dinner at Rachel's house prepared by the Women's Society of the Federated Church.

"So Karl," said Father Crespi. "Your son, Josh here, he is a fine young man."

I was enjoying my dad's further discomfort.

"Yeah, he is. A fine young knucklehead—I mean, a fine young man."

"You have raised him well. By yourself, I understand?" said Father Crespi, between forks full of tuna casserole.

"Yes, so anything he does wrong, you can blame me for it," answered Dad.

"And whatever he does right, you can claim credit for it, too." said Pastor Kate.

"I wouldn't go that far," said Dad. "I'm only his father."

"So does Josh get his curiosity about religion from you?" asked Father Crespi.

"Like I say, I'm only his father. That is an area where he can take all the credit for himself," said Dad. He was really in over his head now. I noticed that from the head of the table, silently, Rachel Parmenter was watching Dad, her eyes smiling with soft wrinkles. "So it's my turn to ask a few questions," Dad continued. "Why are you religious folks so interested in *mojados*?"

Pastor Kate was ready with an answer. "Because that is what we are called to do as Christians: to stand with the poor and oppressed. So we formed an interfaith, ecumenical covenant group to address the issues of migrants, and came up with a plan of action."

"You think this is going to solve the problem? Putting water out there for them to drink? Hey," said Dad, waving his fork for emphasis, "I don't think the U.S. immigration policy makes any sense either. Not that I have any alternatives to propose. But let's get realistic here. You put water stations in the desert, that just attracts the *mojados*. More of them come across, more of them die. You make it hard for them, deny them water, fewer come across, fewer of them die. It sounds harsh, but when you look at it practically …"

"Karl," said Rachel, "when you are dealing with human beings, when you see them suffering, sometimes you do things for them that aren't entirely practical."

***

I sat across from Seedless in the library, reading a book about the legal rights of undocumented aliens. Seedless crumpled a piece of paper, tossed it a few feet into the trash can by the librarian's desk, startling her. He pulled out another sheet of paper and resumed writing.

Another of his letters, this one to a girl in Brazil:

Dear Paula:

I read about the floods in your country. Terrible! I am writing just to tell you I'm thinking about you and your family a lot right now. Let me know how it is going. I sure hope nothing bad happened to your village during the hurricane.

I wish I could send you my raincoat. I don't use it much here, since I live in the desert. But I'll bet you could use it, though it's probably too big for you. It sure does a nice job of keeping a person dry.

But since I can't send it to you, I hope you can find other kinds of protection from the bad weather. If you don't have anything else to put on over you, I hope you find some love and care to put on over

*your heart from all the fear and confusion that
must be going on around you. It's what everybody
needs. I need it, too. It doesn't rain much here, so I
don't need that kind of protection very often. But
there are a lot of times when I get sad and need
protection for my heart. And then I think about
how much harder life is for you guys, and I stop
feeling so sad for myself.*

Your friend,
C.D. Thompson

After a game of chess with Seedless, which I won,
I left the library for a walk under the *portales*. There
was a storefront on the plaza I had never checked out
before.

Nobody else was there but an older woman sitting
at the front desk.

The room had the air of a place seldom entered;
the stillness of books never opened; carpets never
soiled.

I had passed by the Christian Science Reading
Room many times, on my way between the ice cream
shop and the Chavez Market. It was a little space on
the plaza, off in a corner under the *portales*. Long ago
I asked Dad about it, but all he said was, "Those guys
are really crazy. They don't believe in going to the
doctor when they're sick. Please leave them alone."

"Hello, young man. How can I help you?" asked
the woman. She was a big, cheery person in her late
60s. She pulled her reading glasses off her nose and
let them hang by their chain over her dress.

"I don't know anything about Christian Science," I said. "So I want to find out."

She was eager to help me, giving a brief introduction to "Science", as she called it. The woman's name was Glossie Protheroe. "Actually, my name is Glossolalia. I was raised Pentecostal, and 'glossolalia' is the Greek word for speaking in tongues. But I go by Glossie."

I knew no more about Pentecostalism than about Christian Science. Yet another religion to explore.

"Why is this place always empty?" I asked. "I heard that you guys don't go to doctors. Do most Christian Scientists die young, and that's why there are so few of them?"

Glossie laughed. "No, we don't die any younger than other people on average. I think we probably live longer."

"Then where is everybody?"

"In time, we believe all shall come to Truth," she answered.

She proceeded to outline the teachings of Mary Baker Eddy. Yet another religion founded by a woman with health problems, I noticed. But at least this one still had women in its leadership.

Glossie read aloud a passage from Science and Health: (S&H 252:32) "I am Spirit. Man, whose senses are spiritual, is my likeness. He reflects the infinite understanding, for I am Infinity. The beauty of holiness, the perfection of being, imperishable glory—all are Mine, for I am God. I give immortality to man, for I am Truth. I include and impart all bliss, for I am Love. I give life, without beginning and without end, for I am Life. I am supreme and give all, for I am Mind. I am the substance of all, because I AM THAT I AM."

"Wait a minute. I AM THAT I AM. That's in the Bible. God said it to Moses in the burning bush," I declared.

"Very good. Most of Science and Health is based on the Bible," said Glossie. "It is a spiritual explanation for the Bible, revealing its inner meaning."

Glossie explained that Christian Science is based on the principle that mind is real and matter is an unreal illusion. As a person cultivates his or her spiritual nature and becomes more aware of it, the corruptions of matter fall naturally away. Disease is a manifestation of belief in the reality of matter, which is unreal.

"But if mind is all that is real, and matter isn't, then doesn't that mean that what we think of as matter is really part of mind, and therefore mind and matter really are the same thing?" I asked.

Glossie tried to explain that matter is an error in thinking, and that once corrected, truth and love can prevail. "That's what the story of Moses and the burning bush is really all about," she said. "When God says I AM, it means that God is real being, which is mind. Matter has no being, so when God says I AM, God must be referring to mind or spirit."

I felt like the conversation was going in circles. "But there is a difference between what I think and imagine and what is real," I said. "There is a difference between thoughts and, well, hods," I declared. "Know what a hod is?"

"Not exactly," replied Glossie.

"Neither do I. But my dad says hods are bad. He says you have to carry them all the time if you don't do your schoolwork. Whatever a hod is, there is a difference between my idea of a hod and an actual hod. They aren't the same thing. And if the idea of a hod is mind, and the actual hod is mind, then there must be two kinds of mind. One that you carry all the time, that hurts your arms, and one that you just think about carrying. It seems like you've just redefined words, that's all."

We talked in such loops for a while longer before I decided to leave, but not before Glossie invited me to come to the Christian Science Church sometime for worship.

***

It was a little building at the edge of town, simple, with a small steeple. Inside, there were a few rows of pews facing a panel in the center that was blank except for the words "God is Love" in the center. On one side of the panel was this quote from Mary Baker Eddy: "Divine love always has met and always will meet every human need", and on the other was this quote from the Bible: "Ye shall know the truth and the truth shall make you free." There were about ten people in the church. The hymns were old and stale, the Lord's Prayer was passionless, and the soloist's tremolo was like dragging a patio chair across cement.

There was nothing original about the sermon: two people stood up and read out loud from the Bible and from Mary Baker Eddy's Science and Health for too long. But the very boredom of it induced me into a meditative state. Random words from the Bible and Mary Baker Eddy somehow lodged in my consciousness and worked on me, giving me a sense of serenity.

I reflected upon the idea that all that is real is Spirit or Mind, and that matter is a falsehood, an illusion. Just what is reality? I wondered. Just a bunch of mental experiences, with nothing physically real upon which they are based? What if my brain is really in a bottle in a laboratory with electrodes coming out of it, feeding it inputs that trick me into thinking that what I experience is actually real? What if everything I think is real is actually an illusion, put into my mind by God or by some other being more powerful than I am? If Spirit is all there is, then what I saw in the cholla cactus was every bit as real as …

My meditation was interrupted by that old familiar feeling. What caused it? I wondered. The absolute stillness of the room? The lack of inputs into my sensorium? Or was it the attractive woman who was reading at the podium? Was it her precise and deliberate diction as she read and turned the pages of the text dictated by the Mother Church, and then swept back her long black hair? Or was it all in my mind—the throbbing, and my interpretation of what

I saw and heard of the woman? Were these errors of thought, or did they serve some mysterious spiritual purpose?

***

At that moment I remembered something that Seedless told me one night at the library when we were playing chess.

Seedless asked me if I had really meant to put my queen diagonally in front of his pawn.

"Oh, no—" and I moved it back from certain doom. "No, I didn't mean to do that."

"Well if you didn't mean to do it, how did it happen?"

"It was a mistake—I wasn't looking," I said.

"Your eyes were open. I saw you looking. You thought about it for a long time," he said.

"But I didn't see the pawn."

"Even though your eyes were open and your brain was on?" Seedless challenged me. "How is it that people do things they don't want to do, when the consequences are plain to see?"

"I guess we don't really have complete control of ourselves," I answered.

"St. Augustine said that, too," replied Seedless. "It's still your move."

I played it safe and shifted the position of my knight instead of moving my queen. "Who was St. Augustine?"

"Augustine was a Christian philosopher from the fourth century."

"How did he figure out that people don't have complete self-control?" I asked.

"From his own observations. He wrote about them in his book, *City of God*. He knew that men get erections sometimes when and where they do not want to get them. And when they do want to get a hard-on, sometimes it doesn't happen. He said it was all because of the sin of Adam in the Garden of Eden. If Adam hadn't eaten the forbidden fruit, men would be able to control their penises just as easily as I can control my index finger." Seedless poked his finger in the air, raising and lowering it, to demonstrate.

"Jesus, Seedless, quiet down," I whispered, as the librarian scowled at us.

***

Just what was this information under my pants telling me, as I worshipped in the pew of the Christian Science Church? Was it real? Or was it just an illusion, a figment of my mistaken belief in the reality of matter? If I stopped believing in its material existence, would this illusion pass away? I tried to meditate on the words that the woman was reading, instead of focusing on the woman herself, but she kept being there no matter how hard I tried to deny her material existence. I was transfixed by the way she pursed her full lips when forming words. I tried to believe that the throbbing under my Levis wasn't real, but that just made it more insistent in its claim to actual existence.

When the service was over, my difficulty wasn't. I waited in the pew for a while before standing. I pulled out the *Christian Science Sentinel* magazine from the pew rack in front of me, and, as gracefully as I could, covered my groin with it as I shuffled with the crowd out the front door.

Sure enough, as soon as I was in my truck and out of danger of embarrassment, the throbbing subsided. "What was that all about?" I asked as I drove away.

On the way home, I thought about the nature of reality. The part that made sense to me in Christian Science was the idea of taking the mind seriously, treating thoughts as if they were real things. I realized that I didn't spend much time considering my own thoughts. I just thought them without really looking at them. What a waste of my life, to fail to notice my thoughts. What an amazing opportunity I had to examine them, to fully appreciate and experience what was going on in my own mind. My inner world seemed like a vast and trackless wilderness begging to be explored.

***

Glossolalia Protheroe called me to ask if I'd wash her place at the Rancho Nolontomo mobile home park outside of town. "I heard through the grapevine that you are in the business," she said.

When I was done with the job, she invited me in to her mobile home and fed me a lunch of tuna sandwiches and lemonade. "I saw you at the church. You left awfully fast," she said, smiling.

"Had to get back to work," I lied.

"What did you think?"

"Well, if you really want the truth, even though it was boring, I got a lot out of it. I meditated during the service and thought a lot about the idea that thoughts are real, not just floaty things that disappear after you think them."

"Very interesting," declared Glossie. She was watering plants in pots hanging in macramé holders, dangling from the acoustic-tiled ceiling of her kitchen. Her glasses were tipped up and tucked into her gray hair.

"That is the part of your religion that I like," I said. "It makes me think about thought. But tell me something. You said you grew up Pentecostal. What is that religion all about?"

"In Acts chapter 2, the disciples of Jesus got together and started talking in different languages, and everybody understood them, even though the disciples didn't know all the languages before. That was when the Holy Spirit came to them, as Jesus promised would happen. It happened at Pentecost, which means fifty days after Passover, when Jesus and the disciples had the Last Supper. The Pentecostal churches believe that the coming of the Holy Spirit is marked by signs and wonders like performing healings and speaking in tongues."

"So why did you quit that church and become a Christian Scientist?" I asked.

"My father was the treasurer of the church where I grew up," she answered. "He caught the preacher embezzling money from the congregation. We were so disgusted that we never went back to that kind of church again."

"Are all Pentecostal people embezzlers?" I wondered.

"No, of course not. There were wonderful people there. But there was too much drama in it for me. It started to feel like more of a show than a serious church. People falling on the floor, rolling around and blabbering. Preachers yelling and crying. I think that when you get swept away with emotions it is easier to be tempted to do things like stealing. You see, emotions aren't the same thing as Spirit. I wanted something with more discipline and order to it, but that was still very spiritual and focused on healing. That is what I found in Science."

***

I went to the library to check out a book by a historian about the origins of the Christian Science Church. Seedless nodded at me, then went back to work on his letters.

This one was to a boy in Jordan:

Dear Hamid:

I'm so glad that you are my "adopted son"! You have come a long way in a short time—passing the test to get into a really good high school after being in elementary school for only a few years. You are my glory and joy!

I remember that only a few years ago, you couldn't go to school because you had to help your grandfather take care of his goatherd. You worked very hard and very fast to be able to pass the test for high school. Sure, I helped with paying for the elementary school fees. But you did the work, and you earned every penny of it!

I feel lucky to know you. I appreciate your nice thank-you letter, but really, I'm not proud of myself. I'm proud of you; knowing about your graduation makes me happy.

Your friend,
C.D. Thompson

9. Who Is Elder Brother?

I read Acts chapter 2 in the Bible when I got home that evening. The part that resonated with me had nothing to do with speaking in tongues. Rather, I was fascinated with verses 44–47, which said that the followers of Jesus "had all things in common; and they sold their possessions and goods and distributed them to all, as any had need. And day by day, attending the temple together and breaking bread in their homes, they partook of food with glad and generous hearts ...." If sharing everything with each other was also something that Pentecostal people did, then it was time for me to pay them a visit.

The chance came soon. At the Chavez Market, I ran into a friend from the Cuprite Baptist youth group meeting, a Papago kid named Ben Jose. He told me that on Wednesday night he and his family were going to "tent meeting" out on the rez. I asked Ben if I could go along.

The road from Portales to Tucson cut right through the middle of the reservation. I passed by the concrete grottoes filled with plastic flowers and pictures and surrounded by little patches of green AstroTurf, reminders of the carnage that regularly occurred on that stretch of highway. Ben once told me that one of his uncles had died on that road. "Fell asleep and crashed his pickup into the mesquites."

I turned onto the side road to meet Ben at his family's place. The road was narrow and the pavement was crumbling. I drove about ten miles before seeing the cluster of mobile homes and little houses and rusted vehicles where Ben lived with his extended family.

The family was getting into their battered camper van when I arrived. Ben hopped into my truck and we followed the van back to the main road.

"So your family goes to the tent meetings and to the Baptist mission, too?"

"Yes. Pastor Bob doesn't think we should go to tent meeting because he says that is not the Bible way. He thinks that we are in a different dispensation than in Bible times," said Ben.

"What do you mean by 'dispensation'?" I asked as we bounced down the road.

"A different time. God has given each part of history its own special purposes. I read about it in the Scofield Bible. Pastor Bob gave one to my dad," said Ben. "Pastor Bob thinks that speaking in tongues was a wonder and a sign for a previous dispensation, but not for the one we are in now. But my family thinks anything from God is good. Holiness preachers are good, and Indian medicine is good, and so is the Baptist mission. And the Seventh-day mission, and the Mormon mission, and the Catholic mission, too. Pastor Bob is a good person, but he doesn't understand the Red path. I think maybe we have our own dispensations, our own time periods, that are different than the white man's."

We turned down another reservation road and drove for another 15 miles until I saw a big tent next to a corral.

The preacher was a black man, and his assistant was a white woman. The song leader and electronic keyboard player had a Spanish accent. Flies made lazy loops in the hot, still air under the canvas as the crowd of about thirty Papagos sat quietly in the wooden folding chairs in the dust.

"They don't call 'em spirits for nothing," exhorted the preacher, leaning over the wooden pulpit at the crowd. "Nuh-uhh. No. They call 'em spirits because they are of the devil, who is a spirit. Alcohol is the physical manifestation of the spiritual reality of evil. But God has the power. The power to cast out evil spirits of every kind, yes, even distilled spirits. The name of Jesus has the power. In the name of Jesus you will be healed of your addiction, set free, as Saint Paul says, to 'obtain the glorious liberty of the children of God'. See what I'm saying? You all hear me?"

The crowd nodded and quietly at first and louder and louder said "Amen. Speak it, brother."

"If you want to be set free, though, you have got to replace one spirit with another. As the Lord Jesus says, when you drive the evil spirits out of a house, you got to get the Holy Spirit in there to replace them. Because if you leave the house empty, then the demons will just come back in and invite their friends. Isn't that how it is, sisters and brothers, with you and me? Tell me something. Have you ever left your house empty? Tried to kick the booze, but didn't put something else in your life to take its place? What happened? Tell me about it, tell me true. Those spirits, those distilled spirits, they came back, didn't they? Come on now, tell me…"

"Yes, yes. Speak it!"

"They came back, didn't they? And invited their demonic pals. Laziness, gluttony, anger, hatred, violence. Like a bunch of bad roommates, yes?"

"Yes!"

"Like distant relatives you didn't want to see in the first place, who come to visit and stay and eat all your food and keep you up at night. Yes?"

"Yes, amen! Say it!" The stereotype that I had accepted about quiet, placid Indians was beginning to disintegrate.

"Yeah, brothers and sisters, you left your houses empty, and sure enough the devil himself moved right back in with all his wicked pals and had a bigger party than ever, and left your house a bigger mess than it was before you cleaned it out in the first place. Tore it up from the floor up. Stained your carpet, burnt holes in your couch, cleaned out your fridge. Trashed your front yard. Somebody say amen."

The crowd was laughing. "Amen! Yes!"

"Am I just talking about houses? No, I'm talking about you. You are the houses that the devil trashed. You are the ones tore up from the floor up by Satan and all his evil angels. So let's clean house, sisters and brothers. Let's clean house now. Let's get those

demons on up out of there, let's invite them to go
straight to hell. Yes, back to hell from which they
came. And let's right now get the Holy Spirit of the
living God to take up residence in your houses, in
you, yes, *you,* right now. If you are ready to clean
house, and invite the Holy Ghost in where the evil
spirits, the distilled spirits, the spirits of sickness, of
poverty, of violence and hatred, had been before,
then come on up. Come on up and receive the Holy
Spirit through the laying on of hands ..."

A line formed to approach the plywood stage. The
preacher put his hand on the first person's forehead
and her head snapped back as if some unseen force
had blasted out of his motionless palm. She reeled
back and fell on the floor in spasms, wailing in low,
unintelligible syllables. The whole crowd started to
moan and mutter as the next person came forward
and kneeled in front of the preacher. The assistant
and the preacher laid their hands on his shoulder and
prayed loudly that he might be healed of diabetes, "in
the name of Jesus, that name above all names. There
is power in the name of Jesus, power in the name of
Jesus ..." and the song leader hit the keys and led
them in a hymn: "There's power in the name of Jesus,
like no other name I know."

I finally stood up and got in line. I was ready to
clean house. I'd had enough words about God lately.
I was ready for the real thing. For the Holy Spirit to
take me over completely. I felt the power in the
name of Jesus, and I wanted it to take the place of all
impurities in my heart.

The preacher's palm seemed hot, unnaturally so, as it rested on my forehead. When the preacher pulled back his hand, I was gone. There was only light.

***

When I returned to my usual senses, I looked up and saw Ben and his family standing around me. The revival was over. We were the last ones in the tent. Ben's father, Leonard Jose, a big round man with a ponytail, took me by the hand and pulled me up. "Elder Brother got you good, young man," he said gravely. "You come with us. Ben, he'll drive your truck back to our place. We got to watch over you for a while."

Nobody said a word as the camper van bumped along the road back to the Jose family compound. Ben's older sister Betty silently offered me some fry bread. I nibbled at it; it tasted good. The people in the van looked unspeakably beautiful. The fry bread was God, the people in the van were God.

They ushered me into the largest of their mobile homes, an old one with half of its aluminum skirt missing. Inside they cleared a sofa and asked me to sit down in it. They handed me a cold Pepsi. Ben's little sister turned on the television and channel-surfed.

Leonard eased back in his recliner chair with his Pepsi and turned to me. "I hear you have visions. But has the Holy Ghost ever got you before?"

"This is very different than my visions," I said.

"Elder Brother visits in different ways. Visions sometimes, possession sometimes. And no wonder

154

you saw him in a cactus. Cactus is sacred," said Leonard. "Cholla is for healing. Eat cholla buds and they will help you take care of the diabetes. Ever eat peyote cactus?"

"No. I've heard of it, but never tried it," I answered.

Leonard laughed, and the whole recliner chair started shaking. "Hah! You don't *try* peyote! You don't *try* Elder Brother! No, no, young man. Elder Brother tries *you*."

"Who is Elder Brother?" I wondered.

"Holy Ghost, God, Elder Brother, Jesus: all the same," said Leonard.

"Are you saying that when you eat peyote you see the Holy Ghost?" I asked.

"Sometimes. But only when Mescalito wants you to see him."

"Who is Mescalito?"

Leonard laughed again. "Who is Elder Brother?"

***

About a month later, there was a knock at the door.

"Josh, it's a kid named Ben," said Dad.

I went to the door, shirtless. It was Saturday morning, too early for visitors to just show up without calling first. "Ben, what's up?" I asked.

"We're doing a sweat today for the equinox. Maybe you want to come along," said Ben.

Later that day we drove about sixty miles down to Baboquivari, on the other end of the Tohono

O'odham reservation. Ben and Leonard Jose took me in their van up a dirt road to the base of the mountain. Leonard explained to me that Baboquivari was the place where the world began. "Elder Brother I'itoi lives there. The mountain is the umbilical cord where human beings came out of the earth after the great flood at the beginning."

The peak was an enormous stone plug stuck into the crimson evening. It looked like the world both began and ended here, the place was so remote. The van pulled up alongside a bunch of other vehicles. We walked a few hundred yards into a thicket of mesquites. Between the trees, ropes were strung and blue plastic tarps were thrown over them, with big rocks holding down the edges. The makeshift tents surrounded a big bonfire. Flames curled around the rocks that were heating in the fire, and steam emitted from the entrance of each makeshift tent.

Ben, Leonard, and I took off our clothes and entered a tent, where we sat in the fading light. We passed around plastic water bottles and took swigs to replenish ourselves, sweat pouring off our skin and down onto the rocks upon which we sat. Every so often, one of us would go out with a pair of sticks and bring in a new, red-hot rock from the fire. Leonard would periodically splash some water onto the stones, and then I would feel a blast of steam burning my skin, and another wave of sweat would pour out of me. I thought I could take no more, but somehow I stayed until the next splash of water on the rocks. Time passed. How many minutes? How many hours?

Without words. Now and then, Leonard would groan as he shed sweat off his rolls of fat.

When it was over, as we were standing in front of the tent, enjoying the relief of fresh air at midnight, we heard drumming. We walked around an outcrop of rocks and saw a group of people gathering about half a mile away, farther down the base of the mountain. "Let's see what is going on," said Leonard.

The people were mostly white folks, some of them wearing long colorful robes, some naked, one mostly naked with streaks of paint all over his body. One woman, with long, graying hair streaming over her natural fiber dress, held a knobby wooden staff. At the top of the staff was a rose quartz crystal upon which I fixed my eyes.

Some of the people were using a compass to mark out the four directions with stones on the ground. Others were drumming improvisationally, building up a strong beat. At the ends of the points on the ground, they placed big candles. In the center, someone was lighting a bonfire.

"Hail and welcome," said the woman with the wooden staff. "How did you find us?"

"We were doing a sweat further up the mountain," said Leonard.

"Are you Papagos?" asked a shirtless man smeared with oil and wearing buckskin pants with leather fringes.

The Native Americans, all wearing western shirts, Levis, and cowboy boots, nodded. "Tohono O'odham," Leonard gently corrected.

"Cool. We'd love to have you join our Vernal Equinox ceremony," he said eagerly.

The woman with the staff introduced herself as Earth Fire, a priestess from the Institute for Spiritual Convergence in Sedona, Arizona.

"Is this some kind of Wiccan ceremony?" I asked, staring at the rose quartz on her staff. I had been warned by Pastor Bob to stay away from Wiccan people.

"It's a universal ceremony and dance for peace and unity with the Earth and all its beings," replied Earth Fire. "We welcome Native Americans, Christians, Wiccans, pagans of all kinds, people of all religions and no religions. We came to Baboquivari because it is a holy mountain, a sacred place where spiritual energy is concentrated, especially at the solstices and equinoxes."

"Do you worship Satan?" I asked, getting the question out of the way.

"We don't worship evil. There is no evil in the universe. Think of it this way: darkness has no reality; it's only the absence of light. We don't worship darkness, because it is nothing. We worship the good. We invoke the powers of the earth and the sky and work with them to bring balance and peace. What people call Satan or the devil is just a natural force with which we must live in harmony, just as we must live in harmony with all other earth spirits. We must bring the male and female forces into balance, the darker and the lighter forces into harmony."

Ben, Leonard, and I and the others lined up behind the group as it marched and swayed into a circle around the points of the compass. They kept swaying as they continued walking slowly in the circle, clockwise, chanting, "Oh Great Spirit, earth, sun, sky, and sea, you are inside, and all around me."

Earth Fire lit the first candle, for East, and flicked salt and water in that direction as the drums pounded. Everyone lifted their arms and aimed them east, then turned their arms to the center and yelled "Ho!" Then she lit the candle for South, and then West and North, repeating the ritual each time. Then she lifted an earthenware chalice and took a knife and stabbed its blade into the liquid in the chalice and gave a whoop, and everyone whooped with her, and then the drumming thundered and everyone danced wildly. There was a big Native American wicker basket of grain near the fire. Every so often, one of the dancers would run up to it, gather a handful of grain, and toss it into the fire. Everyone would yell "Ho!" and the dance would go on.

A naked man ran up with an earthen bowl of pigment and marked green circles with his finger on our foreheads. I started to dance. Faster and faster I whirled. I looked up at the fire sparks merging with the stars forming spirals as I spun. "Ho!" I yelled, with a power and volume I'd never yelled before. My arms and legs flew like palm fronds in the wind. I felt the drumbeats in my bones. "Ho!" I howled, over and over, as I leaped and turned. I felt like I was plugged into the electrical grid of the cosmos.

On the way back to the Jose's place, I asked Leonard what he thought of the circle ceremony.

"Indian wannabes," he said. "We get a lot of visitors like that, coming out to the rez, trying to practice native ceremonies. It's okay. They mean well, and mostly they don't cause any problems."

"So those folks weren't violating the sacredness of Baboquivari?"

"They did their ceremony just outside the reservation boundary. Some people might think they were too close, but I think they showed enough respect. These people were a little crazy, but I think they were sincere. They were trying to find their way to Elder Brother. I think they are lost in the labyrinth he made to confuse people who look for him. But then, who isn't?"

"Is that the labyrinth on the gate in front of the church at San Xavier?" I asked. A wrought-iron gate with a distinctive pattern on it guarded the entrance to the beautiful Catholic mission on the reservation near Tucson. I had visited the church on a school field trip when I was in the fourth grade. The teacher had explained that the labyrinth was a sacred symbol of the Tohono O'odham.

"Yes, that is it. Elder Brother makes it tough for you to seek him out. So maybe we should not have a lot of judgment about the ways people try to find him," said Leonard, as the van bumped along the road.

***

"Well, how was the sweat lodge?" asked Dad.

"It was hot. Really, really hot, for a long time."

"Any visions?" asked Dad.

"Nope. I got kind of dizzy part of the time, but didn't get any visions."

"How about the Papagos? Did they get any visions?"

"If they did, they didn't tell me about them," I answered.

"So what was it all about?"

"Maybe it wasn't about anything," I mused.

"Pointless, then?" Dad baited me.

"I don't mean pointless. I mean that maybe it wasn't *about* anything. There is a difference. For these people, sitting in hot steam under a weird-looking mountain is the thing to do now and again. They don't seem to need any reasons. They've been living on that land, visiting that mountain, for a long time. I don't know, maybe they forgot the reasons for doing what they do, but they wouldn't be who they are if they didn't do what they do, so they keep doing it," I said.

"That would define pointlessness for me—having no idea of why you do something. That is why I think religion is pointless; when you get down to it, there is no way to explain why anybody would want to do all those rituals and believe all those beliefs," declared Dad.

"This is a pointless conversation," I said.

"Maybe it's pointless for you, but not for me," said Dad. "I think it is useful to reflect on these

161

matters. Maybe you want to quit talking, but I am not done yet."

"No, I don't mean I want to stop talking. I just mean that by your definition, this conversation is pointless," I replied.

"Okay. How so?"

"Because you can't explain why we are having it," I answered. "It's just a ritual. Kind of like religion. You know, you talk, then I talk, and then you talk, and then I talk. You try to figure out why I care about spiritual stuff, and I try to explain. Nothing gets resolved. Neither of us really changes his mind. So it is a pointless ritual. But I think it is still worthwhile. It keeps our relationship going. It connects us to each other in a special way," I said.

"But you just contradicted yourself. If it connects us in a special way, then it does have a point, and therefore it isn't pointless."

"And you contradicted yourself, too, Dad. If this conversation isn't pointless, then religion isn't pointless either. Because religion also connects people to each other in a special way. In fact that is what the word 'religion' means: it is Latin for 'binding together'," I said. "I looked it up in the dictionary."

"Have you looked up 'hod' in the dictionary yet? Because if you keep spacing out on religion instead of getting better grades at school, carrying a hod is the only job you'll be able to get," scolded Dad, with a wink.

***

Dad and I adjusted to the interruptions of pilgrims coming to Portales to visit the sacred cactus of the Virgin of San Lorenzo. The numbers went down steadily, to our relief. But every so often, I was ambushed by people with cameras as I went in and out of the house. People knocked at our door occasionally, begging to talk with me. I learned how to refuse them firmly but politely.

One Saturday morning, when I went outside, I saw Magdalena Gonzales, Grandma Greta's friend, with a group of about thirty pilgrims. When the people saw me, some of them took pictures.

"Can I talk with you privately?" I asked Magdalena. I ushered her into the kitchen of our house and invited her to sit. She was a heavy-set woman, somewhat younger than my Grandma Greta had been. I saw how hard it was for her to climb the trail to the cactus.

"Have you ever had a vision of the Virgin at the cactus?" I asked her.

"Yes, she has spoken to me four times. The first time was just a week after you took us there. She told me to tell everyone that those who are separated from their loved ones, those whose families are kept apart by the border, should pray to her. San Lorenzo was holding up the crescent where she stood."

"Thank God," I said. "Okay. From now on, when anybody asks me about the visions, I'm going to talk about your vision, okay? I can't handle all the attention I'm getting. So from now on, this is all about your vision, not mine. Do we have a deal?"

"But you had the vision first," she answered. "It would not be right to deny that."

"I like your vision a lot better than mine. Yours has some specifics to it. Mine was not clear at all. What does it mean to follow the Virgin? Who is she, anyway? I'm still trying to sort it out. You have no idea how much work I've done to make sense of what I saw and heard. Your vision gives people something to do, it gives directions. So from now on, let's focus on what you heard and saw. All I did was direct you to the cactus."

Reluctantly, she agreed. But the cult of the Virgin of San Lorenzo was not something either of us could control. Not long after that, I learned that a graphics company in Mexico had printed up thousands of *La Virgen de San Lorenzo* prayer cards and car-mirror medallions and key chains. Migrants were carrying them across the border and kissing them as they prayed to her. The images were showing up in more and more roadside grottoes in southern Arizona and in Sonora. I'm sure they littered the migrant trails through the desert.

But there were fewer knocks on the door and fewer paparazzi encounters. The attention had shifted to *La Virgen* herself. One day Magdalena left me a prayer card with the Virgin of San Lorenzo's image on it, on our doorstep, with a post-it note: "Thank you".

10. *La Virgen de Las Vegas*

It was one of those days when teachers have conferences, so Mike and Ronnie and Eddie and I decided to meet for a late breakfast at the Rinconada Cafe on the south corner of the plaza. We packed into the window booth.

"Look," said Ronnie. "There goes one of those ragheads." It was one of the women from the nearby Dar al Islam community outside of Portales. The women wore white scarves and the men wore white lacy skullcaps. They were white people who were members of an Islamic commune.

"Fuck her," said Mike. "I ought to get my pistol and pop a cap in that bitch. She's just another one of those terrorist sympathizers."

"There's no bag limit on terrorists, you know," said Ronnie. "Open season, all year long. Waste her!"

"And then what?" I asked.

"Then she'll be dead, that's what," said Ronnie.

"And then what?" I asked.

"Then the rest of them will get out of here, that's what," said Mike.

"And where will they go?" I asked.

"Back to Arabia, or wherever," said Ronnie.

"But they're terrorist sympathizers. Shouldn't you kill all of them right away?" I asked.

"Sure. But hey, one at a time, right?" said Mike.

"One at a time?" I asked. "You might miss some of them that way. I mean, if these are such bad people, why don't you get serious and do something? I mean, here you are, sitting in the Rinc waiting to get a milkshake when the United States of America is in grave danger because some lady walked by wearing a white scarf on her head on her way to buy groceries. Scary. This is serious, you guys! Come on. You have guns. What are you waiting for? Or is your milkshake more important?"

"Fuck 'em!" said Ronnie.

"Yeah, fuck 'em!" said Mike. "They are so fucked, they aren't even worth us getting up to go shoot 'em."

"Yeah," said Ronnie.

"Yeah," I said, mocking their swaggering voices. "Wimps, that's who you guys are! Too busy drinking milkshakes to protect America."

Finally, the waitress came by our booth. One look at her and a rush of energy exploded up my spine. It was *her*. The pale, pretty girl I saw in my vision on Cobre Mountain the first time. There was the small scar on the right side of her nose, just under the eye.

How do you order breakfast from God? I wondered. Finally the words fumbled out. "Uhh—OJ, yeah. And—uhh. Yeah. Eggs over hard, biscuits, home fries. Yeah, and some coffee ..."

There was softness about her face, serenity. As she wrote down the order she smiled for a moment, revealing double dimples. She was quiet, reserved. The other guys tried to banter with her as they made their orders, but she just smiled without otherwise responding.

I fell far behind in the conversation with the guys. I kept sneaking looks at the waitress. She moved with a quiet grace through the restaurant. There was something almost sad about her expression. She had long black hair and a soft, ample, but not fat body. She seemed absolutely unaffected, somehow mature, yet young. She was the one. My heart was in two places at once, mystically enabled to stay inside my chest, but at the same time wander around the restaurant and merge with the waitress' body and soul.

***

She was there on Saturday mornings, too, I discovered. I was there the minute the place opened. I took a spot at the counter and when she came by to take my order, I found the courage to say "Hi."

"Hi," she answered as she filled my coffee cup.

"My name is Josh. What's yours?"

"Martha."

"Nice to meet you, Martha. You new in town?"

"Yes, pretty new."

"Pretty, for sure," I quipped. "Where from?"

She smiled wide at me, her dimples in full bloom. She had one tooth that was out of place in her upper row of teeth. It gave her smile an adorable asymmetry. The wildfire in my chest was uncontained.

"From Vegas," she said.

"Now why would anybody move here from Las Vegas? Out of the frying pan, into the fire. In Vegas you can fry an egg on the hood of your car in the summertime, but here, the egg hard-boils the minute you take it out of the carton. So what is it? You like the Indian casinos better than the ones in Vegas?"

Martha covered her mouth as she giggled. "How long have you lived here?" she asked me.

"Since I was six years old. I don't know any better."

"Well this place may be hotter, but it is better than Vegas," said Martha, her face sobering as she moved on to fill the next customer's cup.

***

Short day at school? I was at the Rinconada Cafe. Saturday morning? I was there. My mouth ran off on its own, disconnected from my mind, saying anything to maintain a conversation with *La Virgen de San Lorenzo* herself.

It took a lot of breakfast and lunch, but in bits and pieces I learned from Martha that her mother and father split up when she was a toddler. Her mom remarried, to an alcoholic. Martha got pregnant and left home with her boyfriend when she was 16. She had fraternal twins: Dana, the girl, and Leon, the boy. Parenting was not her boyfriend's idea of a good time. They got into an argument and he smashed her face with his fist, leaving a permanent scar and giving her a concussion, and she wound up in the hospital

for a month. Her mother's oldest sister, Esther
Young, then came up from Portales. Esther stayed
at a hotel in Las Vegas with the infant twins until
Martha was able to leave the hospital. Martha and the
twins then went with Esther to live in Portales. The
Youngs treated Martha like a daughter, and the twins
like their grandchildren. L. D. and Esther Young had
one of the biggest houses in Portales, out by the
nine-hole golf course at the north end of town. I
knew L. D.'s name well; it was mentioned in the
Portales newspaper, *The Pit*, pretty often. L. D. Young
was the Mormon bishop, the chairperson of the City
Planning Commission, the past president
of the Portales Chamber of Commerce, and the
owner of the heavy-equipment dealership
in town.

I had to do something. But what? Take her and
her kids to the Dairy Queen for a milkshake? How
was that more intimate than chatting with her over
the counter at the Rinconada Café?

***

It was time to play the Mormon card in my game
of Go Fish with Martha.

I went to the LDS ward one Sunday morning, and
Martha and the twins were there, sitting with the rest
of the Young family in the second row of pews. The
twins were dressed in their Sunday best and behaved
pretty well for such little people. Martha's face looked
peaceful as she vaguely smiled at the proceedings of
the service.

Souljourn

It was the most un-churchlike church service I'd
attended yet. It was chatty, with announcements,
supposedly inspirational talks, interrupted by some
pretty dull hymns. Nobody in particular seemed to be
in charge. It felt more like a family reunion than a
sacred occasion.

Was it God, or my own conniving cleverness
that put it into my mind? Either way, I knew what
I must do.

After the worship service, I walked up to Martha's
uncle and asked him a question. "I would like to learn
more about the Mormon religion," I told him. "I
wonder if I could talk to you about it?"

"Absolutely, young man." He was a tall, balding
fellow with a long nose and bright blue eyes. "I'm
L. D. Young."

An hour later, I was sitting at the table in the
dining room of the Young's house. L. D. excused
himself. "I need to make a phone call, but when I'm
done let's keep talking," he told me.

The twins came tumbling into the dining room,
and I asked them: "Okay, which one of you is Dana,
and which one is Leon?"

"I'm Dana," said Leon.

"I'm Leon," said Dana.

"Do you guys like stories?" I asked.

"Yeah, sure we like stories."

"Well, I know where all the stories come from.
I've been there," I declared.

"What do you mean, mister?" asked Dana,
wagging her curly hair at me and making a face.

170

"I mean, I have been to where all the stories come from. That means I can tell you absolutely any story you want to hear."

"For reals?" smiled Leon.

"For reals," I said. I sat down on the carpet with them. "All the stories come from the story mine."

"What?" they asked.

"You know there is a big mine, a big hole in the ground here in Portales, right?"

"Oh yeah. Teacher Ella took us there," said Dana.

"Well they used to dig copper out of that mine. But there is another mine, not too far from here, and it is where they dig up all the stories. It is a secret mine, and only certain special people can see it. And I'm one of them. I dug up some stories out of it just the other day. I brought them with me," I said.

"Where?" asked Leon.

"Right there. I put them on a secret bookshelf on the wall." I pointed to the blank dining room wall near the kitchen. "See all those books? See the one with the blue cover and the gold letters? And the one with the orange cover and the black letters? Go ahead, pick one out."

"The green one," demanded Leon, smiling. His smile included the same out-of-place incisor as his mother's.

"No, no, I don't like that one. I want the red book," demanded Dana.

By the time L. D. Young returned to the room, the twins were sitting on either side of me as I read them the story from the imaginary book that they had picked from the imaginary bookshelf. L. D. took a seat at the table and listened to the last half of my story. When I was done, the kids dashed out of the room. I pulled up a chair to continue my conversation with L. D.

"That was a great story!" said L. D. "Where'd you hear that one?"

"I just made it up."

"When did you come up with it?"

"Just now," I said.

"How do you do that?" asked L. D.

"I pretended that I really had the book in my hands, and I just read it. If I didn't pretend like I had the book in my hands, I don't know if I could have made up the story," I said.

The subject turned back to the Church of Jesus Christ of Latter Day Saints. L. D. was pleased that I had already learned a lot about its doctrines, but was eager to answer the objections that were implicit in some of my questions.

In the middle of L. D.'s discourse on temple marriage and the ritual of sealing of families for eternity, heaven herself walked through the room on her way to the kitchen. She bit her lip to hold back a laugh when she saw me. I tried and failed to keep my eyes off her, and wasn't sure if L. D. noticed my preoccupation.

Two hours later, Martha passed through the room again. This time, I said, "Hey Martha, would you mind sitting down? Your uncle and I were just talking about the Aaronic and Melchizedek priesthoods. I was just about to ask him why women can't be in the Mormon priesthood, and I wonder how you feel about that."

She laughed and raised both her hands and shook her head. "No way! Don't get me trapped on that subject. Let Uncle L. D. explain it to you. I'm new to this stuff," she said as she walked toward the kitchen.

"No, come on, Martha. Sit down here, if you would, and join us. I think you, as a woman and a recent convert, ought to explain it to him," insisted L. D.

She rolled her brown eyes and grinned her double dimples and sat down next to me. My body basked in the subtle heat radiating from her.

"Okay, Mr. Josh. Why are you so interested in this subject?"

"That would be Mr. Stoneburner to you, Ms. Kopecki," I replied.

"Well, excuse me, Mr. Stoneburner."

"Do you wish you could be in the priesthood?" I asked her.

"No. I'm just fine with things the way they are. Look, I don't know that much about LDS teachings. I'm still learning a lot of the basics. But I'll tell you something I am sure about. These people, and this church, saved my life. If it wasn't for L. D. and Esther here, and all the good people in this ward, I'd still be in Las Vegas with no money and nowhere to live and two little kids tugging on my skirt. So let me tell you something, Mr. Stoneburner. When people you love and trust tell you something, you take it seriously. I love and trust these people, so when they say the LDS church is true, I take that very seriously." She stood up, patted her uncle on his back, and went into the kitchen.

"Does that answer your question?" asked L. D., with a chuckle.

"Enough for now. But I have another question for you. A personal one. I can't help but ask. Does your name—L. D.—mean Latter Day?"

L. D. laughed. "No, but plenty of people have called me that. I don't care what you call me, just don't call me 'Late for Dinner.'"

"So what do the initials L. D. stand for?" I asked.

"I am named after Lorenzo Dow Young, who was a distant relative. He was the brother of Brigham Young, who led the Latter Day Saints into Utah."

"Lorenzo? You are Lorenzo?" He was startled by my raised voice.

"Yes. Why are you so excited about that?"

"I'm sorry. You just don't look like a Lorenzo to me," I muttered.

"I don't look like a Lorenzo to me, either, which is why I go by L. D.," he laughed.

***

My hair went on end again when I got home. On the internet I read that Brigham Young's brother was named after Lorenzo Dow, an itinerant preacher in America in the early 1800s. I read that the original Lorenzo Dow had white, flowing long hair and beard, wheezed with asthma, and had visions as a child and young man. In one dream, Dow encountered the late John Wesley, founder of the Methodist church. Wesley, an old man in the dream, told him to go forth and preach the gospel.

Lorenzo Dow was poorly educated. He was rejected by the Methodist church in which he started out as a preacher. Church leaders considered him to be mentally unbalanced. But his visions and his conversion experience were compelling, and drove him to preach where other preachers would not go, from the frontiers of upstate New York and Ohio down to the backwoods of Alabama. He was known as "Crazy Dow" because of his idiosyncratic style, including his habit of leaping off his horse to preach spontaneously to whomever would listen, on city street corners or in remote settlements. I read that the religious establishment of Lorenzo Dow's day wanted nothing to do with him. But he had such a powerful impact on people in so many parts of the U.S. and Great Britain that about 20,000 baby boys in the early 19th century were named after him.

And clearly, his version of Christianity had a big effect on the parents of the second most famous Mormon of them all, Brigham Young. So, why was I chosen for an encounter in a cholla cactus with this counter-cultural spiritual hero from the deep past?

***

I was at the door of the cafe when it opened at 6:30 in the morning on Monday. Inside, I found Dana and Leon eating breakfast in the first booth.

"What are you guys doing here so early?" I asked.

"We're going to kindergarten," answered Dana.

"Mind if I join you?" I asked.

"Did you get any more stories from the mine?" asked Leon.

"Yes indeed. Ahh, biscuits. Smell that!" I breathed deep. "I'm starved."

"Want some Cheerios?" asked Leon.

"No, I'll just wait for my usual," I answered.

"Whah?" asked Leon.

"I always have eggs and biscuits and hash browns," I said. "It's my usual. I wouldn't want to mess up your mother's routine, you know."

"Why do you eat that stuff?" asked Dana.

"Because it is the best breakfast in the world," I announced, with a flourish of my arms and hands, in an affectation of a Mediterranean accent. It worked. The children laughed.

"Is it time for a story?" I asked, hunching over the table toward them.

"Yeah!"

"Okay. Pick which one," I told them.

"The blue one with the gold letters—" said Dana.

"You mean this one, on the first shelf?" I asked, pointing to the blank wall above them.

"Yeah, that one."

Martha Kopecki's hand appeared in front of my face. Smooth, pale, delicate, it was wrapped around the handle of a coffee carafe. "Cup of coffee, Josh?"

"Yes, thanks." Oh, that hand … My eyes followed it as it glided, blessing the air of the Rinconada Cafe.

"Please finish your Cheerios," she said to Leon.

"Okay, Mom," grunted Leon, slapping his spoon on the surface of the milk in the cereal bowl.

Martha floated over to the next booth.

"Read it." demanded Dana. "The story!"

"Oh yeah." I snapped out of my trance and picked up the book, my fingers opening its etheric pages. "It's called The Baker of Rrrrrrinconada. Once upon a time there was a baker. He lived in a town called Rrrrrrrinconada, high up in the mountains. Early every morning he baked the best bread in the world." I lifted the imaginary book so they could see the imaginary pictures.

"The baker's name was Rrrrrrrrramon. His bread was so good that all the kids in town woke up early every day. You know why?"

"No, why?"

"Because the smell of the bread was so wonderful that they could not wait to go get some and eat it. And Ramon loved kids. Every kid that bought a loaf of bread got a miniature loaf of bread for free. So every day the kids in each family would fight over who got to go down to the store and buy bread. Whoever got the job would go down and buy a loaf of the best bread in the world from Ramon, and he would give them an itty bitty loaf, and they would eat it right then and there, *'orita ya*, because it was so good. But one day all the kids in town slept in and were late for school. You know why?"

"No, why?"

"Because they couldn't smell the bread. Ramon didn't bake it that day. And you know why he didn't bake it that day?"

"No, why?"

Tommy the cop hoisted his pants up by the pistol belt and pushed open the glass door into the cafe.

"Because he wasn't there. Somebody had kidnapped him. Terrible. Hey, Tommy."

"Yeah, Josh."

"Did they ever figure out who kidnapped Ramon the baker?"

"What are you talking about?" Tommy shook his head and kept walking.

"See? Even Officer Keady doesn't know what happened to Ramon. A big mystery. Nobody in the town of Rinconada knew what happened to Ramon. He just disappeared. But what really happened was that the King of Sonoyta heard that Ramon made the best bread in the world, and he wanted all of it for himself, so he sent his soldiers over the mountains to kidnap Ramon in the middle of the night and bring him back to Sonoyta to bake for him and his lords and ladies."

"King of Sonoyta? They have a king?" asked Dana.

"Not Sonoyta, Mexico, silly. Sonoyta, Spain!" I carried on. "So they brought Ramon into the king's court. Ramon was so scared. His legs were shivering so much he could hardly stand up. See the picture here, of Ramon? Look how upset he is, in front of the king. The king said, 'Ramon, I have brought you here to bake me the best bread in the world. I love the aroma of bread, and I sent my spies to find the best bread in the world. It took them many years, but, finally, they found your bakery.'"

Glossie Protheroe slung her macramé purse over her shoulder and opened the door of the Rinconada Cafe.

"Mrs. Protheroe, isn't it true that Ramon is the best baker in the world?" Behind my hand I mouthed the words "Say yes."

"Yes, it is true." She smiled and shook her head and proceeded to join her friends Marge Bessemer and Bertha La Bounty at their usual booth. The kids' mouths hung open in amazement.

"See? It's true. The king's spies were right. The king said to Ramon, 'Now that I have finally found you, I present you with the best bakery in the world. Here, you will bake bread for me for the rest of your life. You will have a place of honor in my court, for all time.' The king showed him into the brand-new bakery they had built just for Ramon. Ramon said, 'Yes, your majesty, this is a magnificent bakery. So much finer than my bakery back in my humble hometown of Rrrrrinconada. But, your lardship, I mean, your lordship, I don't think I can bake the best bread in the world here. I will try to please your majesty, but I must warn you that the taste of my bread in Rrrrrinconada cannot be matched anywhere else, no matter how excellent the equipment in the bakery may be.' Can you kids guess why Ramon couldn't make the best bread in the world in the bakery of the king of Sonoyta?"

"Maybe they didn't have any stuff to make the bread out of in Sonoyta," answered Dana.

I shook her hand. "You are right. They had most of the stuff to make bread out of in Sonoyta, but there was one little thing missing. One itsy-bitsy, tiny, eeny-weeny thing. A thing so small, you cannot see it with the naked eye. See? This is my naked eye…" I pulled my eyelids apart to reveal my right eyeball in all its blood-vessely roundness. The kids squealed. Glossie Protheroe, seeing it with her not-so-naked eyes, sighed. I pointed at my other eye. "And this is my 'clothes' eye. See? My eyelids are the clothes for my eyes - that's why we say 'clothe' your eyes!" More squealing.

"Anyway, this thing that was missing was yeast. Yeast is what makes bread fluffy, and what gives it taste. And the yeast for the bread he made in Rrrrrinconada lived only in Rrrrinconada and could not live anywhere else, not even in the glorious, marvelous kingdom of Sonoyta. The air in Rrrrrinconada was just right for that special yeast. That's what Rrrrramon told the king of Sonoyta, but the king didn't believe it. He sent his soldiers to bring back the yeast. They snuck into Ramon's bakery in Rrrrrinconada in the middle of the night and scraped here, and scraped there, and gathered up all the gooey stuff they could find in his bakery that might have the special yeast in it, but when they got back to Sonoyta all they had was a blob of goo that smelled terrible.

They brought it to the king, who said, 'Get that stuff out of my court at once! It smells like … like …"

Paul Blewett, owner of Copper City Auto Parts, stepped in just in time for me ask him, "Mr. Blewett, what is the stinkiest thing you ever smelled?"

"Do I gotta talk about this before breakfast?" He slicked his hand over his slicked-back hair, but he was grinning a bit, and the kids grinned back. "Okay, okay—lemme think. Oh Lord, I'll tell you, the God-awful-est thing I ever smelled was a dead coyote in a black plastic bag in our dumpster behind the shop. Musta been road kill, I suppose, and some fool put it in the bag and tossed it in there. Well, after a few days at 110 degrees, that coyote carcass just swoll up that bag so big that it exploded, right there behind the intake for the swamp cooler, and it stank so bad we had to close up the shop."

"That's it," I declared. "That's just what the king of Sonoyta said. He said to his servants and his soldiers, 'That stuff smells like a dead coyote.'"

Paul grinned again, shook his head and moved along to join Tommy, the cop, for breakfast.

"Well, Ramon the baker said to the king, 'I told you so, your hugeness. I told you that with the best bakery in the world, with the best oven in the world, with the best flour and water in the world, I still can't bake the best bread in the world here in the kingdom of Sonoyta. I beg the pardon of your magnificence, but I can only bake the best bread in the world back home in my little town of Rinconada.'"

"Leon," I leaned over the table. "When you were little, did you ever have a tantrum? Scream and yell because you couldn't get your way?"

"He has tantrums all the time," declared Dana.

"You shut up," Leon snapped at her.

From the other end of the restaurant, Martha firmly responded. "Leon, don't ever say things like that, here or anywhere else."

"Okay, Mom," he grumbled, slapping his milk again with the spoon.

"Well then you both will understand what happened next. The king of Sonoyta had a tantrum. He was furious that he had gone to all this trouble and still couldn't get the best bread in the world. So he threw Ramon in the dungeon where he dangled in shackles and had nothing to eat but bad bread and water. The king, upstairs, stomped around and yelled for a while. Finally after a few days of being mad, he told his servants to bring Ramon back up to him. Ramon was dirty and hungry and was starting to smell like a dead coyote himself, but he was grateful to get out of that dungeon. The king said, 'I'm sorry I threw you in the dungeon. I was having a bad day.' Ramon said, 'I'm sorry I can't make the best bread in the world here. But you know, if you let me go back to Rinconada, and if you come visit me, I'll make you all the bread you want.'"

Martha's lovely hand, holding a plate full of breakfast, hovered over me as I moved orange juice glasses and scattered Cheerios out of the way. I tried to make naked eye contact with her, but her eyes were mostly clothed, and turned toward her kids. "Thanks, Martha." She was already on her way to Paul and Tommy's table.

"So. Where was I?" I asked the kids.

"Ramon told the king to come to Rinconada." said Dana.

"Oh yeah. So, the king thought about it for a while and finally said, 'Okay. Ramon, you can go home to Rinconada and open up your bakery again and start baking bread. Only if you promise never to tell anyone that you were ever here or that you ever saw me.' Ramon said 'I swear on a stack of bread loaves, I'll never tell anybody about it.' So Ramon went home, and the town rejoiced and had a big party to celebrate his return. Ramon told the people of Rinconada that he had taken a long trip, and had been asked to start a bakery someplace else, but that he loved Rinconada so much that he just had to return. He said that the reason he came back was the kids—he loved to see them in his store every morning. He didn't say anything about being kidnapped by the king of Sonoyta. In other words, he lied."

An elderly couple came in the door, people I had never seen before. "Excuse me," I asked them, "Have you folks ever told a white lie before? You know, something that wasn't entirely true, but if you told the whole truth it might hurt somebody needlessly?"

The old man said, with a twinkle, "I have never told a lie in my entire life."

"Liar," said the old woman, giggling, poking him in the ribs with her elbow.

"See?" I said to the kids. "This gentleman just told us a white lie. When he said he had never told a lie in his life, he was lying. He didn't want you kids to think that lying is okay. Good for him." I turned to the couple. "Thank you folks, very much, for setting a good example for these kids. Thank you, sir, for such a sensitive and thoughtful white lie. And thank you, ma'am, for telling the real truth."

The bemused and bewildered couple walked over to a booth.

"So Ramon reopened his bakery and started baking bread again, and the marvelous aroma filled the air of the town of Rinconada once more." I lifted the biscuit off my plate, waved it in front of the kids' noses, and then broke off chunks for the kids and then ate a chunk myself. "Ahhh," I sighed, revealing a mouthful of biscuit mush. The kids *ahhhed* back.

"And then one day a stranger showed up in Ramon's bakery. He was a simple peasant, with rough clothes, a bag over his shoulder, and holding a walking stick. 'What can I do for you, stranger?' Ramon asked him. The peasant said, 'I hear you have the best bread in the world. I'd like to buy a loaf.' Ramon immediately recognized the peasant's voice. It was the king, disguised as a poor person. He was the fattest *campesino* Ramon had ever seen. Ramon pretended not to recognize the king, because there were other customers in the shop, and he had made a promise on a stack of bread loaves never to say a word about what had happened in Sonoyta. So Ramon sold the king a loaf of bread, and the king, in peasant's clothes, left the bakery. Ramon heard a loud yell from the plaza outside: 'This is the best bread in the WORLD!' The next day, the king was back for another loaf, and every day after. The king loved the bread so much, he decided to give up being a king, and live in a little cottage outside the town of Rrrrrinconada, happily ever after, so that he could always eat the best bread in the WORLD." I slapped my hands together as if slamming shut the covers of the book.

Martha had two little brown paper bags in her hands as she approached the booth. "Okay, you two, off to school." She kissed her son and daughter on their heads, gave them one of her crinkle-cheeked smiles, and patted them out the front door.

I clothed my eyes for a moment before finishing my eggs, mentally comparing and contrasting the curves of Martha's dimpled cheeks and the curves of her dimpled hands.

11. Why Camels Smirk

I spent entire class periods at Portales High School completely lost in thought, considering what to do next. If I would just join the Church of Jesus Christ of Latter Day Saints, I'd be a lot closer to her. But I wasn't ready to do that. I could keep on talking with L. D. Young, learning more about Mormonism so I could stay close to Martha. But was that really right? How much more did I really want to learn about it right now? There were so many other things I wanted to explore. My latest obsession was about Lorenzo Dow. Was he really the person I had encountered in the vision? And who was John Wesley, the guy Lorenzo Dow saw in a dream? Were these old men in the visions really just old men, or were they just God taking the form of old men for the sake of giving Lorenzo Dow and me the messages we needed to see and hear? If only Lorenzo Dow would show up and tell me what to do.

During English class one day, when I was supposed to be writing an essay, I wrote a letter instead:

Dear Martha:

I have so much I want to talk with you about. I just couldn't stand it anymore and had to write you this letter. I hope you won't think I'm nuts or something, but I have some really important things to say, and I would really like to talk to you about all this stuff sometime really soon. Tell me a time when just you and me can talk somewhere that you feel comfortable. Here's what is on my mind.

When I was 14, I went walking one morning behind Cobre Mountain and I looked at a jumping cholla cactus and all of a sudden I saw a vision. I saw a girl in the cactus that looked just like you. I felt this amazing feeling all through my body, and the vision went away. Whatever I saw was real, and it was important, at least to me.

When I saw you for the first time at the cafe, I was so blown away, I didn't know what to say. It was so intense, seeing you for the first time after the vision I had when I was 14. I had to get to know you, to find out what you were really like, to find out who you are. Maybe I've been kind of a pest to you. I hope you don't mind it too much. I had to be kind of pushy to get to know you.

I get it that you are a real person, not just a vision-person. I think the better I get to know you the more real you will be, and the less it will matter about the vision I had. Whether or not you really had anything to do with my vision, I feel like you are a very special person, and that I need to make friends with you.

For the last couple of years I have been trying to figure out the vision. I have learned a lot of things that are pretty interesting, that I want to tell you about. I have been visiting and learning about a lot of different religions. Each one has good things in it. The Mormon one, too. I started out trying to understand my vision, but it seems like the more I learn about religion, the more I need to learn. I am starting to think that it will take forever to figure it out.

You know I like you a lot, but really, I love you. I know this must be embarrassing because we don't know each other very well. And the confusing thing is that you were like a messenger or an angel in the vision I had, and now I am falling in love with you for real. Is it right to fall in love with an angel? I need your help to figure it out.

Your friend,
Joshua T. Stoneburner

I felt relieved when I got home and sealed the letter in an envelope and put it in the mailbox. Finally, I was getting honest with Martha. If she couldn't deal with it, well, that was a risk I had to take.

***

"Josh," said Dad from behind his *Arizona Republic* newspaper.

"Yeah?" I answered from the kitchen, where I was making a peanut butter sandwich for a late-night snack.

"Why have you been leaving so early in the morning lately?" asked Dad.

"Uhhh, I've been hanging out with a friend at the Rinconada Cafe."

"Are you eating a decent breakfast there?"

"Yeah, Dad."

"Kind of an expensive habit, doing that every day, isn't it?" asked Dad.

"Yeah. But hey, I work, I make money, I spend money."

"So what's her name?" asked Dad.

"Whah?"

"Her name," insisted Dad.

"What makes you think it's a she?" I asked.

"Why else would get you up so early in the morning?"

"Dad, I gave up sleeping a long time ago. What do you think I am, a punk kid?"

"Exactly. You aren't a punk kid, you're a punk teenager with a crush on a girl who shows up at the café at seven in the morning. Right?"

"Is it any of your business?" I sneered.

"Yes. And what's her name?"

"The Virgin of San Lorenzo," I answered.

***

My answer from Martha finally came in the mail. I opened the envelope and pulled out the note before the screen door swatted shut behind me.

Dear Josh:

Thank you for your letter. It was good to know what is really on your mind. I think you are a

*really nice and fun person. My kids love your
stories. They tell them to me at home. They're
great stories. It would be great if everything was
different, but I don't know how anything can
change. I can only be your friend if you are okay
with only being my friend. I hope you understand.
If your life were like my life, you would
understand.*

*So don't waste a lot of money buying breakfast at
the Rinconada if you think it is going to change
things. I will understand if you stop coming. If we
can just be friends, then I will always be glad to see
you there.*

*I'm not an angel or anything like that. I am not the
Virgin of San Lorenzo, I'm sure of that. Keep
looking and maybe you will figure it out. I don't
know if the Mormon way is the right way for you. I
only know it is the right way for me, for a lot of
reasons that maybe don't make any sense for you.
You are a smart guy and you will figure it all out. I
am sure.*

*Your friend,
Martha*

***

The next morning, a Saturday, I drove the old
pickup out of town to go to work. By 8:15 that
morning—starting to clean a doublewide mobile
home with two big, dirty aluminum awnings—it was
already too hot. It was May, getting close to the end

of the tourist season: I'd be washing the permanent mobile homes through the summer.

As I blasted a fine spray of water against the ridges of aluminum siding, I began to notice my thoughts, something I had resolved to do after visiting the Christian Science church. I observed my own obsession about Martha Kopecki, my constant rehearsal of what I wanted to say or do with her. I observed that I was hopeful that things would change, despite her declaration that they would not. I observed that this hopefulness felt good. I observed that it made my mind race ever onward with schemes to win her over. Then I observed that I had no idea what I would do with her if we really connected. She, with two little kids, and I, with another year of high school? She, living with her aunt and uncle, and I, living with my dad? I observed my thought that a romance with her did seem far-fetched. I observed that my emotions rolled and coasted with these differing imagined outcomes.

As the day went on, I became more fascinated with my mind. I observed that it was hard to keep observing my mind. It was so easy to get completely consumed with my thoughts and feelings, rather than observing them. But each time I slipped, I was able to pull back and observe again. I noticed the strain it took to get myself out of the powerful flow of my mind, to pull myself up onto its banks, and watch it from above instead of being swept away by it.

I realized that most of the time, what I called being awake actually was a form of sleep. Mostly, I thought and acted automatically, reacting to things according to instincts of which I was not immediately aware. This exercise of watching my thoughts was a new kind of wakefulness. I felt more alive, more aware, more capable of choice in thought and action.

In the evening, I coiled the hoses and draped them over the back of the compressor in the bed of my pickup. The hoses felt wonderfully cool on my hands and arms. I'd just finished the last job of the day, a 40-foot Excelsior motor home on the far end of the Snowbird Roost recreational vehicle park.

Out in the desert beyond the park I noticed a cholla cactus glowing brilliantly in the setting sunlight. I saw it, and I noticed that I saw it. Maybe my visions of the Virgin were meant to wake me up, to move me from living like a robot into living like a fully aware human being.

***

The next morning I got a call from Father Crespi. "Got some time to go fill up water tanks? I'll come with you to show you where to go."

I picked up Father Crespi at the rectory. We filled up the tank on the back of my truck from the hose in front of the church.

Father Crespi was wearing a white cowboy hat, a western shirt, and a pair of faded Levis with a turquoise and silver belt buckle. "Father, you know the rodeo's not till August," I laughed as he hopped into the cab in his nicely tooled cowboy boots.

Father Crespi flashed his gold teeth at me. "What you didn't know is that I really am a cowboy. I grew up on a ranch down in Sonora, and went on cattle drives with my dad, who was a *vaquero*. I roped and branded and fixed fences till I went to the seminary when I was 16 years old. I earned the right to wear this stuff any time I want."

I saw a road sign along the way through the desert. At the top, it said: "Adopt a Highway." Below, it said: "AVAILABLE."

As we rode through the Tohono O'odham Reservation, heading down dirt roads close to the border, I got an earful about how American cowboys are just wannabes, and that the Mexican *vaquero* was the real thing. "My dad wove his own lariats from rawhide he skinned himself," said Father Crespi. "He was an honest-to-God desert cowboy. In drought times he used to light fires around clusters of cactus, to burn off the spines so the cattle could eat it."

I was captivated by Father Crespi's stories of life on the range down in Mexico. But my curiosity about another matter led me to change the subject.

"Father Crespi, I know it is none of my business, and I hope I'm not insulting you. But I want to know. How can you stand having a job where you can't ever have sex?"

Father Crespi took off his cowboy hat and smiled. "Let me ask you this, as a way of answering you. How do *you* stand not having sex?"

"What do you mean, Father? I mean, I've kissed girls, and stuff, but it's not like I have gone all the way or anything."

"Yes, I get that. But what I'm asking is how you can stand not having sex when you are a young guy full of sexual energy," asked Father Crespi.

"Well, I think about it all the time, and sometimes it does drive me wild, I guess. But I can hope to have sex someday, and that keeps me going. But you can't hope to ever have sex. I couldn't handle that," I answered.

"But you don't know when you are going to have sex, and you can't even be sure you ever will. So what keeps you going?"

"Well, I do have other things to do. I mean, I gotta get out of high school, and go to work, and stuff."

"Well, it's the same for me, Josh. I have to go to work, too. It's just that I have been doing what you are doing for a lot longer. I may not have sex, but I do have a life. I have a lot of people who depend on me, and it takes almost all of my time and energy to serve them. I feel like there is a lot of love and friendship in my life. Sure, it isn't sexual, but it is very wonderful. I know I've missed part of life, but I feel like I have received so much more in place of what I have missed. It is tough sometimes, and I don't always feel good about being celibate, but mostly, I feel peaceful about it. I'm grateful for my life just the way it is."

Down the rutted track I could see a blue flag, a piece of plastic tarp hanging from a long piece of electrical conduit driven into the ground. The plastic water tank marked *AGUA* was nearly empty. Father Crespi and I drained out the stale water and filled the tank. Around it were lots of shoe prints, and a few dirty, holey socks abandoned in the dirt.

As I coiled up the hose onto the back of the truck, I heard Father Crespi singing a simple chant as he stood by the water tank, looking off to the south toward the border: "Truly, this is the house of God, holy ground; truly, this is the house of God, holy ground …"

***

On the way back, Father Crespi asked if I'd ever been to the mosque outside of Portales. "Heard of it, but never got there," I said. "Seems like I've been to all the other religious places around. But not that one."

"Want to stop there?" asked Father Crespi. I have friends there, and I'd like you to meet them."

The Dar al-Islam Mosque was the butt of a lot of jokes in Portales. Some folks were suspicious of its people, thinking they might be Muslim terrorists. There had been a few incidents of vandalism against their cars when they came into town to shop. I remembered that Pastor Kate had collected money from the local churches for a fund to fix their cars after the attacks. If anything went wrong in Portales, people half-joked that the Dar al-Islam guys had caused it. But in fact they had lived peacefully in their isolated compound south of town for decades.

Most of the people of the mosque home-schooled their kids, so I had never met any of them.

We arrived just in time for evening prayers. In the enclosed courtyard outside of the mosque, men in one area and women in another were bowing down to the east. They prostrated themselves on a patchwork of oriental carpets laid out on the stone patio, muttering in what I assumed must be Arabic. But only a few of them looked Middle Eastern or East Asian; there were plenty of light-haired, blue-eyed people in the crowd. We kept our distance and watched and listened from outside the beautiful latticed gate of the courtyard. Beyond the mosque I could see a cluster of houses perched against the side of a steep hill. The shadowed side of the white dome of the little mosque was backlit by reflected light, making it look surreal and evanescent.

After the prayer time, one of the men, a tall, pale fellow with a red beard, wearing a long white jacket and a white-laced skullcap, approached Father Crespi with arms outstretched. I listened to them talk about a lecture that Father Crespi was going to give at the mosque in a few weeks. "Ibn Shams, I'd like you to meet Josh Stoneburner, a friend of mine from Portales," said Father Crespi.

"*Salaam w'aleykum*," Ibn Shams put his hand over his heart and then shook my hand with both of his. "Peace be with you. Welcome to Dar al-Islam, which means House of Islam."

Father Crespi and Ibn Shams talked as they walked inside the mosque, while I marveled at the beautiful tiles on the floors. Along one of the curved walls was an elegantly carved wooden stand with a big illuminated book lying open on it. The hand-written letters were formed in sinuous brushstrokes, colored and gilded and interwoven. I imagined the time that would have been necessary to produce such a book. "The glorious Koran," said Ibn Shams, interrupting his conversation with Father Crespi to explain. "You read it right to left, like this." He followed with his finger across the open page and read aloud. "That was the Arabic. In English, here's what it says: "The words of the Prophet, peace be unto him: What would make you comprehend what the uphill road is? It is the setting free of a slave, or the giving of food in a day of hunger to an orphan, having relationship, or to the poor man lying in the dust. Then he is of those who believe and charge one another to show patience, and charge one another to show compassion."

"It sounded prettier in Arabic," I said. I had been captivated by the lyrical sound of the language.

Ibn Shams' face brightened immediately. "Yes, you understand. There is really no way to appreciate the Koran fully except in Arabic. It is a thing of such beauty that no translation can come even close to expressing it. The poetry of it is sublime, but it cannot be experienced very well in English."

Ibn Shams explained that the Dar al-Islam community was studying about Jesus, and had asked Father Crespi to speak to them on the subject.

"Why would Muslims study Jesus?" I asked. "I thought you guys worshipped Mohammed."

"For one thing, we don't worship Mohammed, peace be upon him. He was God's prophet, but he was not God. We are interested in Jesus because he is mentioned quite a bit in the Koran and other writings of Islam," answered Ibn Shams.

"Muslims have a lot of respect for Jesus," explained Father Crespi. "They don't think he was divine, but they think he was a great prophet. I have been studying the Arabic Muslim texts about Jesus with Ibn Shams here recently. I've learned a lot about Jesus from our work together."

"You should also know that Father Crespi is quite a scholar," said Ibn Shams. "He is a student of Muhyiddin Ibn Arabi, as I am."

Father Crespi explained that Ibn Arabi was one of the Spanish mystics. In the medieval era when the Moors occupied much of Spain, Muslim, Christian, and Jewish people shared many ideas about the inner experience of God. Father Crespi said he was very interested in the Spanish Christian mystic, St. John of the Cross, and that his studies led him to learn more about the Islamic thinkers who had influenced Spanish Christians.

"Why don't we ever see you guys in town, except at the Chavez Market?" I asked.

"We are a spiritual community. We are dedicated to lives of devotion to Allah, and set ourselves apart to serve Him," replied Ibn Shams. "Let me tell you about our community."

I learned that there were about 75 people in Dar al-Islam. Ibn Shams told me that they were followers of a Sufi Muslim teacher or *sheikh* from Tunisia. Sufism, said Ibn Shams, was a mystical school of Islam that taught people to have a direct experience of Allah, "in mind, soul, and body." The community found land near Portales where they could live and work and pray together in the same place. Ibn Shams showed me the print shop the community owned, which produced books about Sufi teachings. This publishing business was the main source of income for Dar al-Islam. I was fascinated by the physical beauty of the books they produced; the textured paper, the elaborate geometrical designs, the artful way that the writings and poetry were laid out on the pages.

Dar al-Islam was a peaceful place. No one seemed to be in a hurry. The few children in the community were happy and playful, despite being dressed in such an odd fashion. The low adobe buildings were spotlessly whitewashed, and the grounds were graciously planted with cacti and flowers. It seemed like a sort of heaven.

"Tell Josh about the dances, Ibn Shams," suggested Father Crespi.

Ibn Shams described the whirling dances that were held after Friday prayer at Dar al-Islam, through which the participants reached spiritual union with Allah.

"You are welcome any Friday night to come watch the dance," offered Ibn Shams.

These people have it one up over the Mormons,
I thought. It's one thing to hold a dance in your
church, but must be quite something else to dance
your way to God.

And then I thought of another comparison with
the Latter Day Saints. "I hear that Muslims have lots
of wives," I said as we walked through the courtyard
back to the mosque.

Ibn Shams laughed. "That would be too much
work. It's hard enough to keep one wife happy. Yes,
there are places in the world where Muslim men have
more than one wife, but this isn't one of them."

A woman was sitting in the shade of the
courtyard, fingering the beads on a necklace and
whispering something to herself.

"What is she doing? Looks like she's saying the
Rosary," I whispered.

"That's right, only it's the Islamic version," said
Father Crespi.

"That's right. Rosary beads started long ago
with the Hindus, got picked up by the Muslims,
and then the Catholics copied the idea from the
Muslims," said Ibn Shams. "The beads correspond
with the names of God. She touches a bead, and says
one of the names, then touches the next, and recites
the next name."

"How many names are there for God in Islam?" I
asked.

"Really only one: Allah. But Allah has many
qualities, which are the names that go with the beads.
Like the Merciful, or the Almighty, and so on. One

hundred attributes. But only 99 are known by human beings," said Ibn Shams.

"What about the hundredth?" I had to ask.

Ibn Shams smiled. "It's known only by camels. Which may be why camels have that funny smirk on their faces all the time."

***

"So what do you think of those people, Father Crespi?" I asked as we bumped down the long gravel road that led back to the highway.

"I have a lot of respect for them. They are very serious about their spiritual devotion. I think they are sincere and kind people. But I think they are out of the mainstream of Islam, maybe even of Sufi Islam, and my other Muslim friends would agree with me. The Dar al-Islam folks are good people. But there is something to be said for being part of a larger community of faith, and they are pretty isolated. They are a small sect. I think it is really great that they are willing to have people like myself come speak to them, and that they participate sometimes in interfaith efforts. They show up sometimes for the Immigrant Justice Covenant meetings. The good thing about Catholic monasteries and convents is that they may be physically isolated, but they are part of a much larger community of faith that gives them support and provides a wider perspective on things. If something goes terribly wrong at a Catholic monastery, the wider church steps in and, sooner or later, makes it right. I don't think the folks at Dar al-Islam have that kind of protection. I wonder if they really have enough balance in their lives, whether maybe they are too involved in their religion. My friend, an Islamic scholar, says that the Dar al-Islam people are a classic example of convert syndrome."

"What's that?" I asked.

"That is where people from a non-Islamic culture convert to Islam, and become far more pious in the religion than most people who grew up in Islamic societies. Same thing happens in Catholicism. People who convert to Catholicism sometimes become sort of fanatical about it. They say the Rosary all the time, join the Right to Life movement, and want to go back to the Latin Mass," replied Father Crespi.

"I guess you aren't like that," I said.

"I grew up Catholic. I take all of it with a grain of salt." Father Crespi's gold-glittered smile brightened his dark, leathery face. "But I think humor makes me a better Catholic, a better Christian. I think God loves a good laugh."

"You know, Father, you seem way too smart to be working in a nowhere town like Portales," I said. "Why aren't you in Rome, getting ready to be the next Pope? If you ran for Pope, I'd vote for you."

"Thanks. But I'm afraid the church is a monarchy, not a democracy, so you won't get to vote for me any time soon." laughed Father Crespi. "The reason I'm in Portales is because it is as far away from Rome as I could get. Here I can do more of the things I enjoy, like studying Islamic mysticism and working on border justice. You know, since I grew up in Sonora, I've got some feelings about the border," he smiled.

"So tell me, Father Crespi. If you were God, how would you solve the border problem?"

"My Jesuit friends in Mexico say it's mostly the fault of U.S. capitalism and imperialism. Those are problems, but it's much more complicated than that. If I were God, I'd have a lot of work to do. I'd have to clean up all the terrible corruption in Mexican business and politics. Corruption holds back economic development that would prevent underemployed Mexicans from wanting to cross the border. If I were God, I'd have to convince all the drug users in the U.S. to stop buying the cocaine and heroin and marijuana that gets smuggled across the border. The *narcos* who smuggle it are the source of a lot of the corruption, and there are entire towns in northern Mexico that are controlled by violent *narco* gangs. If I were God, I've have to convince the Americans to have a liberal guest-worker program so that *mexicanos* here would not have to live in an underground economy with no benefits or protections. If I were God, I'd have to convert Americans away from the racism and the fear and the small-minded politics that dominate this country today."

"And the list goes on," sighed Father Crespi. "But we are God's hands and feet. We need to pay attention to the injustices, pay attention to the still, small voice of God, guiding us from within, and act.

God depends on each one of us to do our part. If we all do our parts, things can change."

"I want to do my part," I said. "I've been looking for a way to do it, ever since I met Rosa."

"Yes, when you had that vision and when those two pieces of the crystal came together, you were given a mission," declared Father Crespi. "It will not be easy. But you have been given great gifts to do this work. Whatever I can do to help you along your way, let me know. *A su servicio*—at your service." He touched the tip of his cowboy hat and bowed a bit in my direction.

As Father Crespi hopped out of the truck at the rectory, he invited me to a meeting at 6:30 on Wednesday morning. "It's our lectionary study group," he said. "I think you might enjoy it. Come by for a while before school and see what you think."

12. From Two to One

I showed up the next Wednesday in the Fireside Room of the Federated Church. Around the table were Father Crespi, Pastor Kate, Glossie Protheroe, and a woman I had not met before. "This is Alice Kahn from Beth Israel, the Jewish community in Portales," said Pastor Kate. "Meet Josh Stoneburner." From Alice I learned that there were not many religious Jews in town, but those few met at her house every week for Shabbat service and Hebrew school for the five or six kids in their congregation.

Alice told me she also practiced Buddhism.

"Then why do you have a Jewish service in your house?" I asked.

"I wanted my kids to learn their tradition," she answered.

"But if you are Buddhist, wouldn't you want your kids to be Buddhist, too?"

The rest of the people around the table were smiling at each other.

"Being a Buddhist makes me a better Jew, and being a Jew makes me a better Buddhist. I do Buddhist meditation practice with my kids, too."

The lectionary study group read three passages from the Bible, and talked about them. From the discussion, I learned that a lot of different Christian denominations use the same set of readings from the Bible on each Sunday, changing them each week and covering much of the whole Bible over the course of

three years. The upcoming Sunday was Pentecost,
Pastor Kate told me, the day when the people
of the early Christian church had an experience
of the Holy Spirit. The members of the group
were impressed when I said, "Oh, yeah, the
speaking in tongues thing." The group first
read from the book of Numbers in the Hebrew
Scriptures, chapter 11, where Moses said "Would
that all the Lord's people were prophets, that the
Lord would put his spirit upon them." Alice Kahn
came up with her own translation of the passage
from Hebrew, explaining the numerological
significance of the number 70, the number of elders
who received the spirit of prophecy in the story
from Numbers. Glossie talked about how someday
all people would give up faith in Matter and come to
the knowledge of Spirit. Pastor Kate said that what
she got out of the passage was Moses' hope that all
people, not just the 70, would learn how to speak for
God. Father Crespi said, "I think it is interesting that
there were 70 elders gathered around the holy tent
who received the spirit of prophesy, but it only
lasted for a short time. Meanwhile, two men also got
the spirit, but they were still back in the camp with
the rest of the people. They weren't part of the
power elite of the 70. But these two didn't stop
prophesying like the rest. The spirit of prophecy
isn't just for the clergy. It can happen to anybody."

Finally, I offered my commentary. "It is a good
thing that only a few people got the spirit of
prophecy. If Moses had it his way, everybody

would be a prophet, and then there would be as many different religions as there are people. Religion would be even more confusing than it already is."

***

A leaky radiator hose led me to visit the auto parts store near the plaza after school. The only other vehicle in front of the store was a big, shiny king-cab truck with a National Rifle Association bumper sticker. It belonged to Paul Blewitt, the owner of the store. There was an official-looking decal on the cab window that read "Terrorist Hunting License." A rifle hung from the rack visible through the window.

Paul smiled as I came in. "That's an old-timer, that truck of yours. Did you get it from the Phelps Dodge? Looks like the kind they used to run from the corporation yard," he said.

"Yeah. My dad got it for me. He bought it from the company a few years back."

"Well, you and me will be seeing plenty of each other for as long as you own that thing," laughed Paul as he used a long stick to pull down a new radiator hose off the wall. "Say, didn't I see you at the Baptist Church?"

"I've been there a bunch of times, yes," I said. "You belong to that church?"

"Well, yeah, in a manner of speaking," laughed Paul. "I'm on the books, but I don't go there much. My wife is real involved there, though."

"So why don't you go more often?"

"Oh golly," said Paul. "I got a business to run, you know, and there's always something doing on Sunday morning. But, I'll tell you the real truth of it. Truth is," he said, slicking back his black hair with his hand, leaning over the counter and grinning. "Truth is, church bores the hell out of me. I swear, I'd rather go to the dentist and get me a root canal than to sit through a couple of hours of church. But, now and again, you'll see me there with my wife," he chuckled. "Makes her happy to have me sit with her. And she's a good woman, and religion done her a lot of good, so the least I can do is sit with her there sometimes."

"So where are the men?" I asked. "The churches and temples I visit are mostly full of women."

"You're right about that. It's Pastor Bob, and a bunch of women, and a few fellas like myself who come now and again because their wives told 'em they'd better. Which is kinda backwards, I guess, 'cause Pastor Bob always says the Bible teaches that the man is the head of the household, and that women should be obedient to the men. Oh, it isn't that bad. There are a bunch of guys who go to that church pretty regular. But there are a lot more women than men in the pews, for sure. So do you go often?" asked Paul.

"Not to that church. But I do go to a lot of different churches," I answered. "I guess I'm checking all of them out, one by one."

"That's pretty unusual for a young guy like you. You could be out having fun, but there you are, sitting in church. I admire you for it. Wish I could do it as much as you do," said Paul, shaking his head.

"It's just something I feel like I need to work out for myself. So tell me, Mr. Blewett, how do you work it out? I mean, what do you think about religion?"

"Well, you gotta have it. You gotta have religion. You have to get saved and you have to follow the Good Book. All the problems of this country, they're all because we don't follow the Good Book. Those homosexuals think they ought to be able to get married, when it's a sin against God for them to be homosexual in the first place. They are bringing God's judgment down on America. Because they hand out condoms to kids, because men aren't in control of their households like God meant them to be, because abortion is legal but people want to take away our God-given right to own any gun we want to protect our families. God is trying to straighten out America, but we aren't making it easy for him. That's what I believe."

"Whoa. Really? You think America's troubles are caused by gay people having sex?" I asked. "They must be having some powerful sex. And are you saying that if we don't let people go *javelina* hunting with machine guns, God will judge America? I've been wondering. Isn't it a lot of work to get all those assault rifle bullets out of the meat so you can cook it? Who can do taxidermy on a pig with its head blown to bits?"

"Quite the jokester, aren't you?" grinned Paul. "Well, Pastor Bob says floods and earthquakes are

God's judgment for immorality in America. And I think there's some truth to it. Mind you, I'm not so smart about what is in the Good Book. I just try to do religion here in my business. I try to be godly. I try to be helpful to the folks who come in here, and I try to treat my employees the right way. Do unto others, like the Bible says."

***

At the oak table, Seedless, the only patron present in the library, was writing another letter.

This one was written to a boy in India:

Dear Rahul:

You ask a very good question: when will there be peace? I have no idea. I wish I did. I wish I could tell you when peace finally comes and we won't have to worry about wars anymore. I hope it comes fast in your part of the world. Doesn't your country have enough to worry about, with rampant poverty and sickness? Does it need the extra threat of a terrible war? I don't think so.

When I was younger I was in a war myself, and I spent some time with bullets whizzing past, hoping for peace. I remember wanting the Persian Gulf War to be over by my birthday. I imagined coming home and finding that my mom had baked me my favorite birthday cake. I imagined blowing out the candles on the cake. When I left the army, I was all screwed up in the head and never even went home to my family at all. Never did eat that birthday cake I was hoping for. I guess I'm still waiting for peace, even though that war has been over for a really long time.

Some people are waiting for Jesus to come back again and save the world. I don't think it works like that. Getting peace is not like waiting for birthday cake or for a savior dropping out of the sky on a platter of clouds. It's more like you have to let peace happen inside of yourself. I'm still working on it. I hope you will work on it, too. You deserve better than this. I'm sad that a person so young as you has to worry about a war.

Your friend,
C.D. Thompson

He folded his letter into an envelope, addressed and stamped it, and put it carefully into his leather briefcase. Out of the briefcase he pulled his chess set, and started playing alone.

I had gone to the library to do research for a history paper. Moving between the book stacks, I watched as Seedless finished a game of chess with himself. Seedless' odd, scarred face curled into a weird grin as he made his next move. When he was done, he turned the board around and scowled.

"Dirty son of a bitch," he sputtered, too loud.

"Jeez, Seedless," I whispered. "Can't you even play quietly with yourself?"

"Back off, kid," snapped Seedless, louder. "Can't you see? That jerk Thompson has backed me into a corner. It's all your fault. I got distracted when you came in the door. He took advantage of the fact I wasn't paying attention, and tricked me into losing my last rook." With a huff he moved his knight ineffectually, knowing that his rook was doomed.

"I've discovered that my self is a tough opponent, too," I said, approaching the oak table.

"What's that?" asked Seedless, again too loud.

"I've been trying to pay attention to my thoughts. I discovered that it is hard to do it. I watch my thoughts, like I'm on the outside of them. I can do it for a while, but then the thoughts take over again and I get lost in them. It is hard to get outside of them and watch them again," I said.

"I work really hard at not watching my thoughts, ever. I don't want to know what I'm thinking. It would be way too scary!" exclaimed Seedless as I grimaced and put my finger to my lips. Seedless went on, pointing at his own head. "There's stuff going on in there that nobody, including myself, should have to look at."

"I don't know, Seedless. It's different for me, I guess. I really want to pay attention to my thoughts. Something good happens when I am able to do it. Feels like I'm living my life then, instead of being lived by it. I just read this poem by a guy named Rumi. A poem about the self."

"Oh, yeah. Rumi, the Sufi," said Seedless, taking his white rook with his black queen.

"You know about him?"

"Oh yeah. I like the stories about him and his friend Shams, how they would get together and talk and laugh for weeks, communing with Allah."

Shams? I remembered Ibn Shams, who had introduced me to Rumi when I had visited Dar al-Islam.

"I learned about Rumi at the mosque," I said.

"You're hanging out with those Muslims?" blurted Seedless. "Here's what I think," he declaimed as the librarian glared at us over her reading glasses. "I think they are working with the terrorists. They set themselves up here along the border with Mexico so they can smuggle their people into the United States."

"But Seedless. They make their money by printing books of Rumi's poetry," I pleaded. "It's really hard to believe that they are working for terrorists."

I made reassuring hand signals to the librarian as I took Seedless by the shoulder and ushered him outside. Seedless loudly carried on as we stood under the *portales*.

"Not only are they terrorist sympathizers," yelled Seedless, "they are polygamists. Any guy who thinks he can have more than one wife is just plain nuts. Why, they'd be at each others' throats all the time."

"The people at the mosque are not polygamous." I tried to cut short Seedless' diatribe before it gained too much momentum. "Sure, women are challenging, but for me, it's for other reasons. I'm trying to watch my thoughts about women, and it is pretty hard to do. I get sucked into those thoughts more than any others. I get completely lost," I confessed.

"Don't bother trying to watch what you think about women," advised Seedless. "Just don't think about them at all. If they get into your mind, hurry up and do something else to distract yourself. Once you get going thinking about them, you are lost. It's too powerful. You can't win. Play a game of chess. Rebuild a carburetor, anything that requires your total attention so you can put them out of your mind."

"I don't want to put her—er, *them*—out of my mind," I said. "I just want to be able to stand outside of my thoughts about them, and watch my thoughts. It feels so different when I can do that."

"Forget it. Don't bother. Take my advice. You will save yourself a whole lot of pain and wasted time," bellowed Seedless.

***

I got an email from Alice Kahn, inviting me to *sesshin* at her house the following weekend. I at first thought she'd misspelled the word, but figured out from the context that it was some kind of Buddhist thing.

Alice's front yard was nothing but perfectly clean sand, raked in an even pattern, surrounding a big rough rock. There was Hebrew writing on a brass plaque on the front door. Inside, the living room was a big empty room with a slate floor with a bunch of woven reed mats in rows. On the wall, I found a framed document done in beautiful calligraphy in English and Hebrew: a marriage certificate. Another frame had a picture of a round figure marked with quadrants surrounded by images of blissful praying people and purple monsters with fangs and lots of arms. A brass Buddha sat in an alcove in the wall, hand upraised in a peaceful gesture.

I spent most of the day sitting on a mat on the floor with ten other people, all of them a lot older than me. We did forty-five minute stints of silent sitting, broken up with short walking meditations, going around the room in circles very slowly. Lunch was a broth-y soup with a few bits of vegetables and some spongy stuff that felt weird on my tongue but tasted pretty good. The proceedings were directed by an older man named Walt, who wore a black robe and was particularly good at sitting absolutely still for long periods of time. Alice had introduced him as a Zen teacher and a member of the Quaker meeting in Tucson. Every so often, Walt would walk among us as if inspecting us to see if we were doing it right. In so many words, he had instructed us to sit still and pay attention. To what? To everything.

At first, I felt ready for this experience. I'd been trying to pay attention to my thoughts for the past month, and finally, here was a chance to get serious about it and do it all day. It went well initially. But by the third sitting session, I got really uncomfortable. My butt itched. My thigh muscles were twitching. Then I started thinking about thinking about thinking, and so on to infinity, and the thought of that kind of infinity bored me. Then it appalled me. Then I got into a kind of panic, thinking that I would not be able to stop thinking about thinking about thinking. Finally, I was able to have compassion on myself, kindness took over, and I noticed that I was feeling it not only for myself, but for others. I thought compassionately about Martha Kopecki, feeling an unusual openness to loving her not for myself, but for herself. What did she need, and not need, from me? I showered compassion on Dana and Leon; on my dad; on my buddies at Portales High School; on Emily Luis. Then I found myself focusing on Seedless Thompson. I sensed a great need in Seedless, and I felt a great warmth for him in my heart.

When I left Alice's house, and looked outside toward Cobre Mountain, with shafts of sunlight breaking behind it, I radiated compassion at all that I saw. The mountain received my caring gaze, as did the brilliant sky. I felt like I weighed nothing. There was no difference between me and anybody or anything else. I remembered something I had read in the writings of Rumi: "Please come in, my Self. There's no place in this house for two."

Alice Kahn came up behind me as I stood in front of her house, staring at the mountain. Smiling, she asked me if I was okay.

"Yeah. It was good, really good. Thanks for inviting me," I said. "I got a lot out of it. Tell me something, though. Walt is a Quaker, but he teaches Buddhism. You are a Jew, but you practice Buddhism. Are there any just plain old Buddhists around here?"

Alice laughed. "Buddhism isn't a religion in quite the same way that Judaism or Christianity are religions," she explained. "When you get down to it, Buddhism is nothing but practice. It helps me be a better Jew. I think Walt would say that it helps him be a better Quaker."

"So who are Quakers?" I asked. The spell of the day's meditation was wearing off.

"You ought to ask the Quakers," she answered. "They are Christians, but their religion is pretty much all about practice, too. They keep silent in their worship, and speak only when the Spirit moves them. I've been to their meeting in Tucson. It is a really wonderful group of people."

***

For a few Saturdays, I showed up at Alice's house for Hebrew school. I was seven years older than the oldest kid in the class, but I was hopelessly behind them in understanding the language. But at least Alice taught me some basics: the letters of the *aleph-beit,* the fact that words were formed by putting different vowels in root words consisting of three consonants, and that the root words gave hints of the deeper meaning of the words from which they were formed. Each letter was also a word in itself, and each letter also stood for a number, and the shapes of each of the letters had special symbolic meanings as well. The number values of the letters also corresponded to events written in the Scriptures: 5 for the books of the Torah, the first books of the Hebrew Bible; 40 for the number of years the people of Israel wandered in the desert, and so on. Therefore every letter and every word had many layers of meaning: numerological, representational, symbolic, and historical.

It seemed like the Hebrew Torah was a vast labyrinth in which every letter and every word was connected in some meaningful way to every other word and letter. You could follow the connections endlessly, and never find all the meanings of the text.

At Hebrew school, I discovered a new dimension of my own name. "You might be interested to know that the name 'Jesus' is a translation of the Hebrew name 'Yeshua,'" she told the class. "We have a 'Yeshua' in our class. 'Josh' is short for 'Joshua' which is another transliteration of the same Hebrew name," she reported. She went on to explain the background of the biblical names of other kids in the class.

***

Piles of books about quantum mechanics and theoretical physics, ones he'd special-ordered from the Tucson library, surrounded Seedless on the oak table as he wrote.

Another letter to a boy in India:

Dear Ravi:

I liked the picture of you with your brothers and sisters. I never saw such wonderful smiles before. You look like such a happy family.

My family wasn't so happy. My older brother ate 10,000 micrograms of LSD when he was a freshman in high school, and was never quite the same after that. He moved out onto the streets and wandered around talking to himself all the time. My little sister got mixed up with the wrong crowd and wound up in jail because she drove the getaway car after her boyfriend killed a rival gangster. My dad was an alcoholic, pretty useless as a father. My mom tried the best she could to take care of us herself, but she was depressed a lot and didn't have the energy to discipline us. I didn't do very well in school. I was kind of a misfit, and didn't have many friends. So later I joined the Army and then got sent to the Persian Gulf War. That was not a good place for a kid who was as mixed up and immature as I was. I went crazy in Kuwait and started acting weird, so they kicked me out of the Army.

I tell you all of this for a reason. I want your family to stay happy. Do whatever you can to be nice to each other, to be kind. Try to stay out of trouble, because it doesn't just make trouble for you, it hurts everybody around you. I don't know if I would have had all my problems if my family had been happier. That might have made a big difference. We all have to remember that we depend on each other. If one person in your family does the right thing, it helps everybody. If one person in your family does the wrong thing, it hurts everybody. Remember that! It's a big deal.

Your friend,
C.D. Thompson

Seedless was licking the envelope to seal the letter when I went over to talk with him. "Good idea to come in here," Seedless bellowed in greeting. "It's so hot out there, your shadow will evaporate before it hits the sidewalk." The librarian sputtered a giggle, trying to restrain herself. I hushed Seedless as he sat down at the table.

"Seedless," I whispered. "I'm glad to find you here because I have a question. I'm still thinking about reality. What is it?"

"Still trying to sort out whether matter is real, or only spirit?"

"Yeah, I guess so."

"Why do you care?" asked Seedless. "What's the problem, did you fall in love or something terrible like that?"

"Why would falling in love make a difference in understanding what is real?"

"You have to ask me that?" Seedless slapped his hands on the table, and I winced. "How obvious can it be? Of course, when you fall in love, you begin to question reality. That's why I don't fall in love. I don't want to have to question whether or not things are real."

"Come on, Seedless. You question reality all the time."

"I'm not in here to question reality. I'm in here to deal with the reality of 115 degree heat outside. My trailer only has a little swamp cooler, but this place has the real thing: good air conditioning."

"Come on now, Seedless. Talk to me. I know you have thought about this stuff a lot. What is the real difference between physical and spiritual reality? Don't they really have to be the same thing? I just can't believe in miracles, like practically every religion seems to ask me to do. Even though my visions in the cactus were kind of like miracles. It doesn't make any sense to me to have nature, and then have super-nature, too. The supernatural must really just be a natural thing that is super-unusual. If there is any spiritual reality, doesn't it have to be one and the same thing with physical reality? Isn't it just a material thing in a different form? Aren't hods and souls just different manifestations of the same reality?"

"Hods?" wondered Seedless.

"Dad says hods are real, but they're bad," I answered.

"Okay, okay," Seedless answered, quieting down. "Let's talk about reality. First, you tell me something. Does the number two exist?"

"Uhhhh, sure, I guess," I answered.

"No 'I guess.' Does it exist or not?"

"Okay, it exists," I declared.

"So it is real?" asked Seedless.

"Sure," I said.

"So then tell me. If I use the number two in one arithmetic problem, and then use the number two in another arithmetic problem, are the two two's different from each other?"

"Hmmmm. No. There is just one number two, used in all sorts of situations."

"That's right," said Seedless, leaning his lumpy balding head over the table toward me. "There is only one number two. You can use it here or there, now or then, but each appearance of the number two isn't any different than the next appearance of the number two. All number twos are the same, no matter how you write or use the number. Two is two is two. Two is a universal concept."

"So what's that got to do with reality?" I asked.

"Well it turns out that just like different instances of the number two have no personality, nothing different about them, so it is with the building blocks of matter," said Seedless. "You know that molecules are made of atoms, and atoms are made of subatomic particles. It turns out that any one kind of subatomic particle is the same one thing, no matter where you find it. Let's call one of these fundamental particles 'Particle A.' It is the same thing no matter where you find it, no matter what atom it's in. The 'Particle A' in 'Atom X' is exactly the same as the 'Particle A' in 'Atom Y' and it is the same as the 'Particle A' in 'Atom Z.' 'Particle A 'is a lot like the number two. It has no different personality from place to place. It is exactly, precisely, the same thing no matter where it is.

"There are no bumps or freckles to make one 'Particle A' any different from the next 'Particle A.' Each kind of particle is a universal concept. Just like each number is a universal concept. So it can be said that there really is only one 'Particle A.' It just appears, or manifests itself, in many ways, times, and places.

Just like there is only one number two, which appears or manifests itself in many ways, times, and places."

"So what does this mean?" I wondered.

Seedless slapped the table with his hands, and I winced again. "This table is made of subatomic particles. The particles are the same kinds of things as numbers: they are universal realities that are the same wherever you find them. It turns out that the substance of this table is real in the same way that the number two is real. Both of them are universal ideas. The physical universe is made out of universal concepts.

"Mental reality and physical reality are each made out of the same kind of reality, the reality of ideas. The universal concepts you think about are just as real as the gray blob of brain matter you think them with. The number two, and the brain cells that think the number two, are made out of the same kind of reality."

I fell silent for a moment, absorbing it all. "My teachers never talked about this in science class. But I think you are on to something. It sounds true."

"It sounds true because the universal concepts in you are the same universal concepts in me. When we learn something is true, we are just discovering the universal truths that are already within us," said Seedless. "So you fell in love, right? Isn't that what got you started with this problem?"

"Well, yeah, I did fall in love," I admitted.

"Did she fall in love with you?" asked Seedless.

"I don't know."

"And how can you know?" asked Seedless. "How will you ever know she loves you? Will you know if you kiss her, and she kisses back? Will you know if you ask her to marry you, and she says yes? How can you ever be sure? There are all sorts of people out there kissing and getting married, but does that mean they love each other? You fall in love, and logic goes out the window. One plus one equals two, but when you are in love you think that one plus one equals one, which is crazy. Falling in love is a recipe for unreality," bellowed Seedless. "I recommend against it."

"Okay, okay, Seedless." I whispered. "Calm down, would you? We're in the library, remember? Look. You say that we learn about the universal concepts that are already within us, the concepts even our bodies are made out of. So if love leads me to a universal truth, doesn't that say a lot about love? So maybe someday Martha—I mean, this woman I'm in love with—maybe someday she and I will discover we have the same concept of love for each other."

"Too many maybes. More likely, you'll be fooled into thinking you feel the same way about each other. Look around you. Fools everywhere. People who think they are in love, people who thought they were in love, but they just fooled themselves with wishful thinking. Just because we humans are capable of discovering universal truths, that doesn't mean every thought we think, or every feeling we feel, is true," declared Seedless, slapping the table again.

I stood up. "Well I'm going to find out if it is true love or not. I'll let you know when I know."

13. Wet Ones

Pastor Kate invited me to come to a Saturday meeting of the Immigrant Justice Covenant in Tucson. "You'll meet people from all over the state who are concerned about the migrants," she said.

I drove my old truck across the Tohono O'odham Reservation to get there. Just as I rounded a bend that afforded a glimpse of Baboquivari, I saw someone up ahead standing along the road waving something in the air. It was a common sight along the highway. I knew that *mojados* came up from Sonora, walking through the hottest and driest part of the Arizona desert with plastic water jugs in hand, and when they got to the road they waited for rides from their coyotes. But if the coyote failed to pick them up, an all-too-common outcome, then there they stood, hiding in the mesquites along the road, leaping out to hitchhike when there were no *migra* vehicles passing by. This one was waving his empty water jug, pleading for a ride. I stood on the brake pedal and skidded the truck to a dusty stop by the side of the road. The *mojado* hopped in the passenger seat and I put the pedal to the metal and rooster-tailed the truck back onto the pavement, continuing on toward Kitt Peak and Tucson.

Though I had made a lot of progress with the language, I still didn't know enough Spanish to understand much of what my passenger, who introduced himself as Rogelio, was trying to express.

A scrawny young guy with a gold front tooth, he reeked of sweat. He was holding his nearly empty water jug upside down in his lap. The jug had a label with a picture of a cactus on it and the words *Sahuaro–Agua Purificada*. *"Una espina,"* he explained, pointing to a little hole in the jug. He had bumped it against a cactus as he was walking the miles from the border to the road. In my best Spanish, I told Rogelio that I was on my way to Tucson. Rogelio shrugged his shoulders and smiled and kept on talking, with me comprehending only the occasional phrase.

I asked *¿adonde vas?* wondering where Rogelio wanted to go next. I couldn't understand the response, so I pulled over and got out my map of southern Arizona and showed Rogelio where we had started and where we were now. It was evident immediately that Rogelio couldn't read in Spanish, much less in English. He kept talking about California. Slowly, I began to realize that my passenger had no idea where he was, other than somewhere in the United States. And I wondered, if I went over the border right now, I might not know what state or town in Mexico I was in, either. But at least I could read enough to find out. Rogelio pointed toward the city and said, "California, *p' aca.*" I shook my head and said, *"No,* California *esta p' alla,"* pointing the opposite direction, back toward and beyond Portales.

I was concerned that if I let Rogelio out at that spot, looking so road-worn and carrying the telltale water jug, he'd get picked up by *migra* right away. So I just kept driving to the meeting of the Immigrant Justice Covenant, which was being held at a Presbyterian Church in the Tucson barrio.

At the church, Rogelio gulped refrigerated water from the social hall drinking fountain, and then went into the bathroom to wash up with soap, water, and paper towels. I had given him a clean shirt to wear; Rogelio stuffed the dirty one into the trashcan in the bathroom. Then the two of us went into the sanctuary and slid onto the *banco* built into the wall that served as the back pew.

The church was constructed to look like a kiva, an ancient Anasazi ritual center. It was round, with heavy adobe walls, with wood *vigas* and *saguaro*-spine *latillas* holding up the roof. Heavy wood pews formed a semi-circle around the altar.

A woman was speaking at the altar. Rogelio nodded as she recounted in Spanish, translated every few minutes by another woman into English, her own encounter with *coyotismo*, the abuses perpetrated by the people she paid to smuggle her across the border. The coyote got her across the border, all right, but then held her in a house for a month, demanding money. "They told me it would cost $800, so my cousin paid the $800 to the coyote when I got across. But then he told my cousin that I owed them $2,000 more. She didn't have the money, so there I was, stuck in a little house with about ten other people, not knowing when or how I would ever get out." Finally, she escaped one night, slipping out a window and hopping over a fence. She didn't know where she was; she didn't even know she was in Phoenix. She stumbled into a convenience store and asked the Spanish-speaking clerk if she could use the phone to call her cousin, and was finally rescued.

The crowd was a most eclectic assortment of humans. There was an old white man with a long white beard wearing a bolo tie; Hispanic women with children leaning on their knees; earnest-looking middle aged women with long salt-and-pepper hair and no makeup; Hispanic men in business suits; a few men wearing yarmulkes; a man with a turban on his head and a long black beard. I could see Pastor Kate sitting stiffly near the altar. Father Crespi was there in his black clerical shirt.

After more speeches, it was time for lunch. The crowd poured out into the courtyard, which was fenced with living ocotillo stalks planted and wired together. Tables were set up under the awnings of the Sunday school wing. Rogelio filled his paper plate to overflowing with church potluck food. I glanced at him as we ate at the table, and just about spit out a mouthful of tuna casserole, laughing, as I watched Rogelio shovel food into his mouth.

Pastor Kate sat down across from us. "So who is your friend?"

"His name's Rogelio. I picked him up on the road on the way here."

Rogelio put down his plastic fork and put out his hand. "*Con mucho gusto*," he said to Pastor Kate. She talked to him in Spanish, which she spoke with what I presumed to be a New England accent. I could only pick out a word or two of what was said. "What did he say?" I asked.

"He said he's trying to get to Santa Rosa, California, to work at a chicken ranch. I told him he was in Arizona, but I don't think he really knows where California is. I told him he had a very long way to go. He said he doesn't mind."

"He'll need somewhere to stay tonight," said a man sitting near us. "He can stay at my place."

The man was an older white guy with a drooping gray mustache and a weathered face. His eyes looked sad but kind. He talked to Rogelio in what sounded like real Mexican Spanish. "What did he say?" I asked the man when the conversation took a pause.

"He says thanks, yes, he'd like that a lot."

The man introduced himself as Cal Redfield, member of the Pima Meeting of the Society of Friends, otherwise known as Quakers, in Tucson. I was amazed that a perfect stranger would open his house to a perfect stranger. But then, I was also amazed at myself for opening my truck to a perfect stranger, too. I realized that I had not given it a second thought when I pulled over. It just seemed like the right thing to do.

I asked Cal to find out more about Rogelio's story. Pastor Kate and I listened as Rogelio talked and the old man translated. Rogelio had come up from Veracruz state in Mexico, riding the rails north. In Monterrey, he got thrown in jail by the railroad police and had to spend all his money for food. I didn't understand the concept. Paying money for food in jail? Cal explained that this was common practice south of the border. The prison kitchen was run as a sort of restaurant. Families of inmates either had to deliver food or pay so that their incarcerated relatives could eat decently. When Rogelio got out of jail, he had to ride the rails south again to Veracruz to put together some more money and for another try at crossing the border.

Once at Nogales, Rogelio found a cheap coyote who took him to the middle of nowhere along the border between Nogales and Sonoyta, dropped him off, gave him directions, and told him he'd meet him at such-and-such a time on the road between Portales and Tucson. The coyote took the down payment, $500, and drove away. Rogelio walked alone across some of the most arid land in the United States. When he got to the road, at the appointed time, nobody was there to meet him, till I picked him up.

***

We returned to the sanctuary for the rest of the conference, which was focused on the response of faith communities to the government's tightening of border controls. As the meeting progressed, I got lost in my own thoughts while speakers were talking. What is the point of the border? Why is it there at all? What would happen if everyone ignored it? Would America collapse, overwhelmed by an invasion of immigrants?

Outside on the patio, during a break, I asked Cal Redfield the question. "Did I do a bad thing to America by giving Rogelio a ride? What do you think?"

Cal grinned under his mustache. "Maybe. You did break the law. But are we citizens of America, ultimately? Or are we citizens of the kingdom of heaven on earth? Look at the book of Revelation, chapter 21. The gates of the New Jerusalem are wide open all the time. No *migra* waiting to catch you if you come in. Everybody's a *mojado*—a "wet one"—in the kingdom, because the river runs right through the middle of the New Jerusalem, flowing from the throne of God. This is it, right here. This is the kingdom of heaven … if you have eyes to see it."

"So you think we're in the kingdom of heaven here on earth? What about the kingdom of heaven in heaven?" I asked.

"Well, maybe there's no border between heaven and earth. Maybe earth is part of heaven. Maybe what is happening in heaven is connected to what is happening on earth," replied Cal. "Jesus says in his prayer 'thy will be done on earth as it is in heaven'. I think he was all about breaking down the boundary between the two. And I think that is what we are doing here, too. Sure, there's a border between the U.S. and Mexico, but there is no border in the kingdom of heaven, where both gringos and Mexicans live. If enough people act like we're all citizens of the kingdom of heaven, eventually the border fence will come down."

"I don't think it will be coming down any time soon," I said.

"Really?" Cal answered, his crow-footed eyes twinkling under his battered Stetson.

***

After the meeting, Cal invited me to stop by at his place outside of Tucson, since it was on the way back to Portales. Rogelio got into Cal's pickup and Cal led the way. Beyond the tract houses of Tucson's suburbs the desert took over again, and I found myself bouncing along a dirt road within sight of the glowing white dome of the Mission San Xavier church to the south.

Cal's place was several dusty acres of chollas and bunch grass with goats, and a couple of horses, nibbling on the sparse vegetation, and a beautiful fenced garden full of native desert plants. An eroded adobe house with a corrugated iron roof and a long porch was set back from the powdery dirt driveway.

While Rogelio enjoyed a long shower in the bathroom, I learned more about Cal. He was a former civil engineer whose wife had died a few years back. He had devoted his retirement to working with the Immigrant Justice Covenant, and to being an active Quaker.

"So what do Quakers believe?" I asked. "I met a guy named Walt who teaches Buddhist meditation, but supposedly he's a Quaker. What's up with that?"

Cal grinned. "I know Walt pretty well from our Friends Meeting."

"What's a Friends Meeting?" I asked.

"I'm sorry. That's the name of a Quaker congregation. We're officially known as the Society of Friends. I've been to some of Walt's weekend Zen workshops. He's a really good meditation teacher. I got a lot out of those sessions."

Cal continued, leaning on the weathered kitchen table, "As for the beliefs of Quakers, there are as many of them as there are Quakers. We aren't so much interested in beliefs as we are interested in seeking the light."

"How did you become a Quaker?"

"Well, I grew up out near Bisbee, on a ranch by the San Pedro River right near the border. There wasn't much to do there at night but read books. Somehow I got my hands on the Journal of John Woolman, a colonial-era Quaker who went a long way toward convincing his fellow Quakers to give up slaveholding. He was constantly trying to bring his way of life into alignment with the light that was being revealed to him."

"What is this 'light' you keep talking about?"

"We believe that the light of God shines in every human being, so we must patiently wait for that light to shine out from within ourselves and others. Because there is something of God in every human being, human life is sacred and must not be destroyed. That's the ultimate reason for the Quaker position against violence."

Speaking of the sacredness of life, I knew the road back to Portales would be more dangerous by an order of magnitude as soon as the sun set beyond the *saguaros*. I offered a *buena suerte*—good luck—to Rogelio as I left. Receding in my truck's rear-view mirror, I saw Cal smiling by the gate to the dirt road.

***

My truck shot past the little stone grottoes, the Styrofoam crosses, the wooden crosses, the plastic bouquets that marked the places where so very many had died in auto accidents along the road across the reservation. The day had impressed on me the fragility and the supreme value of human existence. Every shrine along the road represented a universe, an entire cosmos that had vanished out of reach because of too much booze or just one wrong move at the wrong time. Here one minute, gone the next in a flash. I thought of Rogelio, a human being who could so easily have become another dried carcass along the trail from Mexico to the United States, picked apart by the circling *buitres*. The thought of that light, glowing from Rogelio's smile, being extinguished; it was too much for me. I cried as I drove into the sun, the visor down to shield my face from the brilliance.

And then I started to sing, louder and louder, the Buddhist chant that Alice Kahn had repeated: "*Gate, gate, paragate, parasamgate, bodhisvaha.*" Gone, gone, gone beyond; gone utterly beyond. Beyond myself; beyond selfishness; beyond birth; beyond death.

***

I filled my truck water tank from the spigot near the garage in front of the house.

"Where to this time?" asked Dad.

"We're going down to Organ Pipe Monument. We have some new water stations out near there," I answered.

"Home before dark, eh? All those fishermen, drunk out of their minds, coming home to Phoenix after the weekend in Puerto Peñasco …"

"Yessir. And I'll expect you home before dark, too. Don't stay up too late with Rachel, now."

"What are you talking about?" laughed Dad. "Where'd you get that idea?"

"Hey, Pop," I answered, "I heard you talking to her on your phone the other night."

"I'll start managing your love life, if you start managing mine," retorted Dad. "You might not like that."

***

When I got home, I found a note on the kitchen counter: *Josh—I took your advice. See you about 10 pm—Dad.* At first, I was delighted that my matchmaking effort had worked so well. Dad had a date for Saturday night.

But then I wasn't.

I paced back and forth on the screened porch that faced the town below as it glowed in the fading twilight.

Finally, I got on the phone. "Mr. Young, could I please speak with Martha?"

"Well, let me see if she's available," he said coldly.

I could hear what was happening.

"Martha, it's Josh Stoneburner. Shall I tell him you are busy?"

"Josh? Mom! Uncle L. D.! Can we invite him over to tell us a story? Please? Please? He tells the best stories in the world!" I could hear Dana and Leon begging.

"I don't think that's appropriate," said Martha.

"What does 'apopiate' mean?" asked Leon.

"It means it isn't a good idea," answered Martha.

"Because? Is something wrong with Josh?"

"No. It's just that we don't invite anybody over here just to tell stories to you guys."

"Why not?" asked Dana.

"Let me talk to him." I heard her say. "Josh, why are you calling?"

"Is this a good time to talk?" I asked.

"I don't know," said Martha.

"You're putting the kids to bed, right?" I asked.

"Well, yes—"

"They'll be in bed in half an hour, right?"

"Well, yes—"

"So in exactly forty-five minutes I'll be parked in the alley right behind your bedroom. You'll find a ladder up against the fence. Just climb it, hop over, and there I will be. How about it?"

"You've got to be kidding."

"I am not kidding."

"This is crazy," she laughed.

"It's *seriously* crazy," I said. "Just tell L. D. and Esther that you told me to bug off. And then when you are putting the kids to bed, tell them that you have a headache and that you need to sleep it off, and if they need anything in the night they should knock on L. D. and Esther's door."

"That's outrageous."

"Yup. But this might make you more willing to consider the first idea I had, which is less outrageous."

"Which was?" she asked.

"Which was that you invite me over to tell your kids a bedtime story, right now. And you let me in through the front door. And then we hang out for a while and talk."

"Like the first idea wasn't bold."

"Well, everything is relative ..."

"Josh ..."

"Yes?"

"Okay, Josh. Get on over here and tell the kids a story. Yes, knock on the front door. Just come and tell the kids a story and then leave. Otherwise I'm going to have a real problem here. Okay?"

"Okay. I'm on my way."

Dana and Leon leaped out the door and grabbed my legs before Martha could even muster "Hello." As Dana and Leon giggled, I waddled into the living room with them hanging on my Levis, dragging them along the carpet.

"Did you bring us a story from the story mine?" they asked.

"Yup. I was just there today, getting a fresh one for you. Are you guys ready?"

"Yes. Yes!"

I sat with them on the floor. Martha sat and watched from the sofa. Behind her, in the doorway to the kitchen, L. D. and Esther stood and listened.

"I brought it with me. So here it is," I said, opening the imaginary book to the first page. "You guys see the picture here? The picture of the boy letting go of the balloon?"

"Yes! Yes!"

"What color is the balloon?"

"Red!" yelled Leon.

No, it's blue, silly," said Dana.

"You are both right. See, it's purple, between red and blue. And look at the shape of it. It's pretty big. It's actually a little blimp that looks like a big balloon. And it has fins on it, and a bloopy thing at the bottom. Let me read what the book says:

"Once upon a time there was a boy named Luke. He loved balloons. He decided to build one himself, a fancy one. He decided to make a little blimp with a cabin on the bottom, where his stuffed monkey, Theo, could ride. He wanted his stuffed monkey to have a special adventure.

"So he started building the blimp. He took drinking straws, toothpicks, coffee stirrers, and string and glued them all together to make a frame, see? And then he put plastic wrap on it and glued that tight around the frame. The bloopy thing on the bottom had a place for Theo to sit. Then he filled it up with helium from a helium tank so that it would be lighter than air. It was attached to a string that went down to a big spool, so that he could let it go very high in the sky and then pull it down.

"At first, the blimp leaked out all the helium and came falling down right away. See Theo, all sprawled out on the ground?" Leon and Dana were transfixed, looking at the imaginary picture on the imaginary page. "Luke had to rebuild it, and make it stronger. See, he put in more straws and coffee stirrers this time.

"Finally, he got it so that it would float up in the air. Theo was the proud captain of a zeppelin blimp. Luke took it outside to see how high it would go. He let out all of the string, until the blimp was so high up in the air that it seemed like just a speck in the sky. See the little speck on the top of the page?" Dana and Leon smiled and nodded.

"He was so happy that his blimp went so far into the sky. Finally, Luke rolled up the string and brought the blimp back down to earth. He asked Theo how he liked the trip. 'Oh, Luke, I never had so much fun in my entire make-believe life.' He was so thankful that he gave Luke a monkey hug on his neck, just like this—"

And I tickled Dana and Leon on their necks until they gleefully rolled on the floor.

"But Theo had something else to say after he gave Luke a monkey hug. He said 'Luke, I want to take a long trip in the blimp. I want to travel farther than any string is long.'

"But Luke said, 'I can't do that. You are my monkey and this is my blimp. I can't let my two favorite things get away from me.' But Theo answered: 'But I'm not a thing. I'm Theo, your friend. And you have made a blimp for me that is perfect for taking a very long trip.'

"Look how sad Luke is now, in this picture. See, it says that Luke went to his room and closed the door and sat on the floor and thought about it. 'Theo is right. He's not just a thing. He's my friend. And the blimp is just right for him. I can't take a ride in it; I'm too big. But if I let him go on this trip, I might never see him again, or the blimp I worked so hard to make. What should I do?'

"What do you think? What should he do?" I asked.

"Let Theo go on the trip," said Dana.

"No, those are his favorite toys. He should keep them," said Leon.

"Well, let's see what happened. On this page it says that Luke came home from school every day and found Theo sitting on the edge of his desk with his floppy legs hanging over, looking at him, wondering what he would do. Finally, on Sunday afternoon, Luke took the string off the blimp, put Theo in the basket at the bottom, filled the blimp with helium, and went outside to the back yard. Theo looked at Luke with his big brown eyes and said, 'Luke, you are a real friend. I know how hard it is to let me go on this trip. Who knows if the wind will blow me back around the world to you, or if the wind will blow me somewhere else, and I'll never see you again? You must love me a lot to let me go, and not know whether you will ever see me or this blimp you worked so hard to make. Think of the stories I'll tell you if I return. But think of the things I'll see and do, and imagine them, and enjoy your imagination, if you never see me again. Goodbye, Luke. You are the best friend a little monkey could ever ask for.' And Luke let go of the blimp, and it floated higher and higher into the air until it was a little speck, see? And then the speck disappeared, and then Luke sat down on the grass in his back yard and cried."

From the corner of my eye, I saw tears run down L. D.'s cheeks as he stood in the doorway.

The children's mouths hung open as they stared into the vacant space in my lap where I held the imaginary book.

I turned and could see that Martha's lip was quivering as she watched.

"Luke was sad for days, for weeks, even for a month, but then he found other things that made him happy. He thought about Theo sometimes, wondering where he was and what he was seeing and doing.

"Then one day while he was walking home from school he saw a speck moving in the sky. It got bigger and bigger and closer and closer and he chased it as it landed in a vacant lot. He picked it up: it was a shriveled-up rubber balloon with a plastic rabbit tied to it. He took it home, cut off the balloon, and put the rabbit on his desk where Theo used to sit. He started asking it questions. 'Who are you and where do you come from?'

"The rabbit answered: 'I'm Reginald Rabbit and I come from Sheepdip, Wyoming. I asked my friend if I could have a ride on a balloon, and she was afraid I'd never come back, but I kept asking and finally she said it was okay. I had the most wonderful adventure. I saw the snow-capped Grand Teton Mountains gleaming in the morning light. I saw the banded canyons of Utah. I saw the Colorado River shimmering like a silver necklace at the bottom of the Grand Canyon. And down below, far down below, I saw a hod.'"

"A hod?" wondered Dana. "What's a hod?"

"I don't know, but it's bad, and that's why the rabbit flew past it as fast as he could," I explained.

"But let's keep reading what the rabbit said: 'But the most amazing sight I saw, which I will never forget, was a little blimp with a monkey riding on the bottom. The monkey was so happy, he was howling with joy as he looked down at the earth and all its wonderful sights. We waved at each other as we passed by. I never saw such a happy creature in all my life. He was more interesting, more delightful, more exciting than anything else that I saw on my trip. Oh, it was all a great adventure, but now I'm very content to sit right here on your desk. All I ask is for a fresh carrot now and then, and I'll be glad to stay right here and be your friend.'

"See how Luke is smiling on the last page? See how happy he is, that his friend Theo was having such a good trip? That's the end of the story. Okay, you guys, off to bed."

I ruffed their hair and patted them on their backs and wished them a good night.

Martha got the kids up and headed them toward their bedroom. On the way, she turned to me and said, "I'll be back in about 15 minutes." L. D. and Esther looked at each other and whispered and went upstairs.

In about five minutes, Martha returned to the living room. "Okay, Josh. They want you to tuck them in. Otherwise they'll pester me all night."

I went in to their bunk beds, pulled their covers tight around each of them, and said, "May you both pay a visit to the story mine in your dreams. Let me know what stories you find there while you are sleeping, next time I see you, okay?"

"Okay! Okay!" And I slowly pulled the door closed.

Back in the living room, Martha and I sat on the couch. Mormon picture books for children covered the glass table in front of us.

"Your kids are great. I really love them."

"They really love you," said Martha, turning her eyes toward the carpet. "A lot. What can I say? You are their hero. They've never met anybody like you. Of course, neither have I. They talk about you all the time. It's getting to be a problem."

"What's the problem?"

She swallowed and turned toward me carefully. "Come on now, Josh. You can see the problem. We live here. You don't. You can't come over here every night and tell them stories and tuck them into bed."

"Why not?" I grinned.

"Come on. How would that work? You are in high school. I live with my uncle and aunt, who would never go for it."

"Where are they now? Why are they leaving us alone? Something tells me this is okay with them."

"Well of course they like you. But they aren't going to like it if you are here all the time."

"What about you? Would you like it?" I asked, putting my hand on her shoulder.

Martha looked into my eyes and her tears welled up in big droplets that didn't just fall down her cheeks, but were springing out and away from her eyes and onto her upper lip. She held me tight.

"It's going to take time. Probably a long time," she said, as her sobs subsided. She stood up and escorted me to the door.

14. How to Get a Cholla Spine Out of a Dog's Nose

Back home, about midnight, I found my father cleaning the kitchen.

"Dad?"

"Yes?"

"It's midnight. You never do stuff like this at night. You're always reading some book about rocks by this time. What is going on?"

"Well, the kitchen is kind of dirty."

"Dad, the kitchen's always dirty. Something is up, I can tell."

"There's nothing up," answered Dad, scrubbing the linoleum floor.

"Let me guess. You are getting ready to invite Rachel over for dinner, huh? You don't want to have her see our dirty kitchen," I said. "Terrible." I pretended to fuss, "See over here. A flyspeck on the kitchen window. This won't do. Oh my! What will Rachel say? Let's clean it right away."

"All right, all right. It's true. So, are you pleased with yourself?" said Dad, still scrubbing, not looking up. "And since you are being so nosy, where have you been? Isn't the Rinconada closed on Saturday nights? Or did you get together with your waitress someplace else?"

"You gotta tell me where you went with Rachel tonight, first," I said.

"We went to the bar in the rec room at Rancho Nolontomo. Pretty romantic, huh? So where did you go?"

"I went to the Mormon bishop's house and told a bedtime story to some little kids," I answered.

"The bishop's kids?" asked Dad.

"No, the waitress' kids," I answered.

"You are dating a woman with children? You are only 17 years old," whined Dad, who was still on his knees but was now turned around waving the scrub brush at me. "Good grief, son, you're having enough trouble getting through high school. What are you doing, mixing it up with some gal who has children? I swear, kid, you're doing life upside down. You're supposed to study the basics, get decent grades in high school, then later you can get into high-flying stuff like theology and philosophy. You're supposed to go to school, you graduate, you get a good job, then you get married and have kids. You're bombing out in high school English while you read the philosophy of Whitehead. You're dating a woman with a couple of kids, when you are supposed to be going to the junior prom with a girl and get your teeth stuck on her orthodontic braces.

"What am I going to do with you? How can I get through to you? I am so confused about you. Because I like you a lot. Not only are you my son, whom I love, but you are a really interesting and extremely fun person to live with. So it's hard to get very upset at you. It's just that I worry about you all the time. I want to help you make something of yourself, but

I see you getting stuck. The worst of it is that I am afraid you are going to trap yourself here in Portales. Never make it to college, never leave town because you are living with a waitress, cleaning RVs in order to feed her kids, living in a trailer, like Seedless Thompson."

"'Mobile homes, Dad. Not trailers. People have been beaten senseless around here for making that mistake," I said, with gravitas.

"Yeah, right," said Dad. "But I want you to get my point."

"That you don't want me to be carrying hods?"

"That's right. I don't want you stuck in Portales, being a hod-carrier."

"I got it, Dad. Hods are bad, hods are bad."

"Look, I just don't want you to get stuck here," said Dad.

"Like you, you mean? Stuck being a bachelor in a beat-up old house at the end of the road, with a dusty rock collection?" I retorted. "If you don't like the idea of me being stuck here, what are you doing here in this crummy little town? You're doing life backwards, too. Look at you, on the floor, trying to impress your new girlfriend. It's time you acted your age, really. I thought teenagers were supposed to impress their dates, not old men like you."

"Well, if I can dish it out, I guess I better be able to take it," Dad chuckled, scrubbing scuff marks off the linoleum.

***

At the oak table in the Portales City Library, Seedless Thompson's right eyebrow twitched and his lower teeth bit into his upper lip as he concentrated on writing a letter.

This one was to a boy in Peru:

Dear Francisco:

Congratulations on winning the race! I would love to see you run sometime. I like to imagine you, speeding up and down the mountain trails. It must feel good to be strong and free like that. Ever thought about running in the Olympics? Maybe I'll see you on TV someday, getting a gold medal!

I think it must be nicer to run cross-country, like you do, than to run around a track in circles. A lot of what I do is like running around in circles, and I don't like it. I am a janitor, so I have to do the same stuff, over and over again. People don't clean up after themselves like they should. So I have to pick up after them, over and over. Around and around. Sometimes I wish I was "running" through a different scene every day, doing something different every day, instead of the same old stuff. But then, when I think about it more, I realize that I don't like change that much. Especially I don't like having to deal with a lot of different people all the time. If I was doing different work every day, I'd have to deal with too many different people. It's all I can handle, just putting up with the people I am already used to seeing!

*So I guess I have to run a different kind of race.
One that goes around in a lot of circles. Maybe I
can get good at it. But I sure like hearing about
your races. They sound a lot more exciting!*

*Your friend,
C.D. Thompson*

***

Dirty socks, plastic jugs, and food containers lay scattered in the brush around the water tank. Against a clear blue sky, the tattered blue flag marking the tank hung limp.

"Whoever gives even a cup of cold water to one of these little ones in the name of a disciple, truly I tell you, none of these will lose their reward" (Matthew 10: 42). This quote from Jesus was written with a marker in misspelled Spanish on the side of the tank.

I looked east across the desert toward the distant thumb-shaped peak of Baboquivari, glowing yellow-orange in the fading sun. My ego was gone: only what I was seeing existed for me. The mountain faded away and in its place I saw Jesus. He was standing right in front of me. I could smell his sweat. He was a tough, wiry little guy, with sun-baked skin, grinning through his rough beard. He offered an earthen bowl of water to me and said something in a language I did not understand. It felt like love was pouring out of him toward me. The rush of energy went up my spine and out of the top of my head. With my eyes locked on his, I stepped forward to receive the cup, and then the vision dissipated. I saw Baboquivari again.

I breathed deeply for a while as the tingling passed from my body. Every shadow, shape, and color on the distant mountain stood out distinctly.

I went back to work, still glowing with joy. I drained the tank and put in the hose from the truck and flipped the valve to fill it. I closed my eyes as I listened to the water gurgling from one tank into the other. I realized I was joining Jesus in offering the sacrament of water to the thirsty. I was in an unbroken line of his followers, going back two thousand years. For me that afternoon, Jesus indeed had come to America, just like the Mormons said.

***

When I got home, I walked in through the kitchen door. I heard muffled voices and looked in the screen porch room. The back of the sofa faced me. I saw Dad's arm holding up a woman's outstretched arm above the top of the sofa.

"Dad?"

With a look of panic, Dad's face popped up. His hand was still holding the arm in the air.

"Dad? Whatcha doing?"

From the sofa, out of my sight, a woman's giggle turned into a full-throated laugh.

I caught my breath. "Is that Rachel?"

She popped up from behind the back of the couch and quickly said "Yes!" and then ducked her head down again.

"Dad," I yelled. He still held Rachel's hand in the air. "Dad, tell me you guys are playing and not fighting."

"Uhhh, playing." said Dad, still holding up Rachel's arm.

Rachel popped up her head again and said, "Playing," and ducked again out of my sight, laughing loud.

I could see it was time for me to leave and pay a visit to the library.

I met Seedless there and we played a game of chess. For a change, we barely said a word. It was a good game, a cliffhanger. I almost won.

This is a letter from Seedless to a boy in Albania:

Dear Enver:

I'm very glad that you are learning from your brother's mistakes. Life is hard enough without making it harder the way he has done, getting involved in drug dealing. It was brave of you even to tell me about it. I learned from my brother's mistakes, too. He got mixed up with drugs, big time. I stay away from that stuff, because I saw what it did to him. I'm a nutcase as it is. I don't need drugs.

Sometimes I think I want to control the world. I get really mad at our president for screwing things up here in this country, and for messing up other countries, too. Then I remember how hard it is for me to control myself. I have a hard time managing my own emotions. I get really angry at the church

*where I work when people leave all sorts of food
out on the kitchen counters, and don't throw it
away themselves. I have to come and pick up all
the stinking filth, all covered with bugs, and I lose
my temper sometimes. I don't think I'd be a very
good president, because I do a bad job of
controlling myself. So why do I think I could do a
good job of controlling the world?*

*It's hard to stay away from temptations. I ought to
know, because it's hard for me. And harder still to
be kind to other people when they do stuff that
ticks you off. I'm trying, even though I'm not very
good at it. Good luck to you!*

Your friend,
C.D. Thompson

***

I went to the Freeze to hang out with my buddies
after school one afternoon. The flies were moving so
slowly in the heat that Eddie Contreras snatched
three of them in midair as they were looping crazy-
eights above the picnic table which was smeared with
the residue of countless milkshakes. It was so hot that
Ben and some other boys from the rez showed up,
too, after a fifty-mile drive from their high school.
Ben and I slapped hands and sat down at a different
table to catch up. It had been months since we'd seen
each other.

"So, Josh. I hear you try to help the *mojado* these
days," laughed Ben. "One of my buddies saw you out

there filling the water tanks close to the rez boundary."

"Really? Where?" I asked, slurping my milkshake off the end of the straw.

Ben laughed again. "Eyes and ears everywhere on the rez."

"Wow," I said, "Really? All that desert and so few Tohonos. Mostly, when I'm out there I don't see anybody at all."

"So you want to help the *mojados*. Well, maybe you want to come with me on Saturday and I'll show you how we do it."

"What do you mean?" I asked, bottoming-up my milkshake while it was still cold.

"I mean we have our own ways of helping. You'll see. Come on out to our place Saturday morning pretty early," said Ben, still smiling.

"Like how early?"

"Like six-thirty in the morning." laughed Ben.

"Okay then. Six-thirty. You got me curious."

"But don't tell anybody what's up. You are my friend, right? You gotta keep quiet about this," said Ben.

"All right. I'll keep quiet."

***

Not even the dogs were stirring when I pulled up in my truck at the Jose family compound. Ben came out smiling from one of the trailers. He had a backpack slung over his shoulder. "We take your truck this time, okay?" he said.

255

"Okay," I said. But there was something in his voice that sounded like this might not be okay at all.

Dawn brought a glory of pink, turquoise, gold, and orange to the heavens as we bounced down a series of dirt roads and up to the base of a steep hill.

"This is the place," said Ben. "Park there, in those mesquites."

We climbed the hill and perched at the top among some big rocks. "Here are your binoculars. You look that way, I look this way," said Ben.

"For what?" I wondered.

"For *migra*. *Mojados* come up this way a lot. If we see *migra*, I make a call."

"Who will you call?"

"To people who will tell the *mojados* to hide. What did you think?"

I stood up and handed Ben the binoculars. "Wait a minute. *Coyotismo* sucks, and that's where I draw the line. No way am I working for those assholes."

"No, don't worry. This has nothing to do with coyotes," Ben laughed again.

"Then what is it about?"

"It's about money. You stay here with me for the day, and do lookout, and I give you a hundred bucks cash money. Not bad for sitting on your butt in a pretty place, is it?" Ben laughed again.

"What are you talking about? Who is paying you?" I demanded to know.

"I don't even know. I just call on this phone if I see *migra*, and some guy answers and takes the information, and then somebody, I never see them, drops an envelope full of cash under a rock by my house. Cool job I got. Good money, huh?"

"If they aren't coyotes, they've gotta be mules. Who else but *narcos* has that kind of cash?" I asked as I took the binoculars back again, to look for cops that might be after us. "Ben, you are crazy, man! This could get you in so much trouble. We are talking jail time, we're talking getting killed by criminals if something goes wrong—this is bad, man." I was so frightened that I suddenly felt the strong urge to urinate. Which I did, behind another rock, while talking. "Ben, I'm out of here, man. I'm not doing this, no way. I'm taking you back home right now, dude."

Ben laughed again. "You know who the chief of tribal police is?"

"No."

"The chief is my uncle," Ben laughed again. "I got nothing to worry about. Neither do you, as long as you stay right here till we're done, and keep your mouth shut about all this. You like to help the *mojados*, right? Who knows, some *mojados* might come by needing some kind of help. If they need a ride someplace while I'm here, I drive them when I'm done with my shift. I give them water, food, whatever. They're just people, poor people who need help, man. Sure, somebody is paying me to keep track of *migra*, but if it wasn't me, it would be somebody else, and it's easy work, and while I'm out here I can help the *mojados*, too. So calm down, man, and start watching your direction."

"Ben, what if *migra* catches us? Then we're in big trouble your uncle can't fix," I pleaded, my heart racing.

"Hey, we're citizens. Right? We're out here hunting for *javelina*, right? What can they do to us? I got stopped one time by *migra* after my shift, and nothing happened. They just told me to beat it. I'm an Indian; they don't mess with Indians. You are just my pal who came along to go hunting with me."

"Except it isn't hunting season, we've got no guns, and no hunting licenses," I complained.

"Quiet down, man. This is the rez. We don't need no stinking hunting licenses. This is our land and we can do whatever we want. We're free here. Nobody can mess with us." Ben gazed out to the south with his binoculars. He saw movement in the brush a mile or so away. "Look out there."

I looked, and saw one, then two, then three human forms moving through the brush, headed our way. "Geezus, Ben." I was so frightened I needed to pee again. "Now what do we do?"

"Hah! Nothing. We just lie low here and they'll walk right by us. Just *mojados*. If they see the truck, then we gotta talk to them. But no big deal. They don't need to be afraid of us, we don't need to be afraid of them. You'll see," said Ben.

I aimed the binoculars to the north. "Holy shit," I hissed, shivering with fright. "*Migra*, over there!"

A faint line of dust was aimed right at us, coming down the same track we had followed to the hill. Ben reached in his backpack and pulled out a whistle, and blew it hard three times. I aimed the binoculars south toward the *mojados*. They stopped and then ran east toward an arroyo full of heavy brush. Then Ben got out the cell phone and made his call. It didn't make any sense to me.

"Call the vet. The dog got a cactus spine in his nose," said Ben, and clicked the phone off.

"What was that all about?" I whispered.

"Man, you don't need to whisper. The *migra* truck is a mile away," laughed Ben.

"What was that all about? What you said on the phone?" I was still whispering.

"I don't know. It's what I'm supposed to say, that's all I know. Look, I don't want to know who I'm working for, or what any of it means. It's just a job, man. Good money for easy work."

"We gotta get out of here."

"No, we don't. We just stay right here. Don't worry, you'll see."

The *migra* truck drove right up to my truck and two agents hopped out. "Okay, where are you? or we'll impound the truck right now …"

"Shit," I whispered. "We're busted."

Ben laughed again. "Don't say anything. Let me handle this. Just come with me and stay calm, all right?"

I saw no choice in the matter. I took a few deep breaths and followed Ben down the hill. I tried to be conscious of my thoughts and feelings, but found it next to impossible.

"We're over here, officers," yelled Ben.

"Hi. I'm Ben Jose, and I live over by Hickiwan. This here is my friend, Josh," said Ben to the officers.

"What are you fellows doing out here?" asked one of the officers.

"Josh here is involved in the water stations thing that the church people are doing, and I was showing him where the migrants come up in this area. I met him at my church youth group. See his truck here? He's got a water tank on it to refill the water tanks," said Ben.

The officers asked to see our IDs. After looking them over, and checking out the truck, they handed them back. "The tribe doesn't want water stations out here. You'll get busted for it if you set one up. Really, you guys shouldn't be out here," said one of the officers. "It's dangerous. There are mules and other bad guys out here. Maybe you think you are helping, but that is our job, to protect the illegals from dying of thirst or when they are abandoned by their coyotes."

"Yeah, I suppose you are right, officer," said Ben. "But hey, my friend here wanted to see this route, so I said I'd help out. We're going to try to convince the tribe to change its policy. Sorry if we caused you any trouble. We'll leave pretty soon, if that is okay."

The officers said no more, hopped back in the truck, and went four-wheeling off the road toward the area where Ben and I had seen the *mojados*. Ben got back on the radio phone and said, "The vet got here and he's working on the dog," and turned it off again.

"Okay, Ben, time to go," I demanded. "Let's put it this way, man. I'm going. If you want to stay out here and do your so-called job, that's your business."

"Can't go. Neither can you."

"What do you mean?"

"I mean I have to finish my shift, or else I'm in really big trouble that even my uncle can't fix. And if I'm in trouble, hey, so are you," he laughed. "But don't worry, I won't make you do it again. And you will get paid."

"But *migra* will be back. What will you tell them if they come back and we are still here?"

"Don't worry. I'll tell them some crap and they have to buy it, because they don't have anything on us."

Sure enough, the border patrol truck came bouncing back. Nobody was in the back seat. The officers questioned us some more. "What are you still doing here?"

"Well, we have to figure out where to put a water station. So we've been out in the brush looking for the right spot. Might take us a while longer. Sorry if that is a problem," said Ben, with a smile.

The officers wordlessly got back in their vehicle and drove away. Ben and I resumed our watch from the rocky hilltop. Ben blew on the whistle; one long "all-clear."

"This is the end of the earth, the place where America dumps out the lint from its clothes dryers. But it's full of people," I observed aloud, shaking my head.

261

A while later, Ben saw another line of dust coming our way from the south. Ben blew the whistle three times, then made his phone call. I pointed the binoculars at the source of the dust. An ATV painted camouflage green raced by below us, dodging the mesquites and the *saguaros*. A chunky guy in a camouflage outfit was driving it, and he had a huge gun with a curved ammo cartridge bouncing over his shoulder.

"Your smuggler, no doubt," I said, ducking lower behind the rock.

"I think it's one of those Border Bouncers," said Ben.

"Who are they?"

"Crazy white guys who round up *mojados*," said Ben. "They think they are protecting America's borders. Really, they just hate brown people. A bunch of gun nuts, those guys. They carry around assault rifles, like it's a war out here or something. We hate them here on the rez."

Ben blew the "all clear" again on the whistle.

About half an hour later, three young men showed up at the truck.

"Go down and talk to them," said Ben.

I went down and met them, all young Hispanic guys. They assumed I spoke Spanish, and laughed when they realized I didn't understand them very well. I offered them some water, and they grinned and accepted. They stank of sweat and their western-style shirts were stained. "*Quieren a llavarse*"—Want to wash? I asked. They accepted the chance to rinse off their faces and hands from the tap at the back of the truck. I choked back emotion as I watched them savor the cleansing water. The border wall must come down so that precious human beings like these men do not have to suffer like this, I thought. My heart poured out to them like the water running over their heads.

They refilled their plastic jugs and thanked me graciously and went on their way, around the hill and to the north. Back up among the rocks, I watched them for a long time with the binoculars, as if somehow that would offer them protection.

I noticed I wasn't afraid anymore.

"Perfect love casts out fear," I remember reading from the Bible during youth group meeting at the Baptist church.

***

In the late afternoon, Ben announced that it was time to go home.

"So, what do you do when a dog gets a cholla spine in its nose?" I asked, after a long silence as we drove along.

"You take a pair of pliers and twist while you pull it out. But then there are usually more little itty-bitty spines stuck in there, too. So you take a soft cloth, soak it with Elmer's glue …"

"Elmer's glue?" I howled.

"Yeah. You take it and put it over the dog's nose and hold it there till it starts to get dry, and then you pull it off real quick and the little spines come right out. The dog hates it like hell. But what else are you going to do? Can't afford the vet."

As we pulled up to the Jose family compound, Ben pulled a roll of bills out of his pocket and handed it to me.

"No way. I'm not taking money from drug dealers."

"Hey, you don't know if it came from drug dealers; neither do I. None of our business. So give your money to your church people to make more water stations," said Ben. "Me, I need my half of the money. You know, my dad, he pawned my belt buckle. He put my turquoise in pawn so he could get money to buy a transaxle. Pissed me off, but hey, we all need that truck to get fixed. That's why I needed a ride today. And that's why I need the money, so I can get it out of pawn. My grandma gave me that belt buckle, and I want it back. You don't need the money, that's your business. But I'm not keeping your half of the dough. You did half the work." He tossed the bills onto the seat as he hopped out of the cab. "Good adventure today? Got you kind of excited, huh?" he said, leaning into the window.

"Yeah, Ben. Promise me you'll never do something like that to me again, would you?"

"I promise. I don't want you to get in any kind of trouble. But I want you to see what's really going on out here. That's the other reason why I took you out with me. I think you ought to know. But keep it cool, yeah? We're friends, right?"

"Can't you find some other way to make money? I don't want you getting all mixed up with drug dealers, getting hurt or even killed, or going to jail, or something," I begged.

"Don't worry. I'm okay. I'm an Indian, right? We're tough people. We've been here for thousands of years, a lot longer than your people. After all you guys are gone, after the white man and the *migra* and the *mojados* and the coyotes and the *narcos* are gone, my people will still be here. So think about that."

"Okay, I'll think about that."

15. The True Name

Pastor Kate drove, Father Crespi was in the front seat, and I sat in the back seat with another member of the Covenant, a quiet fellow named Ajit Singh, who belonged to the Sikh community in Tucson. Father Crespi had offered to take us down to Sonora for a visit with a Catholic group that was providing shelter for *mojados* who had been deported back across the border. I eagerly accepted their invitation to come along.

On the way, I asked Father Crespi a question. "Who was San Lorenzo? Is he a real Catholic saint?" I'd been wondering how the bearded Lorenzo of my vision, who seemed to be Lorenzo Dow the American revival preacher, had been so readily adopted as part of the cult of Cobre Mountain.

"Oh yes, Saint Lawrence is a real saint. He's said to have been the one who took the chalice Jesus used at the last supper, and taken it to Spain for safekeeping," said Father Crespi.

I just shook my head in amazement. "I'd say that the chalice has made it to America to relieve the thirst of the *mojados* at our water stations," I said.

We drove a long way across southern Arizona, out to the border town of Naco.

There isn't much to Naco. It's Portales, without the glitter. It is one very small town sliced in half by the border of two countries. The surrounding vastness of desert dwarfs it. As we drove into town, a

few kids were doing wheelies on their little motocross
bicycles, up and down the main drag, which leads
straight to the border crossing. Into Mexico, the road
was open. But going the other way, from Mexico into
the U.S., traffic turned into a line of cars waiting at
the U.S. Customs and Border Protection station.

"Let's go check out the metal fence," said Father
Crespi.

We parked on the U.S. side and walked down
the dirt road along the border. It was a rusting,
corrugated wall of metal panels, about 12 feet tall.

"The metal sheets were used by the U.S. military
for landing strips for the aircraft during the first Gulf
War," explained Father Crespi. "Recycling, I guess
you'd call it."

As we walked, I fell behind. Father Crespi, Ajit
Singh, and Pastor Kate were walking side by side and
continuing a conversation they'd had in the car. They
were talking about some organizational details of the
Immigrant Justice Covenant, which didn't interest
me much.

The longer I walked, staring at the fence, the
angrier and the sadder I felt. The obscene wall of steel
went on and on, off to the west, bisecting the vast
emptiness of the desert. It was one continuous
magnificent landscape in both directions, and the
arbitrary irrationality of the border impressed itself
upon me.

A spray-painted image of the Virgin of
Guadalupe, the bright rays of effulgence around
her, pierced the dull rust of the metal wall. Father

Crespi, Ajit Singh, and Pastor Kate were so absorbed in their conversation that they had passed the Virgin without noticing her.

I dropped to my knees in the dust in front of the image and held my hands together and bowed my head.

"Holy Mother," I prayed aloud, surprising myself that I was doing it, "I ask forgiveness for this wall and I pray that you will give me strength to do all that I can to take it down."

As we got back in the car and drove into Mexico, I looked at the wall one more time.

"Help me understand something," I said to Pastor Kate and Father Crespi. "How come the Catholic church makes such a big deal about every sperm being holy, and other Christians spend all their time complaining about the existence of gay people, and meanwhile the grossest thing I've ever seen, that metal border fence, is no big deal to them? Why aren't there a zillion Christian protesters here, complaining about it? I don't understand."

"Good question," nodded Father Crespi. "I don't understand it either."

"Josh, a good question can change the world," said Pastor Kate.

The *albergue*, or shelter, on the Mexican side of Naco was a simple stucco home built around an open courtyard. The rooms were tidy and full of metal-framed bunks with neatly made beds, ready for the next wave of deportees. The nun, wearing street clothes, explained in Spanish how the deportees, in many ways, ran the place themselves, following the rules of the shelter. "It's all by word of mouth," she said. "They seem to know the rules of this place before they ever get here." There was a politeness, a cooperative spirit, in Mexican culture; I remembered it from trips to Mexico with Dad. Looking at the blankets on the bunks, neatly tucked and folded by the itinerant guests, I committed myself to make my own bed every morning from then on.

Father Crespi in rapid Spanish discussed the financial needs of the *albergue* with the nun. Father Crespi later explained that years ago, he had preached many times in the Mexican parish church that sponsored the *albergue*, and he had become the broker of most of the shelter's financial support from Catholic churches on the U.S. side.

While Father Crespi took care of business, I struck up a conversation with Ajit. "Okay," I said, "now's my chance to find out about your religion."

Through his magnificent black beard, Ajit Singh smiled. "Just what would you like to know, young man?" he asked.

"First, what's with the turban?"

"*Kesh*," he said. "One of the Five K's of the Sikh Khalsa," he replied. "All Sikh men who go through the Amrit baptism ceremony commit themselves to keep their hair and beards uncut, and to wear turbans."

He then explained the other four K's. He showed me his *kangha*, a wooden comb he demonstrated on his beard. He showed me his shiny *kara,* the steel bangle around his wrist representing God's endless encirclement of the universe. He showed me his little plastic *kirpan*, a fake sword representing his commitment to stand up and defend the truth. He told me about his *katchera*, special underwear he wore as a sign of remaining pure.

"Just like the Mormons," I said.

"Yes, it's something like their special underwear," Ajit said with a grin.

"Did your Savior come to America, too, like the Mormons believe?"

"Our God is everywhere, in the Punjab as well as here in Mexico as well as in America."

"So these Five K's are all about how you look. But what do you believe?" I asked.

Ajit stroked his beard and smiled gently. "Well, maybe our religion is more about what we do than what we believe. I think the most important thing we do is to say and sing the name of God, *Sat Nam*."

"*Sat Nam*?"

"Yes, *Sat Nam* means 'The True Name,'" replied Ajit.

"Just like the orthodox Jews," I said. "They say *Hashem* instead of God. *Hashem* means 'The Name.' They think the real name of God is too holy to say out loud."

"Very interesting!" said Ajit. "I did not know that. But it does not surprise me. God's name is holy, indeed. We have many names for God, but *Sat Nam* is one we use a lot. We think that if you repeat God's name with true intention, over and over, your ego will be put in its place and then it will be much easier to do the right things and avoid doing the wrong things in life.

"One of our favorite ways to say the name of God, or listen to it and meditate on it, is through music. We call our music *kirtan*. It's very beautiful. You really should come to our *gurdwara* in Tucson sometime and listen for yourself. Everyone is welcome, you know. And everybody can stay for very tasty vegetarian food. Here is my card. Please, I am serious. I want you to come visit us."

***

We had to cut the visit short because Father Crespi was scheduled to lead the vigil at El Tiradito in Tucson that evening. Every week, an interfaith circle gathered in a dusty lot near downtown, on the edge of the *barrio*. El Tiradito was a barren lot with a few crumbling adobe walls on the far end, away from the street. The adobe walls were darkened with melted wax from hundreds of *veladoras* placed on them over the decades by people mourning for lost lovers. The original *tiradito*, or castaway, was a legendary lost lover, and this site became a place of remembrance for broken romances or dead *novios*. The vigil was held on the lot once a week at sundown to remember the latest casualties of the border crossing.

About thirty people gathered on the stony, dusty lot as the sky streaked purple and gold and pink to the west.

Father Crespi put his liturgical stole around his neck. He greeted everyone and began with a prayer in English and then in Spanish. Everyone sang a few songs accompanied by a Hispanic man with a big guitar. I recognized several of the people from the Immigrant Justice Covenant meetings. Mostly, they were older white women with lots of turquoise jewelry and long, graying hair, and a few old white men with white beards and bolo ties. There were a few Hispanic people and younger folks.

It came time for the reading of the names and the circumstances of their deaths. Some had died of thirst, others of exposure in the bitter cold of winter nights. Some had fallen behind because they had been injured or had a medical problem along the way, and their coyotes or their fellow *mojados* had left them to fend for themselves. A couple of them had been shot under mysterious circumstances.

One by one, Father Crespi recited the names and the stories, if there were any to tell. He had been given the roster by a volunteer from the Covenant whose job it was to gather the information from the Border Patrol and other sources.

Then he read the name "Ángel Luis Escamilla Hernandez."

"No," I yelled. That stopped the ceremony cold. I stumbled over to the adobe wall, which was streaked with the tears of spent candles, and leaned on it to hold myself up. All the warnings from people in the Covenant group, telling me that it was likely Ángel was dead, didn't prepare me for the final word. Did Rosa know? Had anyone told her? It made me sick.

"DAMN THE BORDER!" I yelled from the bottom of my lungs, as I pounded my fists with futile force on the wall of El Tiradito.

Father Crespi made the phone call. Rosa had heard the news the week before, but she came over to El Tiradito anyway. Father Crespi and I sat with our arms over her shoulders, and Pastor Kate crouched at her knees and held her hand as she cried. I got up and lit a candle and placed it on the wall.

We learned later that Ángel's decomposed body was found, handcuffed, with his face on the ground, hidden near a dirt track frequented by migrants near Baboquivari. His wallet and ID were intact. He had a broken leg. Investigators found fingerprints on the handcuffs that matched those of a felon who belonged to the Border Bouncers. He was apprehended and jailed. A few days after the vigil at El Tiradito, I read the story in the *Arizona Republic*. According to the story, the Border Bouncer said he found Ángel in the desert, injured, and he was trying to take him back over the Mexican border. But the Border Bouncer panicked when he saw a *migra* truck and dumped Ángel in the desert and took off.

Rosa reached into her purse and took out the crystal and asked Father Crespi to pray over it. He said the Hail Mary and pressed his hands over it with his eyes closed.

Then Rosa got up and pinned a plastic-laminated image of *La Virgen de San Lorenzo* on the adobe wall, below the candle.

***

I went to return some books at the library, and then sat down with Seedless at the oak table. He showed me a simple drawing of a man lying on a bed with an IV in his arm. It was drawn with colored pencil on that grainy lined paper used by his kids to write him letters. He said the picture had triggered a memory of his time in the hospital after he had a nervous breakdown in the Persian Gulf War. Other soldiers, mangled physically, lay in their beds with IVs dangling above them. At the time, he was unable to feel what he felt now: gratitude that he was one of the lucky ones. He walked out of the hospital with all his arms and legs and other important appendages intact.

But others weren't so lucky. In the war, all he could think about was the fear and the panic and the rotten luck of having to be there. There, he had not been able to think about much but himself. Now he could think about others. The responsibility that came with survival, the guilt of having failed in courage, weighed on him all the time.

Another letter, this one to a boy in India:

Dear Mohand:

I'm so very sorry that your father is so ill. As the oldest son, this must be a big burden. You have to

*try to do what he can't do for your family anymore.
In one way it is like being a slave; you have to be in
this role whether you like it or not. But in another
way, it is an honor, being the father of your family
for a while, hopefully only for a short while. I
guess that is what it is like to be a real leader. You
become the servant to the people you are leading, if
you are really doing your job the right way. It's a
heavy responsibility. I'm sorry you have to take it
on so early in your life, but it is a good lesson to
learn.*

*I wish you well in this big challenge! I wish I could
be there to make it easier, but since I can't, I'm
sending you some extra money. I hope it helps.*

*Your friend,
C.D. Thompson*

***

The wind stopped after a week of whistling down
Cobre Mountain past our house. Hot air sat on
Portales like the locked glass case over the dead pawn,
the unredeemed jewelry, in the Indian store on the
Tohono reservation. It was awfully hot for an early
March afternoon. I headed to the Rinconada Cafe
after school. Inside, the air conditioner was going
full-blast.

The big, curved Naugahyde booth near the
window was occupied by a bunch of mostly
overweight middle-aged men in camouflage outfits.
I saw that there were embroidered patches on their

shoulders. "Border Bouncers," they read. I walked up to their table.

"Hi," I said. "I'm Josh."

They smiled and said, "Hi, Josh." One of them took off his shades for a moment for a closer look at the kid who had just presented himself, then put his sunglasses back on.

"I've heard of you guys. What are you all about? I'm curious."

They invited me to sit with them. Martha came to the table with the coffee carafe. "Anything for you, Josh?" she asked.

"Sure, Martha. How about one of those great blueberry milkshakes?" She nodded and walked away.

"Cute friend you got there, young fella," said the guy who had taken off his sunglasses.

"I think so. So tell me about you guys. I've never met any Border Bouncers before. Saw something in the papers about you."

"Don't believe any of it. Remember who owns the newspapers," said one of the men.

"I have no idea about that, either," I said. "So tell me, what are you guys trying to do with this Border Bouncers thing?"

"You can't have a free country without real borders," said another of the men. "And we can't have real borders unless citizens stand up to protect them. The government won't do the job, so the people must rise up and do their duty."

"So how do you do your duty?"

"We maintain volunteer patrols to apprehend illegals and then we turn them over to the Border Patrol. That one guy who screwed up, well, he was acting on his own. We are law-abiding citizens," said yet another of the men.

"I hear you guys carry some huge weapons with you. What's that all about? Do you really need big guns to catch a bunch of Mexicans armed with water jugs?" I asked.

"So you are a smart ass," laughed one of the men.

"If I am so smart, why am I pulling C's in high school?" I asked. That wasn't quite true anymore. I was getting A's in Spanish and history.

The men shifted a bit in their seats.

"So what's the deal with the big guns? I mean, those are some pretty cool-looking pieces, from what I saw in the paper. I've never seen a gun like that up close."

"So maybe you want to volunteer for Border Bouncers," said one of them.

"We train recruits in the safe handling of weapons, too," said another. "We're always looking for young people to join us. Especially Mexican-Americans like you."

"Am I a Mexican-American?" I asked. "I think I'm just an American."

"All the better," smiled the Bouncer. "Our kind of guy."

The men turned toward the bearded guy on the other end of the half-round table who was still wearing silvered sunglasses. He spoke:

"Josh, this country is going to lose its freedom pretty soon unless we keep the Mexicans out. Those people have no place up here. They have a herd mentality. They don't understand about individual freedoms. They are superstitious and fatalistic. They just do what they are told. They don't know how to think for themselves. You know, over there in California more than half the babies being born nowadays are Mexicans. That means that if we don't do something about it right now, they'll take over. You think about it, Josh. Use your head. Ever been down in Mexico?"

"Yeah, a lot," I said.

"Nice place to visit, yeah? But you wouldn't want to live there. They don't get it about sanitation. They don't get it about education. They don't get it about democracy; their government is completely corrupt, so voting is meaningless down there. You want to see that happen up here? If you don't, then you'll support our mission.

"It's real simple. We want America for Americans. Mexico is great for Mexicans. Mexicans fit in real well down there; it's where they belong. They don't belong up here. They throw their disposable baby diapers out the window. Ever seen those Pampers all over the parking lots, with flies buzzing all around them? That's what the whole United States of America is going to look like. All the parking lots full of dirty diapers tossed out of cars by the Mexicans who are having all those kids up here. They take over the schools with their kids. The school test scores go down. The schools have to spend all sorts of money to teach them English, which they should have learned at home. They take over neighborhoods, have too damn many people living in their houses. They—"

"Excuse me for interrupting," I said, "but my mother was born in Mexico. So I'm not relating very well to all this talk about how Mexicans don't belong here. But all that aside, I have a question that might help me understand you a lot better."

"Fire away," said the bearded man.

"Why are you guys doing this, but other people aren't? I mean, most other people aren't doing what you are doing. So why do you particular guys do this particular Border Bouncers thing? Did something happen that inspired you to do this?"

"Good question," said one of them.

"Excellent question," said the bearded guy. "I always wanted to be a Marine when I was a kid. My daddy and my granddaddy were Marines."

"Did your dad beat you up when you were a kid?" I asked him.

The men fidgeted in their seats again.

"Well, that is none of your business, young man."

"I'm sorry. I just heard someplace that pretty often, people who are into violence as adults were abused when they were kids. That's pretty sad, if it's true," I said.

"That's the Jew-controlled media for you," said the one skinny guy in the group. "My daddy never beat me, I'll tell you that. That has nothing to do with it. And besides, we aren't into violence. We're into defending our country. Everybody who loves America ought to have a gun. It's not just a right, it's a responsibility. Every godly citizen should have weapons, any weapons they want, and know how to use them. Look at what's happening on the border. All those Mexicans and God knows who else, maybe terrorists, coming across every day, walking right past the Border Patrol. There's proof that the government won't defend you. You have to defend your country yourself."

"So what motivated you to join the Border Bouncers? Anything happen when you were a kid to get you started down this path?" I asked the skinny guy.

"I grew up pretty poor. My dad died when I was six," he said.

I interrupted. "My mom died when I was four. How did your dad die?"

"Well, it was suicide."

"My mom committed suicide with pills. How did your dad do it?"

The men fidgeted some more.

"He shot himself," said the skinny guy.

"Do you think the fact that he shot himself with a gun might have anything to do with the fact that you are now riding around in the desert with a big rifle?" I asked.

The guy with the sunglasses grimaced and leaned over the table menacingly.

I leaned over toward him and said, "Are you mean? Or just ugly?"

Was I idiotic, or just stupid? He grabbed me by the front of my shirt, which I had made so convenient for him to reach, and pulled me over the table on my belly. He was about to punch me out when his pals restrained him and made him let me go.

I and all the Border Bouncers got bounced out of the Rinconada Café by Bernal, the burly Mexican-American cook, who saw what was happening from the kitchen. "Out. All of you," he boomed like desert thunder. "I don't know who started it and I don't fuckin' care." From his reputation around town, Bernal was scarier to me than any of the Border Bouncers, but I didn't stick around long enough to tell them that.

I tucked tail and ran out of there before Bernal was done lecturing.

***

"You'll have to talk to Bernal about it," said Martha, turning away from me when I came in to the Rinconada the next morning. "I don't make the rules here."

I went into the kitchen. "Bernal, I messed up. I should not have talked to those guys. You know who they were? Border Bouncers, those assholes with guns who chase the *mojados* out in the desert. I didn't know how violent they are."

Bernal slammed his spatula down on the stainless counter and got right up in my face. His was an imposing visage with tattoos and scars. "You fucked up, kid. I don't care who they are. I don't care who you are. Don't bring your shit into my restaurant."

"*Entiendo bien*," I whimpered.

"Now go back to your booth. What are you having this morning, the usual?" he said.

When Martha came to my table, I begged forgiveness. "It was all my fault. I upset everybody in the restaurant."

She put down her coffee carafe and stared at me. Her lip was trembling. "Josh, you've got to grow up," she said, poking her finger into my chest. "I need you to grow up."

***

At the next meeting of the Immigrant Justice Covenant in Tucson, I sat in the Presbyterian Church next to a man who looked vaguely Mexican but had a very different accent. He had been identified during the meeting as the fundraising chairperson. As we got up to go to lunch, the man introduced himself as Siva Aggarwal, the representative of a Hindu temple in Tucson. He and I went through the lunch line together in the courtyard of the church, and I noticed that Siva turned down all the meat dishes. We sat together and ate.

"So, do Hindus believe in God?" I asked.

Siva laughed. "Do we believe in God? Indians are the most God-crazy people in the world."

"But you do believe in God?" I insisted.

"Believe? For me that is a strange question. Let me ask you a question," said Siva. "Do you believe in lunch?"

"What do you mean? Do I think I'm eating lunch? Sure," I answered.

"No. Do you believe *in* lunch?" asked Siva.

"Okay, okay. Sure, I believe in lunch, it's obvious. You don't need any faith to believe in lunch. It's just there, in front of us. You can see it, you can taste it, you can smell it," I said.

"And God isn't as obvious as lunch?" asked Siva.

"Uhhh, I guess not," I answered.

"Well, for me, and I think for many Hindu people, God really is as obvious as lunch. We see God, we taste God, we smell God."

"Why is God so obvious to you?" I asked.

"Why is God not obvious to you?" asked Siva. "I mean, look around, my good man. Look around you. We are surrounded by beautiful human beings with love pouring out of their hearts, trying to serve their fellow human beings who are suffering because of borders between countries that keep them apart. They are full of God, every one of them here. Look at the blooming ocotillo in this patio. Every petal of every flower is full of God. Even the flies that are buzzing around us are full of God. Go outside and look at the beautiful jagged peaks north of Tucson in the distance. They are spectacular. The mountains here are full of God.

"You see, where I come from, we understand that God is everywhere and in everything. When we greet each other we say *namaste*, which means 'I greet God in you.' We name our children after God. I myself am named after God."

"'Siva' means God?" I asked.

"It's one name. There are many," said Siva.

"I heard that the Hindus worship lots of idols," I said.

"I wouldn't describe it that way," answered Siva. "We have lots of gods; it is said that there are 333,000,000 of them in the Hindu pantheon."

"That's ridiculous. How can you worship that many gods? I mean, my grandma took me to the Catholic Church, and that's complicated enough, with all those saints."

"To say we have 333,000,000 gods is more of a poetic way of indicating that God has about as many different manifestations as there are people to notice them," answered Siva.

"Wait a minute. Are there lots of gods, or just one?"

"Both," answered Siva with a smile, revealing just about every tooth in his head.

"But it's got to be one or the other," I demanded.

"Oh, does it, young man?" asked Siva, still grinning.

"It's not logical to believe that there is only one God and that there are many gods at the same time," I argued.

"It may not be logical to you, but to me it makes perfect sense. Let me ask you this question. Who is the most important person in the world to you?"

I paused. It was a really good question. A few months ago I would have said it was Dad. No doubt about it. But now …

"Martha." I said it with enthusiasm.

"Very well. Now, you ask me the same question."

"Okay, who is the most important person in the world to you?"

"Sita, my wife. Who, I might add, is also named after God," answered Siva. "So we were asked the same question and gave two different answers, yes?"

"Yes."

"So was one person right and the other wrong?" asked Siva.

"No, of course not." I said.

"My point exactly. Martha is the most important person to you, and Sita is the most important person to me, and we are both right. And what do our answers have in common? You love Martha as much as I love Sita. What we have in common is love. And of course love is who God is, yes? So Hindus worship many manifestations of God, but the devotion and love they feel for that god is the same, no matter what the god's name is or no matter what the god may look like. In India I went often to do *puja* at the temple of Kali, but here at our temple in Tucson we have the images of many gods."

"But you said your name is the name of God. Why don't you worship at the temple of Siva, if that is a god?" I asked.

"My father's family were devotees of Siva. But my mother went to the temple of Kali."

"Wasn't that a problem? I mean, two religions in the same family?"

"No problem. We understand that all gods are really one. We are very accepting of different people having different names or ways of worshipping God. At least that is so among the worshippers of Hindu gods. Unfortunately, there are many Hindus who don't respect the worship of Allah or Christ. But there are also many who do," said Siva. "I like to think of myself as a Hindu who respects all religions. Siva, Kali, Krishna, Allah, Christ, they are all one God, with many names and faces."

"So you worship all 333,000,000 gods?"

"I would if I could. So many gods, so little time," chuckled Siva. "Speaking of which, we are late for the afternoon meeting session."

"So where is your temple?" I asked. "I want to go there."

Siva smiled again. "What do you think? What is more important, seeing the temple or staying for the rest of the meeting?" he asked.

16. 333,000,000 Gods

In Siva's car, riding down the boulevard past strip malls and tire stores, the conversation continued.

"So your temple has lots of gods in it? Why not just one, like back in India?"

"Well, we Indians here in Arizona are from all over India, from many different traditions of Hindu religion. So we had to consolidate and make room for many of our gods."

"Did you start the temple? Are you in charge of it?" I asked.

"No, no. It was started by Americans. Hare Krishnas."

"Who?"

"Hare Krishnas are devotees of Lord Krishna."

"Another god?" I asked.

"Yes. They gave up their worldly lives and traveled in groups through many countries singing *bhajans* and dancing to Krishna with drums and tambourines. They look just like wandering devotees of Krishna in India except they are almost all white people. When lots of Indians started immigrating to the States, some of the only temples we could find were the ones started by the Hare Krishnas."

"Did you give up all worldly things, too?" I asked. "If this is your Audi, I guess you didn't."

Siva laughed. "No, I am afraid I did not. I am a software engineer. I have a wife and three kids. Mine is the path of the householder, not the ascetic."

The car stopped in front of a boxy building next
to an oil changing shop. Over the front door was a
small sign with images of what I presumed to be gods
imbedded in it.

Inside, I was overwhelmed by scents and colors
and forms. Facing the front door was a big mural of a
feminine-looking man with blue skin playing a flute.
Around the first corner was an elephant statue with
human arms and a fat belly, its lap covered with dried
flowers and bowls of fruit, a garland of plastic flowers
around its neck. In front of another large statue of a
dancer with multiple arms and legs were more
offerings of flowers and fruits. Below it was a similar
statue of a half-man, half-woman, with one breast
and four arms. "Ardhanarishvara, the union of Kali
and Shiva," he said. "Or Siva. My namesake."

"Why were you named after a half-woman,
half-man?" I wondered.

"Know any Spanish-speaking people named
Mario?" asked Siva, with a grin.

"Yeah, at school. What does that have to do
with it?"

"Mario is a version of the name Maria. All Marios
are named after a woman, the mother of God,"
answered Siva. "In a way, the Christian God is part
female, part male, because of Mary."

"Mary was the mother of God?" I was transported
in that instant back to that moment on Cobre
Mountain when I first saw the image of the woman in
the cholla cactus. She was God's mother? This was

sounding a lot like the Mormon religion, with its belief that God once was human, and had a wife.

"Mary was Jesus' mother, and Jesus Christ was one of the manifestations of the Godhead. So she was the Mother of God. How can you be mother of God without being a manifestation of God yourself? All of us, men and women, each have both a feminine and a male aspect. So does God.

"One tradition of Siva says he and she were the creator of the universe, so Siva had to have both male and female aspects. Out of him and her came the male force and the female force. After this, Siva was male, and his consort was named Shakti. Together they represented the balance of the sexual energy in the universe. Their physical relationship is the basis of the Tantric tradition."

"So your gods have sex with each other?" I asked.

"Sacred sex. That's what tantric sex is all about. Making love as a spiritual discipline. You might enjoy reading the *Kama Sutra* sometime. A classic of Indian literature."

"So let's break this down," I said. "There are 333,000,000 Hindu gods, but all of them are really one God. Some are male, some are female. They are all the same God as the Christian God, you say, and the Christian God had a mother, who was divine herself. So if they are all Gods, then God makes love to him or herself, and then is born out of herself, or himself. To get 333,000,000 gods, God would have to be having sacred sex with him or herself all the time."

"Well, I don't know that any of our gurus would put it quite that way, but I suppose there's a germ of truth in what you say," replied Siva, with his wide grin.

"So what about sacred sex?" I asked.

"What about it?" asked Siva.

"Is it as good as the regular kind?"

"Much better, if you have the discipline for it."

"Well, then sign me up for that," I said.

Siva led me to another statue, that of Kali, a fearsome looking figure with fangs who held severed heads in her hand, and trampled a man underfoot. "That's gross," I objected.

"No more gross than a statue of a man being tortured to death on a cross," answered Siva. "That's a symbol to be found in every church."

"Yeah, well, that's gross too, if you ask me," I muttered.

Around a corner in the building we came upon a tall white guy in a flowing robe, his head shaved except for a long thin ponytail in the back. He was pushing a mop across the cement floor in front of one of the statues.

"*Namaste*," Siva greeted him, holding his palms together and bowing lightly. The tall man did the same.

"Josh, meet Hari Das," said Siva. "One of the devotees here."

In a blur of motion and words Hari Das gifted me with a big book of floridly colored pictures of Krishna and related deities. It was written by His Divine Grace Swami Prabhupada, founder of the International

Society for Krishna Consciousness, otherwise known as ISKON. Hari Das' presentation had the same sort of well-worn, oft-repeated quality that I remembered from my visit by Jehovah's Witnesses. Why, I wondered, was this white man with an adopted Hindu name so much more eager to proselytize than was Siva, who was raised in a Hindu country? Was this a case of what Father Crespi called "convert syndrome"?

These were questions I posed to Siva in the car on the way back to the Presbyterian Church.

"I wasn't converted to the Hindu religion. It surrounded me from birth. I took it in like mother's milk," said Siva. "But Hari Das is a convert. He had a different experience than I did. So it does not surprise me that he talks about our religion in a different way than I do. And I think there is something about the way Americans relate to religion that is unique."

"What's that?"

"It seems to me that there is an American way of being religious, no matter what the religion may be. Americans convert to other religions in the same enthusiastic manner in which so many Americans embrace Jesus. Whatever Americans believe, they tend to become missionaries for it."

"So instead of accepting Jesus as his personal lord and savior, Hari Das accepted Krishna as his personal lord and savior?" I asked.

"And wants everybody else to do the same. So American," chuckled Siva.

***

The meeting was just ending as we returned to the church. Cal Redfield came out of the sanctuary and put on his cowboy hat. "Howdy, Josh," he grinned under his grizzled, drooping mustache. "It's good to see you've met my friend Siva here," he said. "Were you here at the meeting when we discussed the plan for a Servant Patrol?"

Cal explained that a subgroup of the Covenant had proposed to form a group that would send four-wheel drive vehicles into the desert to seek out migrants who were injured or otherwise in trouble. The group would also monitor and document the activities of the Border Bouncers.

"Is this turning into some kind of war?" I wondered.

"No," said Cal. "Our effort is committed to nonviolence."

"So if you find Border Bouncers beating up on a bunch of *mojados*, you won't do anything to defend them?"

"Nonviolence doesn't mean non-action," replied Cal as we took a seat together on an adobe *banco* in the church courtyard. "When Gandhi led the people of India to shake off the British occupiers of their country, he led them to take very vigorous actions against the oppression. Strikes, marches, boycotts. His word for nonviolence was *satyagraha,* which best translates into English as "truth force."

"*Satyagraha* is a relentless, unending quest for truth. Why do we have *mojados* dying of thirst in the desert? Why must the U.S. put up a wall along the border? The many answers to these questions lead us to ask other questions. Why is there such a difference in economic conditions between Mexico and America? Our search for truth in that question leads inevitably to yet others. Why would a person become a Border Bouncer? What kind of immigration policy does the United States have, and why? What alternatives are there which might result in more humane and just relationships between Americans and Mexicans? But answers to questions aren't enough. Getting politicians and leaders to respond isn't enough. The search for truth leads us to press for justice and peace. Acts of violence seldom get us closer to the truth. But nonviolent action can lead to a fuller revelation of truth," said Cal.

"So what happens if these Servant Patrol people see some Border Bouncers beating up migrants in the desert?"

"I don't exactly know, but one possibility is getting in the way of the violence. It's a very dangerous thing to do, and not always successful in saving the victims of violence. But it is a powerful witness for the way of nonviolence. People have done this: put their bodies between the victim and the attacker, without attacking the attacker. Some folks have been killed taking this kind of nonviolent action," said Cal.

I told Cal what happened to me in the Rinconada Café. "What if it's really obvious that the Border Bouncers will kill the migrants and whoever tries to stop them, too?" I asked.

"Good question, and I don't have a clear answer," Cal said. "Even Gandhi said there are times when doing violence is better than doing nothing, but he believed very strongly that nonviolent action is a vastly stronger power than people usually believe. Try all nonviolent actions first, if you possibly can. There are times when the cause of truth is advanced by self-sacrifice, a willingness to die in the course of nonviolent action.

"Think of what Martin Luther King did in the South. He was a Christian minister who learned much about the way of nonviolent truth force from Gandhi. Much of the civil rights movement adopted Gandhian principles in pressing for an end to segregation and other kinds of racial oppression. Martin Luther King was hit on the head with a brick, he was stabbed almost to death, bullets blasted through his house when he was asleep inside with his family—and, of course, he was eventually shot to death. Other nonviolent civil rights workers were blasted with fire hoses, beaten, and even killed for marching for justice, but people kept marching, even when they knew they'd be attacked,. I got blasted with the hose down in Alabama myself."

Cal then told me how he dropped out of college for a while to work full time in Alabama during the critical period of the civil rights struggle. He was in Birmingham when Dr. King was in jail there. He marched over the Edmund Pettus Bridge in Selma right after peaceful activists for black voting rights were attacked by the police.

"But those police weren't Nazis. What would you do about people like that? Knock on the door of the concentration camp and say, 'Begging the pardon of you Nazi guys, but I'm going to get in the way while you put Jews in the gas chamber.' That doesn't sound realistic," I objected.

"Good question, all right," Cal answered.

"The Border Bouncers I met think they're doing the right thing, just like the Immigrant Justice Covenant thinks it's doing the right thing."

"Well, tell me what you learned from them."

I told Cal what the Bouncers said to me, and told him about my encounter with them when I was in the desert with Ben.

"What were you doing out there in the desert that you ran into them?" asked Cal.

"Ahhhh, well … Actually, I was hoping I'd find you here today, so I could ask for your advice," I said. "It wasn't my idea. I didn't know what I was getting into when I got into it," I blubbered.

"What do you mean?" asked Cal.

"I don't want to put you in an awkward position, but I think you could help me figure out what to do about this. I accidentally discovered something I wish I didn't know. I discovered that a Native American friend of mine was working as a lookout for mules. And I'm pretty sure he is not the only young Tohono getting paid to watch out for *la migra* and help the smugglers get through. God, I hope you won't tell anybody else about this and get my friend in trouble … I'm really worried about him."

"I don't know who your friend is, so I won't be able to get him in trouble. But this is a serious thing. I have not heard about it before," said Cal, lifting off his straw cowboy hat to wipe off the sweat on his forehead. By this time, the meeting was long over and the midafternoon sun had us in its fiery thrall as we sat on the *banco*. "How does it worry you?"

"I'm afraid my friend is either going to get busted and put in jail, or get into trouble with the drug dealers and get killed."

"I'd be pretty concerned about the same things," nodded Cal, gravely.

"What should I do?" I asked. "I'm pretty freaked out about it. I mean, my friend is really poor. His dad pawned his favorite piece of turquoise so he could fix the family's truck. They live out in the middle of nowhere in some beat up trailers with a bunch of skinny dogs running around. My friend needs the money, so he is getting paid by some bad guys to be a lookout. I went out there with him. I swear, I didn't know what I was getting into. It's some kind of really bad business, that's all I know. So what do I do? I trust you a lot. I mean, I trust my dad, too, but you know. He's my dad. So what should I do?"

"I don't know. I can't tell you," said Cal, whose face was softening with compassion. "Wish I could tell you."

"What do you mean?"

"How old are you, Josh?"

"Seventeen."

"Welcome to adulthood," Cal chuckled.

"What do you mean?"

"Adulthood comes in the moment when you realize that you are the one to make your own moral choices."

***

I stayed overnight at Cal's place because I had contacted Ajit Singh about visiting the Sikh *gurdwara* the next day, Sunday. It was a small white building with domes with golden globes on top of them. It looked very much out of place in its location next to a liquor store.

Ajit met me in front and shook my hand with both of his while bowing to me. "Come on in." Exotic music in a minor key floated out the door as we walked inside.

He explained that the Sikh religion began in the 16th century in India in a time when there was a lot of tension between the two major religions of the country. "Our first Guru, Nanak, went around the Punjab in India saying, 'There is no Hindu, there is no Muslim.' In a way, the Sikh religion is a blend of both. We are monotheists like the Muslims, and we have a devotional spirituality like the Hindus."

He ushered me into a room where I removed my shoes and stashed them in a rack on the wall. In a basket was a pile of orange scarves; I tied one over my hair. I washed my hands and then was ushered into the main room. The carpet was covered with white sheets. Men sat cross-legged on the right, women on the left. Front and center was a low pulpit covered with thick cloth, with a huge book on top. An imposing fellow with a long beard and a white turban was waving a wand, something like a limp broom, back and forth over the book in a very slow and deliberate manner.

"What's he doing?" I whispered to Anjit.

"The book is our *Guru Granth Sahib.* You see, when our religion started in India, our Gurus were human beings. Then we took the songs and words of our Gurus and wrote them down in the *Granth,* and the book has been our Guru ever since. In India, in the old days, a *rajah* or a guru or other special person would always have somebody behind them waving a fly-whisk, to chase away the bugs. So we show reverence to the *Guru Granth Sahib* in this way. The words to our music come from the *Granth.*"

We came forward and Ajit bowed and touched his forehead on the sheet-covered carpet in front of the *Granth.* I did the same. Ajit put some money in front of the *Granth,* too, but whispered to me that I was a visitor and didn't need to do it. Then Ajit went up to a man sitting next to the *Granth,* who gave him a little ball of doughy stuff that Ajit then ate. I did the same. It was dense and slightly sweet. "*Prasad,*" he said. "Something like Christian Communion."

Then we went and sat with the other men and listened to the *kirtan* music. Four men with long beards and white turbans sang in Punjabi and played on instruments I later learned were harmoniums. They were like little organs; the musician touched the keys with one hand and pumped air through the

organ with a lever with the other hand. The music
was plaintive and repetitive, and at times the
musicians seemed to be in some kind of ecstatic
rapture. Everyone in the room sat peacefully,
sometimes singing along. "Hymns to God,"
whispered Ajit.

It was the most pure worship I had ever
experienced. Just love for God who is love. Just as the
prasad had melted in my mouth, my ego dissolved as
the music moved through my body. I felt light, floaty,
free from any tension. It didn't matter that I didn't
understand a word that was being sung.

***

Back home, about a week later, just after I had
read the *Kama Sutra*, which I had to special-order
from the county library, I got a phone call from
Martha. I could feel the urgency in her voice.

"I've got four hours. They made a mistake on the
schedule at the café, and I don't need to be here."

Martha's hair streamed toward me in the wind
rushing through the passenger window, brushing my
cheek as the truck rattled down the road toward Organ
Pipe National Monument, while the sun went orange
beyond the mountains to the west. And her hand, that
soft hand, the same hand that held the carafe of coffee
in the Rinconada Café when I first met her, that hand
lay on my thigh, and I turned briefly away from
watching the road, and the golden orange light glowed
around the edge of her silhouette and touched her
slightly opened lips and flashed on her teeth as she

slowly broke a smile and turned toward me with a look that might have been embarrassment mixed subtly with eager longing. And her hand moved up and her other arm came around, glowing in the light, damp with sweat, and her other hand caressed my cheek as she drew nearer and kissed it, and then I felt her breasts softly heaving against my forearm as my eyes took in the sight of *saguaros* standing tall along both sides of the road, a crowd of silent witnesses to all we were seeing and feeling.

I turned down the first dirt road I could find, just north of Organ Pipe, and followed it around a hill out of sight from the highway. I parked, and in no time we were writhing together on a blanket on the ground.

I was gone; only Martha was there. And I think Martha was gone too; for her, only I was there.

"Are you …?" I gasped.

"I AM!" she screamed.

And then, the divine cosmic bliss of all 333,000,000 manifestations of divinity, including the Most High God and the Virgin Mary, sang out of us and echoed off the stony embankment above. And at that sacred moment, I felt a burning energy at the crown of my head, the palms of my hands, and the arches of my feet.

A few minutes later, my cell phone started to beep the alarm.

I sighed and turned off the phone. "It's the kids' bedtime."

"I know," groaned Martha.

"Mmmm," I mumbled as I kissed her neck. "We gotta go back.'

"Yeah," Martha groaned again.

We stared straight ahead as we drove north in the truck, back to Portales. We snuggled close on the bench seat.

"I think I understand things a whole lot better now," I said.

"What do you mean?" asked Martha.

"I think you just showed me a lot more of the meaning of the visions I had," I said. "It is about letting go of yourself and loving somebody else completely."

Martha breathed deep and snuggled closer. "If that was the lesson, I promise I'll never forget it. But in the vision, was the other person supposed to be me or God?" she asked.

"I wonder if there is any difference …" I sighed.

"But Josh, am I God? I don't think so."

"But if God is love, and I love you, then maybe it's all the same," I said.

"Maybe."

"But what does it mean for me to let go of myself and love you completely?" I asked. "Now I have to do right by you and your kids. And I swear I will. But I'm 17 ridiculous years old and I haven't even finished idiotic high school." I shook my fist out the window in frustration. "We can't live on a blanket by the side of a dirt road." Tears welled and flowed and dried in the hot wind before they made it halfway down my cheeks.

17. Growing Up

"Josh, are you there?" asked my history teacher.

"Uhhh, sorry, Mr. Echeverria."

"Josh, you're up next to present your project."

"Oh … yeah … Okay," I muttered as I fumbled to make the presentation. I had to snap out of my meditation on the serious practical consequences of the love between myself and Martha Kopecki and her children, a love I now knew to be as irreducible as the number two, as fundamental as subatomic particles, as real as the oak table in the Portales City Library.

Pastor Kate had lent me her camera to take pictures of the water stations for the email newsletter of the Immigrant Justice Covenant. I decided to make this into my special project assignment for history class. So I wrote the text, took the pictures, and organized a presentation about the history of the Covenant's work. Pastor Kate was very happy with it and shared it with the churches and temples to show to their congregations. Now it was time for me to present it to my history class.

When I was done, I asked if there were any questions.

The quiet made me uncomfortable.

"Josh … you are … like … *really* into this," said Mike, finally.

I imagined what Mike really wanted to say was something like, "Josh … *dude* … this is … like … so far from the kind of stuff we used to talk about when you smoked weed with us every day after school in my backyard."

I didn't feel the need to respond with words that would have sounded something like, "Yeah … *dude* … I had … like … no intention of growing up … but … like … you know, growing up happened anyway."

***

Seedless Thompson rolled his butt against the glass door of the library to open it. His hands were full of books to return. As the door swung shut and he rotated himself into the library he stopped, facing the children's reading area. There I was, sitting on the floor on a pillow with two young kids, one on either side.

"'I do not like them, Sam I Am. I do not like green eggs and ham,'" I read aloud, as Dana and Leon giggled.

Seedless kept on staring.

Finally, I put the book down. Leon and Dana looked up at the big man with warts and dark moles on his face, with its troubled expression, and at the pile of books in his arms up to his chin.

"Dana, Leon, meet my good friend Mr. C.D. Thompson."

Seedless' face went into further contortions. Finally, he spoke. "Nice to meet you both. I … uhh … I need to turn in some books."

"See you a little later, Seedless," I said, lifting up the book again. "Okay, you guys, do you recognize this word?"

***

"Where you been the last couple of days? You are scarcer than green grass around these parts," declared Dad.

"Yeah, I have been pretty busy lately," I said. I was at the old Formica kitchen table with a bunch of scribbled notes in front of me.

"Whatcha doing there?" asked Dad.

"Figuring some stuff out."

"Such as?"

"Uhh ... like ... what to do next."

"That's a pretty good thing to be figuring. Since you just turned 18, and you graduate from high school in a month."

"Yeah. I'm sorry, Dad. I suppose I've disappointed you, with me not applying for college and all. My grades are getting better, finally, but I guess it's too late now."

"So what about the junior college over in Tucson?" asked Dad. "Maybe it's time to go over there and check it out. There's nothing wrong with the two-year schools, like I keep telling you. Finish there and you can go to the University of Arizona."

"I don't know, Dad. My business is going pretty good here, and I think it might be good to take some time off so I can figure out what I want to do about college."

"It's the girl, eh? Martha, right?"

"Yeah, Martha."

"I have a confession to make," said Dad.

"I thought you gave up on the Catholic Church a long time ago, Dad.'

awwKansasMabelEvansarrangementinclinedcargoourselveshorizontalVenkateshsupernatural

"Not that kind of confession."

"Are there different kinds?" I asked.

"Well, I'm not confessing in front of God," said Dad. "Just in front of you."

"Oh Dad, give it up. Love is God, and you and I love each other, so if you are confessing in front of me, you're confessing in front of God."

"Okay, okay," protested Dad. "Have it your way. Anyhow, I have a confession to make."

"Speak, my son," I said, crossing myself correctly. "And when you are done, say ten Hail Marys."

"I want to apologize for having so many opinions about you." I was surprised by his sudden intensity. "You know, for the past few years I've been kind of hard on you. And I feel bad about it. You know, I've been worried about your grades, wishing you'd get more serious about school, wishing you'd be more practical about your future, wishing you'd find yourself a more appropriate girlfriend, wishing you'd stop getting tangled up in religion and in all the confusion along the border, and so on. But I've talked to Rachel a lot about it, and she has helped me see you in a different way. She thinks you are wonderful, and you know, she's absolutely right. I see now that you need to do life your way, and I need to enjoy and appreciate the way you do it. I need to support you, even when you do things that I'd never do."

Dad's eyes blinked as the tears suddenly flowed. "I was blind to how amazing you are, because I was so busy thinking about how I wanted you to be. I'm really sorry about that, because now I see. You care about the world, you have a big heart, you care so much about Martha and her kids, so much about the *mojados*. How can I not be impressed with that?

"I don't understand how you got so obsessed about religion, but it sure looks like your interest in the subject has helped you grow up and become a more responsible and mature and thoughtful person. I guess it is what you needed to do.

"There have been a lot of times when I have looked at you and thought, 'Can this really be my kid?' We think so differently, see things so differently. But right now I am so thankful that you are my kid. You are a really, really interesting person and you make me think about things I would never think about otherwise.

"And one more thing. I really believe that if your mother were alive today, she'd be so proud of you."

He wiped away his tears with the back of his hand. "I'm a lucky man. Thank you for being who you are, for being my son. That's my confession," he sputtered. "And forget about the Hail Marys."

I was transfixed, my eyes on Dad's. It was an out-of-ego experience. I was in and with and for my dad's soul, overcome with awe at the love that was emanating from him.

"So. Now that I have made my confession," continued Dad, "I want to help you any way I can. I want to help you do what you want to do. Even if it's not exactly what I might want you to do."

***

309

Friday morning, first thing, Dad and Rachel and I slid into the booth at the Rinconada Café where Dana and Leon were playing with paper and crayons, waiting for their cereal. Dana had drawn a picture of an especially colorful horse. "Do you kids like horses?" asked Rachel.

"Yeah!" they answered in unison. "Do you like horses?" asked Leon in return.

"I love my horses," answered Rachel.

"You have horses? How many?" asked Dana.

"Depends on how you count. Three of my own, and 15 others that I board on my ranch."

"How many is that altogether?" I asked them.

The children's fingers danced as they computed.

"27,000 million horses," giggled Dana.

"90-90-90 billion horses," giggled Leon.

"You kids like rocks?" I asked. "My dad here; he's all about rocks. He does rocks for a living."

"I like rocks," declared Leon.

"I've got lots of them, mostly in my head," grumbled Dad.

"Rocks in your head?" giggled Dana.

"Yup. Think about them all the time," muttered Dad, with a grin.

"Seriously, you guys. If you want to see some amazing rocks, you should see my dad's rock collection sometime," I said.

Martha glided by with the coffee carafe.

"Excuse me, Martha, but would it be all right if we took your kids to my ranch tomorrow afternoon? I've got lots of horses and rocks there. Better yet, let's all go there for time with the horses and rocks and then barbecue afterward. Would that be okay?" asked Rachel.

***

The dust glowed around the hooves of the horses in the slanting sun as we rode single-file toward the shadowed flanks of Cobre Mountain. Rachel held Dana in front of her on the saddle with one arm and with the other hand held the reins, leading the way through the ocotillos and the chollas and past the thickets of mesquite. Martha held Leon as she rode behind Rachel, and Dad and I sauntered behind. We fell silent, even the kids, as the desert enveloped us, body and soul, with the glory of evening.

The jingle of my cell phone interrupted the reverie. It was Tekla. Pastor Bob had just heard the news that Ben Jose was in jail.

I didn't say much at the barbecue at Rachel's place. But the kids wouldn't leave me to wonder and worry about Ben. "Story! Story!" they said.

"But I read you a story yesterday, remember?" I said.

"No, no. We don't want a library book. You read too many library books to us now. We want a story mine book," demanded Leon.

"I read you library books because you are growing up," I said.

"But now we want a story mine book," hollered Dana.

"Okay, okay." I said wearily. "You guys pick the book." I pointed to an imaginary bookcase on the wall of the barn near the barbecue pit and picnic area behind Rachel's house. The kids ran over to the wall and argued with each other for a moment about which imaginary book to choose. I stared at them in amazement at their innocence, their unworried minds, their joy and eagerness.

I opened the invisible book toward Dana and Leon, and Rachel and Dad and Martha listened along.

"What color horse do you see on this page?" I asked.

"Orange," said Leon.

"Blue," said Dana.

"As usual, you are both right. See, it's a white horse with orange and blue markings. A beautiful horse, too. It's the horse that ran away."

"Ran away?" asked Dana.

"Yes, it ran away. See here, this horse was named Ahhh."

"Ahhh?" wondered Dana and Leon. "Funny name," said Leon.

"No!" I protested vigorously. I wondered at myself, sensing that my worry had evaporated as I entered into the mind, the mine, from which the stories came. "Not a funny name at all," I said with mock seriousness, silencing the children, whose mouths fell open in surprise at my tone of voice. "Not a funny name. Because 'Ahhhh' is the name of God."

"God is named 'Ahhhh'?" wondered Dana.

"Of course. Think of it. The Jews called God 'Yahhhweh,' the Muslims call God 'Allahhh,' the Hindus call God 'Ramahhh' and 'Sitahhhh' and 'Krishnahhh' and 'Shivahhh,' and the Christians pray to Jesus whose name in Hebrew was 'Yeshuahhh,' and the Native Americans pray to 'Watankahhh' and the Jews and the Christians pray by saying 'Ahhhmen,' and the Hindus pray by saying 'Ahhh-om.' And the Buddhists meditate with 'Buddhahhh.' So God's name around the whole world must be 'Ahhh.'"

"How do you spell it?" asked Dana.

"Two different ways. 'A-h-h-h' or 'A-w-e.' Either way, it's the same sound, same idea, same name," I declared. "So this horse was named after God. And she was a beautiful horse. But how did she get her beautiful colors of orange and blue?"

"Born with them, silly," said Dana.

"No. Somebody painted them on her," said Leon.

"Well, let's turn the page and find out how Ahhh got her colors. Once upon a time, Ahhh lived right here in the desert. She was a white horse with no spots or colors. She could run for miles and her momma horse and her daddy horse didn't worry about where she went, because they knew the desert really well and they thought they could always find her. Besides that, they believed that the Gila River and the Mexican border and the tops of all the mountains were the edges of the world, and that nobody could go any further than those edges. So they thought she was safe running around free in the desert.

313

"But she was an adventurous horse. Being free wasn't enough for her. She wanted more. She would go running up the mountains and down the mountains, across the flat lands, all the way down to Baboquivari, all the way up to Kitt Peak, all the way almost to Yuma, and never lose her way back home. But she kept wondering, 'What is on the other side of the edge of the world?' Didn't there have to be something on the other side? It couldn't just be nothing, could it?

"So one day she decided to find out for herself. So she ran all the way out to Baboquivari and ran to the top of the mountain and decided to be brave and run past the top of the mountain."

"She can't do that," said Leon. "A horse can't run past the top of a mountain."

"Oh yes she did," I said. "Look, see the picture? There she goes, running right up into the sky. She ran into the sky and was so happy. Look how much fun she was having, running higher and higher into the air. She was having so much fun that she forgot that it was time for dinner. Her parents started to worry about her and they went looking for her. They looked from Yuma to Tucson, from Sonoyta to Gila Bend, and they couldn't find her. Finally, they went to Baboquivari and saw her hoof prints but they saw that the hoof prints stopped at the top of the mountain. So they stood there and waited and wondered what had happen to their lovely daughter.

"Ahhh kept on running into the sky and went so high that she got to the sun, but the sun was so hot that it burned her and put orange spots all over her hide. So she ran away from the sun, even higher than the sun, so far that she bumped into the blue of the sky. She ran right into the blue of the sky and some of it rubbed off on her hide and put blue spots among the orange spots. She ran into the blue of the sky so hard that she bounced off it and fell back down to the earth on top of Baboquivari Mountain, right in front of her mom and dad. Do you know what happened then?"

"Her mom and dad were mad," said Dana, seriously.

"They gave her a timeout," said Leon.

"That is exactly right. They were mad, and they took her home and gave her a timeout in a circle of mesquite trees. They watched her to make sure she stayed there. But as they watched her, they said 'Ahhh.' And she said, 'Why did you say my name?' And they said 'Ahhh' again. And she said, 'Why did you say my name?' And they said, 'Sorry, we were talking to God. Because your orange and blue spots are so 'ahhhsome.' How did you get them?' And she told them she had run to the sun and got burnt with orange, and had run to the top of the sky and got rubbed with blue. At first her parents didn't believe her, but she kept saying it was true, over and over again. Finally, they said, 'We don't know how you really got those beautiful spots, but we forgive you for running away into the sky, and we love you so much, with or without spots, and are glad you made it back home.' And they hugged her, and when they did, the orange and blue colors rubbed off onto their hides, so her mom and dad had orange and blue spots, too. And they all said, 'Ahhh,' and they were all happy forever after.

"So if you see anything wonderful, just say the name of God—'awe,' 'ahhh,' and what you see will rub off on you, too." I closed the book and laid it on the picnic table next to my plate of pork ribs.

"Can I see the book?" asked Rachel. I picked up the imaginary book, handed it to her, and she took it, dipping her hand a bit as if it had weight. Silently, she leafed through its pages, reading it appreciatively, then closed it. She held it close to her heart and rubbed it against herself and said, "Ahhh."

***

Ben Jose had turned 18 just a few days before he was arrested. The agents pulled guns and badges on him as he turned over the rock near his house to gather his cash envelope from the drug smugglers who had been paying him for his lookout duty. I took a day off school and got up early to take a ride with Pastor Bob to the jail. Pastor Bob volunteered as a chaplain in the federal jail a few days every month.

"I've always had a burden for that boy," said Pastor Bob as we drove through the rez on our way to Tucson. "And for his whole family. They are the kindest, warmest folks you'd ever meet. But they just can't seem to get their act together. It's always something; the alcoholism is the worst. And they don't work very hard, they drop out of school, they don't keep up their trailers or their vehicles; they just collect their casino money and never get ahead." Pastor Bob shook his head.

"But Pastor Bob, I mean, think about it. The Tohono O'odham have been out here in the harshest possible physical landscape for thousands of years. Somehow they have had their act together enough to survive all this time. I don't think it is fair to compare them to white people. They are doing their own stuff and I feel like it isn't our place to judge them," I argued.

"But just look at these crosses by the road, for Tohonos who have died from drunk driving. It's so terrible," answered Pastor Bob.

"Well, I think it's awful that they died. But think of it this way. The Indians care a lot about their dead people. They love each other, or else they'd never put up all those crosses," I said.

"If they loved each other, they wouldn't drink in the first place and kill themselves and each other on the road, and they would feed their children a better diet, and take care of their children's teeth, and not get diabetes from all the liquor and the sugar, and they'd go get educated, and ..."

"So Pastor Bob, do you have a 'burden' for the Indians, or are you a burden on them?" I demanded.

"Look," said Pastor Bob, "you are being a relativist. You think that you can't judge people because their ways are as good as your ways."

"Well, I guess I do think it might be a mistake to judge people," I said. "I'm certainly guilty of it myself.

But does that make me a relativist? I don't think everything has the same moral value. Some things are more humane and kind than others, but that has nothing to do with religion."

"Yes it does. Because God has standards. God has created absolute moral values. And absolute religious standards. I know, you're out there tasting the nectar of all the flowers in the garden of religions, right?"

"Whoa, Pastor Bob. Now we're going down the religion road all of a sudden?"

"I'm always going down the religion road," answered Pastor Bob.

"Well, I suppose I go down that road a lot, too," I confessed. "But where are you taking us?"

"Josh, God has given us moral standards, written once and for all in the Bible, and a standard of faith, who is Jesus. If people stray from these standards, they face the consequences. I'm not the judge of Ben Jose and his family and so many of the other Tohonos. God is their judge, and God has spoken. And they have not heeded God's word, and they suffer the consequences, which are plain for all to see. That's why Ben is in jail, and why the Indians have so many problems. If they would come to God, who loves them and wants the best for them, if they would only return to the truth of the Scripture, their lives would be so much better here on earth, to say nothing of their heavenly reward. But they go to our church one Sunday, another church the next, they take our clothes and food and vitamins, they take the Mormons' help, too, then they go do their pagan rituals, and they open up casinos, then they get drunk. Like you, they're relativists."

"Pastor Bob," I said, attempting to choose my words carefully for a change, "sometimes I'm a smart-ass. Sometimes I am not so respectful of my elders, and I don't want to disrespect you. I respect you a lot just because you are Tekla's dad, and she really and truly is a wonderful, caring person, so I have to take you seriously just because of your daughter. But really, Pastor Bob, I am having a hard time with what you are saying. I actually read a lot of the Bible, because you introduced me to it in the youth group at your church. You got me started on it, and I'm glad I read so much of it. But when I read it, I see all sorts of problems.

"You say that in the Bible God has made the moral standards perfectly clear. But they weren't clear to me at all. I read in the Bible that you should put gay people to death. I have a few gay and lesbian friends at my high school; they didn't choose to be gay or lesbian. I see no reason to stone them to death for having gay or lesbian sex, but that's what the Bible says we should do. I remember your sermon against homosexuality, but it just didn't make any sense to me. The homosexual people I know are nice and don't hurt anybody. You say you obey the Bible, you think every word is right. So how many gay people have you put to death lately?"

There went my careful choice of words.

"You are putting yourself in God's place. You are acting as if you have a right to decide what is godly and what is not. The Bible is the word of God, and God has spoken, and I believe it. I don't understand every word of the Bible, but that doesn't mean it isn't true. It just means I am merely a human being and God is greater in wisdom and understanding than I am."

"So why don't you stone my friends to death? If I gave you their names and addresses, would you get some rocks and go their houses and do what God says you should do?"

"It is not my job to punish gay people for their sexual sin," he said. "God will take care of that. Look at AIDS; it's God's punishment against them for their sin. I don't need to stone them. God will give them the treatment that is just."

"But that's not what the Bible says," I said. "It really does say in Leviticus someplace that a man who lies with a male as with a female shall be put to death. Who are you to decide what is your job and what is not your job? I remember that the Bible said, "Keep my statutes, and do them." There are your orders, addressed directly to you, Pastor Bob. So when are you going to kill my friends? What day? What kind of rocks will you use? My dad has a nice collection. Maybe you could borrow some of his. I promise to see you in jail if you do it. We could have a really interesting conversation together about relativism, in the visiting room."

"I think you already confessed to being a smart-ass sometimes?" said Pastor Bob.

"Sorry," I said. "But really, Pastor Bob. Some of the Bible's moral rules don't match up with what you preach. The Old Testament says that having more than one wife is just fine. The New Testament says that even getting married to one person isn't the best way to go. It says that the best thing is not to have sex and never get married. I mean, there are two very different creation stories in the book of Genesis; the Bible doesn't have its own story straight even in the first chapters. Get honest, Pastor Bob. You are relativistic. Some things in the Bible are relatively more important to you than others. Some things you ignore, like stoning gay people to death. Or the part where Jesus says love your enemies and turn the other cheek. You ignore that part when you give your sermons about how God is on America's side in war because we are a Christian nation."

"You think you can be a cafeteria Christian," argued Pastor Bob. You won't accept the whole Bible as God's word. You just pick out the parts you like, and ignore the rest, like choosing food in a cafeteria line."

"I think you just missed everything I said, Pastor Bob," I answered. "You are the cafeteria Christian. You pick out the parts of the Bible that support your own moral standards that you like, standards that you decided were essential. You ignore the parts of the Bible that don't matter to you. You choose the fruit cocktail, you choose the chicken nuggets, you leave behind the broccoli."

Bob's face squinched into a grimace and his hands stiffened on the steering wheel. "Josh, if you accepted Christ as your personal Lord and Savior, if you accepted the Bible as the infallible word of God, all these supposed problems you have with Christianity would go away. You'd be saved, you'd be right with God, and God would reveal to you the right way to believe and live. Accept Jesus, and your confusion and your searching will be over."

"Well, there's one thing you obey in the Bible that makes a lot of sense to me, Pastor Bob, one thing on the cafeteria line that we both would choose. And that's the part in the Bible that says we're supposed to remember the people in prison. Because I don't know anybody else who visits people in jail, and I think it's cool that you are doing it."

***

Pastor Bob got a contact visit with Ben in a conference room, because of his status as a chaplain. I could only get a window visit. Ben and I spoke through telephone handsets on either side of a thick pane of glass. At the bottom of the glass, a previous inmate had pasted a tiny, hand-drawn, colored-pencil picture of an eye-full, mouth-less Betty Boop in skimpy clothes, her voluptuous breasts bulging toward the visitor's side.

Ben beamed when he saw me through the glass.

"Josh, it's great to see you, man."

"Ben, this is terrible. How did this happen? How did you get caught? I was so afraid this was going to happen to you."

"Doesn't matter now. Hey, don't worry, man. It's all going to be okay. My uncle got me a good lawyer. I'll be fine. These guys can't make it stick against me. I won't be in here for very long."

"But Ben, this has got to be really scary. This place is terrible. I'm freaked out, and I am just a visitor. All these metal gates and doors and cops everywhere—how can you stand being here?"

"It's not so bad. Hey, I'm eating okay, and I work out every day," said Ben, smiling. He rolled up his sleeve. "Check out these muscles. I'll be really buff by the time I get out of here."

"What can I do to help you get out of here?"

"I don't want you to get mixed up in any more of my business. I scared you pretty bad that one time. I'm sorry about that. I just wanted you to see what's really going on, because I knew you were so interested in the *mojados*."

"But what can I do to help?" I begged. I felt so helpless.

"Hey, visiting me is help. It's really cool to see you here. My dad and my brother are taking care of a lot of stuff for me. I think I'm gonna be okay. So tell me, what are you doing these days?"

I filled him in about my love life, about finishing high school soon, about my mobile home maintenance work. "When you get out, come work with me. I've always got plenty of jobs," I said.

"So are you still doing the religion thing?" asked Ben. "You were always so interested in it. Get 'slain in the Spirit' lately? Had any more visits from Elder Brother?" he laughed.

I told of my latest encounters. And I told Ben about my conversation with Pastor Bob on the way to the jail.

"So, Ben. What do you think? Does God have rules about morals, or not?"

"Pastor Bob told me all about it. He's right. You violate the laws of God, you pay the price. I violated, I am paying the price. But I confessed my sin and I accepted God, so I am going to get mercy, and I won't have to be here for very long."

Things weren't simple for Ben at all. I talked pretty often with Leonard and with Ben's brother. Ben's family had been threatened with death by the smugglers if Ben revealed any information about them. And Ben was facing years of federal jail if he didn't turn evidence about the smugglers to the prosecutor. Ben's uncle, the chief of tribal police, could fix speeding tickets on the rez, but he couldn't fix the ambition of a federal prosecutor trying to make a name for himself as a tough guy. The prosecutor was making an example out of Ben, to scare other Tohono O'odham youth away from scouting for coyotes and mules. It was all over the Tucson newspaper and television.

***

Martha grilled me about Ben one evening after the kids were in bed.

"I can't talk about it here," I said. "If you know what I mean."

"Let's go outside for a little walk," she suggested. She told L. D. and Esther she'd be back in a minute. It took some negotiating, but they agreed.

The wind was blowing hard outside. Dust was swirling over the street, making ghostly shapes in the moonlit air.

"Ben tricked me once. He got me to go with him out into the desert to help him be a lookout. I didn't know what I was getting into until I was there. I was completely freaked out, and after that, I was really worried that Ben would get caught."

"Are you worried that you might get in trouble, too?" asked Martha.

"A little bit, but that's not really why I'm so upset," I said. "His family is so poor. He needed money, for himself and for his family. And now he's being used by the federal government to scare other kids just as poor as he is. Instead of helping him and other kids with their needs, so they won't be tempted by smugglers, the government is punishing a nice kid who didn't mean anybody any harm.

"Ben had to make choices I never had to make. My dad didn't have to pawn my belongings to get money. I've never been desperate for cash to help my dad pay the bills. No smuggler ever came to me, offering a bunch of money to be a lookout. And if he did, I would never even be tempted to take a risk like that, because my life is so secure. My dad has a great job and I have everything I need already. That alone isn't fair. Why doesn't Ben have everything he needs so that drug smugglers can't tempt him to do something so dangerous?

"You know what it is, Martha? I think I'm mad at God for making a world where there is so little justice and equality. Why did God make it so that Americans would have all the jobs and money, and Mexicans would be so poor and have to die in the desert trying to get here? How long does it have to go on, all this suffering of poor people? When people with money have it so easy?"

"You think that is God's fault?" wondered Martha. "You really think God made things this way? Wasn't it humans who screwed things up here on earth?"

"I don't know, Martha. I'm lost in Elder Brother's labyrinth," I said.

"I have no idea what you are talking about," she said.

"The Tohono O'odham believe in a god named Elder Brother who hides himself in a labyrinth so it is hard for people to find him."

"Well, it is hard to figure out this world, to understand a lot of things," said Martha. "I'm lost in a labyrinth, too, I guess. Maybe mine isn't so spiritual. I don't blame God that it's so hard to figure out. I figure that I made some mistakes, and got myself lost, and now I get to be responsible and figure out how to get through it."

"But think about it, Martha. Did you choose to have parents who couldn't take care of you? Did you choose to grow up in so much chaos? Whose fault is it? Not yours. It's God's fault. Or the universe's fault. I sure don't blame you for all the trouble you've had."

"But here's what I have learned," Martha said. "I am not to blame for having dysfunctional parents. But I'm responsible for dealing with the consequences I face as a result of having had them as parents. It's useless to blame them, or to blame myself, or to blame God. I just have to take responsibility for myself, for my own actions.

"Ben isn't to blame for all the bad things that happened to him. But he's responsible for what he does now. He can blame others, he can blame the government, he can blame God, but so what? He's got to take responsibility for himself from now on. And that's tough. I feel for him, a lot.

"And what happened to him could have happened to me. Real easy. I was tempted to do some pretty crazy stuff to survive. I got offers. I came close to taking them. To turning tricks. To dealing drugs. Just to make enough money to get by. I had bills to pay, and no way to pay them. I got lucky, really lucky. My aunt and uncle saved my life. If they hadn't, I don't know. I might have taken those offers.

"Now I have to be responsible, but it's still not easy. What does it mean to be responsible, when I have two young kids, a crummy job, and I have fallen in love with a teenager? You know, maybe the best

327

thing you can do for Ben is to make responsible choices yourself."

"So what is the right thing, the responsible thing to do?" I asked. "In two weeks I get out of high school. Yeah, I'm actually going to graduate, after all my bad grades, after spacing out in class for four whole years. I haven't been real responsible in school, that's for sure. Should I stay here to clean and repair mobile homes for old people who come down from North Dakota to escape the winter? And live with you in some cheap mobile home with your kids, and get stuck here and not have enough money to give them a good life?"

"I say the most responsible thing we can do right now is to go back to my aunt and uncle's house, say goodnight to each other, and think about this later," Martha said, clutching my arm and holding me close as we walked into the wind.

18. See You on the Mountain

"I'm ready for you, Seedless. I'm all done with homework. Let's celebrate with a game of chess."
I said as I ran into him in front of the library.

Seedless opened his mouth but couldn't answer. He waved his arms up in the air, as if begging for something I could not see. His face was contorted.

"Whoa, Seedless. What's up, man?" I asked.

No answer. He got on his bike and rode away faster than usual. I walked fast to his trailer at the church. I knocked on the metal door.

"Seedless, it's me, Josh."

"Beat it. Go away!" yelled Seedless.

"Seedless, are you alright?"

"I'm fine. Go on, now."

"I'm worried about you."

"Don't be worried about me. There are plenty of people to be worried about but I'm not one of them. I'm just fine. Now go."

"Seedless, please. Something's wrong, I can tell. I'm your friend. I'll try to help."

"Okay, you care so much about me, do me a favor," bellowed the voice from the inside of the trailer. He opened the door and dragged four cardboard file boxes onto the asphalt. "Take these boxes, take them away, I don't want to see them ever again. Give them away, do whatever you want with them, just don't let me ever see them again. Burn them, bury them, get rid of them, I don't care. Now go. Beat it. Leave me alone," he wailed, and he turned and slammed the door and locked it.

I pleaded with him at the door for a while longer, and finally gave up. I stared at the boxes, wondering what to do with them. Finally, I took them to Pastor Kate's office door and called her on my cell phone. "I'm really worried about Seedless. Can you come to the church right now?"

She and I put the boxes on her desk and opened them. We sampled the contents: hundreds of letters from children addressed to Seedless. All were written on the same kind of grainy lined paper. Some included photographs of the children: charming, hopeful, but sometimes hollow-eyed from living in poor places all over the world. All were full of enthusiasm and faith in the face of all sorts of privations and trials. Seedless Thompson was a very, very important person to these young people around the globe. Seedless had touched the lives of hundreds of kids in need. How was this even possible for a janitor living in a trailer in a small town in the middle of nowhere?

"Incredible," said Pastor Kate as she looked through the letters. "It's beautiful, all the love that is locked in that man's heart."

She was already a pale woman, but suddenly her skin color turned appliance-white. "Oh God. I read something in the paper today. I wonder if Seedless sponsored these kids through the World Christian Children's Fund. It is a famous charity based in

Chicago, and the government has indicted it for mail
fraud. Oh, that is so sad, if that is what happened."

"What happened?"

"They collected the donors' money and never sent
the letters to any of the children. All the letters back
to the donors were phony. The fraud went on for
years. If that is what happened, no wonder he is so
upset. All these letters are fakes." She put her hands
over her face and wept. "Oh, the poor man. What a
terrible thing." When she got her composure again,
she said, "We've got to find out if that is what
happened. We have to talk to him."

Together we went out to the trailer at the back of
the Federated Church's parking lot. We knocked on
the aluminum door and waited for a response, but
there was none. We listened for any sign of life inside.
Finally, the voice of Seedless Thompson bellowed,
"Beat it. Leave me alone."

"Seedless, it's me, Kate, and your friend Josh is
here, too. We want to talk to you. We want to ask
you: those kids, did you sponsor them through the
World Christian Children's Fund? Is that what is
upsetting you, Seedless? We want to help you,
because if it is true it is a terrible thing and we want to
give you some support. You must feel awful and we
don't want you to."

"Beat it. Bug off and leave me alone."

Pastor Kate and I finally backed away from the
trailer. She said she would try again later. "I'll keep
track of him, so don't worry. I'll make sure he is
okay."

I stared at the trailer. I could feel a volcano about to erupt inside of myself. I turned my face into the air and howled. "How could they do this to Seedless?" I let out a furious scream.

Seedless opened the drapes for a moment and peeked out to see us. Then he quickly closed them.

Kate backed away from me. "Josh, calm down, please. Yes, it's a terrible thing."

"It is beyond terrible. Those bastards didn't just steal money. They stole Seedless's heart. It's like killing him," I yelled. I raised my fists skyward and shook them.

"I think we need to back off a bit and give Seedless some time," she said quietly.

"Wait a minute," I said. "Wait a minute." I closed my eyes and in silence I repeated the Jesus Prayer over and over. I breathed deeply with each phrase.

"Wait a minute. Stay right here with me, please, Pastor Kate."

I could feel the words forming within me. I went to the door of the trailer, and in a loud voice I spoke.

"You know who I am, Seedless? I'm not just Joshua T. Stoneburner. I am also Yolanda, in Nicaragua. I am Joao, in Brazil. I am Prajna, in India. I am Lupe and Jorge and Maria in Mexico. I am Kwame in Nigeria; I am Hafez in Mali; I am Rama in Nepal. I am every child you ever loved in every poor place in the world. I am the face behind every letter in those boxes. Even if that World Christian Children's Fund thing was a sham, and all those letters were bogus. May the people who did this to you roast in

Baptist hell for eternity. But you. You. You, Seedless Thompson, are what being human is all about. You are the real thing. We read a bunch of the letters. As I read them, I felt like I had received money and letters from you, from a person I'd never seen in a faraway country who really cared. I couldn't help thinking those kids' letters back to you were real, too. I wanted to believe they were real, because I wished I had written one of them myself.

"But now that I know the story, I realize that I am one of those kids. You reached out to me, too, and shared your kindness and wisdom with me many times.

"So listen up, Seedless. Believe this, because it's the truth, and you know it. I have been sent by Sarla, Kumar, Paula, Rahul, Francisco, Mohand, and all the other kids you loved so much to tell you to come out of your trailer, Seedless Thompson, and accept the thanks you deserve after caring so much for all these years. Today is your day, Seedless. Today, after all these years, you will finally get thanked in person, not just in a letter."

And then we waited.

The trailer door finally opened, and Seedless stood in the doorway. There were heavier bags than usual under the eyes on his lumpy face.

"Thank you!" I said. "Thank you for caring, for sending your money, for writing your letters, for years and years. You meant it, from the bottom of your heart. You sacrificed, because you knew how much it mattered to help. You are my hero. You rock,

Seedless Thompson. You are the *man*. You did it for all of them, and you do it for me."

Seedless Thompson stared at me as his eyes brimmed. Then he turned away. "Nah," he blubbered.

"No 'nah.' It's all true and you know it."

Seedless' face contorted as the tears fell, and he covered his eyes with his big hands. "Oh God," he said, sobbing. Finally, he stepped down and let me embrace him. Then he embraced back, his big body heaving with sobs. We let go of each other and, with a few slaps on each other's backs, in the way of guys, tried to lighten things up. "Wow," said Seedless, calming down. "I haven't cried in a long time."

"Yeah, Seedless," I said. "You earned those tears, man. You earned them fair and square."

"Keep the letters, you and the pastor," said Seedless, suddenly getting serious, and speaking much more softly than I had ever heard him before. "Don't destroy them, okay? But I don't want to see them ever again. You promise?"

"We will keep them safe," said Pastor Kate.

Pastor Kate told me later that the morning after we got the boxes of letters, she carefully packed and shipped them to the postal inspector in Chicago. But not before running many of them through the church office copier.

***

A few days later, after my last class of the day, I was called into the principal's office.

"Who did this?" I asked him, incredulous. "I mean, whose idea was this, to make me the graduation speaker? Promise me it has nothing to do with the Virgin of San Lorenzo."

"No, it isn't about that, Josh. It's pretty interesting but it is not the reason you were chosen. The whole faculty voted on it. You were the first choice of three quarters of the teachers here at Portales High," said Mr. Hawkins.

"But I'm a screw-up. I got rotten grades and I didn't pay nearly enough attention in class. I'm not even a good jock. I'm ... I'm embarrassed to be chosen. I mean, sure, this is a big honor, and I appreciate it, but ... man. I just don't understand it at all."

"All true, what you say about your high school career," laughed Mr. Hawkins. "You bugged the heck out of some of the same teachers who voted for you to be the speaker. But in your own unique way, you are the best student to come through Portales High in a long time. You have touched dozens of lives in the last four years. You don't know it, and neither do many of your fellow students, but you will be an inspiration to them for the rest of their lives. You have served suffering people. You have befriended the friendless. You think big thoughts, you read big books, you ask big questions, you care with a big heart. You are an outstanding person, Joshua T. Stoneburner, and I'm proud that you have walked these halls for the last four years. You are a big reason

I still love my job, in spite of lots of other reasons to hate it.

"You see, there's more to education than tests and papers. More to education than SAT scores and college acceptances. More to education than the achievements that earn medals and certificates. You represent that something more: you represent the value of learning itself. The value of enlightenment. Yes, in class here at Portales High, you screwed up. You didn't pay attention and you were an amazing underachiever." Mr. Hawkins slapped my back. "Out in the desert, with the water stations, we knew what you were doing. We even knew what you've been doing for those little twins. And for Emily Luis. It's a small town here, and it's not entirely a bad thing that everybody knows everybody else's business. You know Mr. Thompson, the janitor at the church?"

"Yeah. You know him?" I wondered.

"Yes, I know him. I was visiting that church one Sunday. And Mr. Thompson came up to me at coffee hour and he said, 'The best student at your school is a kid named Josh Stoneburner. I bet he doesn't know it, but I know it, and I hope you know it.' He made me curious. So I asked our teachers about you. Who is this kid? I saw your face, I knew your name, I knew who your dad was, but that's all I knew. So I asked about you, talked to your teachers. And they all said the same thing: 'Josh has a hard time in class, he can be a wise guy, but he is a deep-thinking person with a big heart.' And then I asked people around town. Who is Josh Stoneburner? And they told me what they knew. Mr. Keady, the policeman. Ms. Protheroe, at the Christian Science Reading Room. Father Crespi, who says you are one of his most important spiritual teachers. Pastor Walker-Thorwaldsen, who has the greatest respect for you. Mrs. Kahn, Pastor Ballard, Bishop Young, all of them respect you a lot, even if you irritated them sometimes. They're all coming to graduation, by the way, to hear you speak.

"So at graduation, you won't get any medals. You won't get any scholarships. You won't wear the special sash for the honor society. All you'll get is the chance to tell us about what matters to you, and why. Because you are a very interesting person and we think you have a lot to say that is worth hearing."

"But Mr. Hawkins, I'm no good at public speaking, really. I am very honored. Mostly I'm just shocked. But what am I supposed to say?"

"I have no doubt you'll give a great speech. You've got a whole faculty of high school teachers willing to help you. To say nothing of all the preachers who'd love to coach you."

***

From Mr. Hawkins' office, I walked off the campus of Portales High toward the plaza. The reflection off the white stucco walls of the school, and the absolute clarity of the air and the sun, bathed the world around me in exceptionally intense light. The edges and textures and colors of everything around me were unusually distinct. But it wasn't clear at all what I would say in a graduation speech. I headed for the library.

Inside, I found Seedless folding a letter into an envelope on the oak table.

"Josh," he said quietly. "You came at the perfect time. This letter is for you."

I sat down across from Seedless and opened it and read it.

Dear Josh:

You saved my life. And I'm glad you did. Because now I see, more than I have seen in many, many years, that my life is worth living.

Thank you,
C. D. Thompson

I looked at Seedless, stunned, wordless.

"And there's something more I want to say to you," said Seedless.

"What's that?" I mumbled.

"Do you need any help with the water stations on Saturday?"

***

I sat at the gold-speckled yellow Formica kitchen table with the laptop before me, writing the graduation speech. This was by far the hardest school assignment I'd ever faced. Each draft of the speech looked absurd. So I would erase it and start over and read that draft, and get disgusted and erase it once again.

"So what do you want for graduation, Josh?" asked Dad. He was sitting in the overstuffed chair on the screen porch, with the *Arizona Republic* open in front of him. "You know how rotten I am at giving presents."

"Hmmm, how about a hod?" I suggested. "I always wanted to see one. And who knows, I'll be carrying them pretty soon, so I better get familiar with hods."

"Yeah, right," muttered Dad. "Well, lucky for both of us, I bet Rachel will have good ideas for a present."

"I do have an idea. A request for a graduation present."

"Oh yeah? Shoot," said Dad, behind the newspaper.

"I want you and Rachel to live together. And I don't care which house you choose."

Dad crumpled down the newspaper. "What?"

"You heard me, Pop. I'm serious. That would be the greatest present you could give me."

"I certainly wasn't thinking that was a possible graduation present," sputtered Dad. "Uhhh … say more about that."

"Say more? What's more to say, Dad? You two are in love, you're old farts, and you should not waste any more time being apart. You should live together. I don't care, get married, don't get married, whatever; just move in together and have a nice life. It's time you did. You deserve it. And it would make me very happy for you two to be happy. I love her a lot and I would love her to be my stepmom or step-girlfriend or whatever."

"Well, I don't know …"

"Bullshit, Dad. It's been over a year. Just do it. You know you're ready. I know you're ready."

"Well, that's nice of you to say. I love her very dearly. I never knew I could be this happy in a relationship. I guess I have you to thank for introducing us. I really am grateful."

"Nice words, Dad. So, I want my graduation present. Actually, I want it now. A week early."

"Yeah, right," muttered Dad with a grin.

"No, seriously," I said, punching Rachel's phone number on his cell phone. "Here you go, Dad. Tell her."

"Hey! Stop that!" He dumped the *Republic* on the floor and stood up, fending off the cell phone being pushed toward his ear. Rachel answered as the two of us wrestled with the phone.

"Josh? Karl? What is going on?" pleaded Rachel on the phone.

"I want my graduation present. I want it now," I yelled.

"Back off, you crazy kid," howled Dad as he flipped over the back of the overstuffed chair onto the dusty carpet. Rachel kept pleading as she heard the thumping and yelling.

"Dammit, kid, turn off that phone."

"Rachel? Can you hear me? Help! Come over quick." I yelled into the phone, pushed away at an arm's length by my father's hand.

Rachel arrived in minutes. I could hear her truck slide in the gravel after she put on the emergency brake.

"What are you boys doing?" she asked, breathless, as the kitchen screen door smacked behind her.

"Oh! You're here," exclaimed Dad, re-sheveling his disheveled hair.

I spoke rapidly. "Thanks for coming, Rachel. You see, my dad has something to say to you. He's going to give me my graduation present tonight."

"Now Josh," warned Dad. "You really are going too far."

"What's the present?" asked Rachel.

"Come on, Dad. Tell her."

"Josh, this is outrageous."

"Hey, you asked me what I wanted for graduation, and I told you. And you would be a fool if you didn't give it to me right here and now."

"What are you guys talking about?" asked Rachel, impatiently.

"Come on. You can do it. Go for it, Dad."

He took a deep breath, sputtered out a laugh, reached his arm around Rachel, and said, "Let's sit down on the sofa and have a little chat. Josh, beat it."

After a few minutes they invited me back into the living room.

"First of all," said Rachel, "I want to thank you for introducing me to your father. Second, I want to thank you for being so supportive, in so many ways, of our relationship. It isn't always easy to add a new person into a family. Finally, while I really appreciate

341

your kindness toward me, I want to remind you that getting us to live together is not an appropriate graduation present. We have to make our own decisions about such things, in our own good time. End of my speech. Your turn, Karl."

Dad cleared his throat. "Uhhh, yeah. Ditto on everything she said. And, uhhhh, fact is, we made our minds up a few months ago that this was a permanent thing between us."

"What do you mean?" I asked, standing up.

"Josh, you are such a male," laughed Rachel. "I knew you'd never notice."

"Notice what?" I wondered.

"Look." She showed me the engagement ring on her finger. "Your dad proposed to me two months ago. We're getting married next December. We didn't tell you because I was waiting to see my kids in person early this summer, so we could announce it to them and to you at the same time."

"You mean, that thing has been on your finger all this time, and I didn't see it?" I was happily astounded.

"We often don't see what we don't expect to see," declared Rachel.

***

Dana and Leon plowed against the glass door and tumbled into the library with their books dropping out from under their arms. L. D. and Esther came in behind them, with their own books to return. They helped the kids put their books into the return slot, and then the twins ran over to see me. I was sitting at the oak table with a stack of books in front of me, writing on a notepad surrounded by sheets of paper crumpled into balls.

"Josh! Whatcha doing?" asked Leon, breathlessly.

"Shhh! Remember? We have to be quiet in the library."

"Josh, tell us a story mine story over in the kids' corner!" demanded Dana.

"Not right now, you guys. I'm writing my graduation speech."

"Story mine! Story mine!" Dana was gleefully pulling on my shirtsleeve.

"Story mine?" I asked.

"Yeah! Give us a story mine story," said Dana again.

"Story mine. Good idea," I said.

***

The next Saturday, first thing in the morning, I picked up Seedless at his trailer.

"Buy you breakfast at the Rinconada," declared Seedless.

"Deal, then," I said, making a left turn at the end of the church driveway instead of a right toward the desert.

Inside the café, Paul Blewett was at the counter sipping coffee next to Tommy the cop when we walked in. "Your old truck still running?" asked Paul.

"Oh yes. It runs great," I said.

"What about that pile 'o metal your old man drives?" asked Paul.

"Still running."

"Hey, Josh," said Tommy. "Bad news."

"What's that?" I asked.

"Emily Luis is in the hospital over on the rez. Doesn't look good. Liver failure, and she's too far gone for a transplant."

"Glad you told me, Mr. Keady," I said. "We're headed through Sells this morning. Okay with you if we go visit her, Seedless?"

"Okay with me!" said Seedless, too loud.

"I hear you work the water stations," said Paul. "I don't know. I just don't know if that is such a good idea." He slicked back his hair and sighed. "It just seems like it won't help. You know, you help out these chile pickers, and then even more of them come across. If more of them died out there, fewer would cross, and after a while, fewer would die. Besides that, who knows how many of those terrorists are coming across and drinking your water? Ever thought about that?"

"Oh, Paul. Give the boy a break," said Bertha La Bounty, sitting in the booth across from them. She was a big, jolly older woman who lived at Rancho Nolontomo and was the head of the evangelism committee of the Cuprite Baptist Church. I had been annoyed by the repeated phone messages she left at our house, inviting me to "come back next Sunday." "Don't be calling Mexicans 'chile pickers.' Josh is half Mexican, himself. That's not polite. Now, Paul, what can be wrong with giving water to people who are thirsty? Does that have to be political? What could be wrong with doing something for these poor people, at least to keep them from dying in the desert?"

Then Seedless got into the discussion, his voice rising. "The poor people have nothing! It's the terrorists who are the problem. Those terrorists can come over that border with gold-plated water jugs, if they want. They got their money from you, filling up the tank on your monstrous pickup truck with gas from Saudi Arabia," he yelled, angrily waving his knobby finger at Paul.

I grabbed Seedless by the arm and pulled. Seedless tried to shake me off, but I wouldn't let go, and kept pulling, until I got him out the door.

"Jeez, Seedless," I complained as we drove to Rachel's place. "You could have started a fight in there. Come on, man, it isn't worth it."

"How can anybody complain about terrorists when they buy monster gas-guzzling SUVs and pickup trucks and pump them full of Middle Eastern oil, I ask you? Who the hell is this guy Paul Blewett, selling auto parts to keep these gas-hogs on the road, and then complaining about terrorists coming across the border? If he wants to fight terrorism, then he better do like me and ride a bicycle."

"Whoa, Seedless. No need to yell. I'm your friend, remember?"

***

We stopped at L. D. and Esther's place to pick up Martha. From there we drove to Rachel's ranch. At Rachel's place, everyone got into Dad old gas-guzzling Dodge Power Wagon crew truck he had bought from the mine and rebuilt years before. The back end was piled with blue plastic barrels full of water. Its knobby tires rumbled deeply as we drove into the rez.

"I need to stop at the Indian hospital. I gotta visit somebody there," I said.

We all went into the room where Emily Luis lay, her body wasted, tubes feeding her oxygen and water and drugs, monitors flashing above her. She was asleep. She looked even smaller than I remembered her. Her hair was thin and wet with sweat. A vein bulged on her forehead.

Seedless' face twisted and twitched as he fidgeted and rubbed his head. Rachel held Dad's hand tight as they stood against the wall near the door.

I went up to the bed with trepidation and touched her hand. Martha stood behind me.

"Emily. It's me, Josh Stoneburner. Can you hear me?"

Her sunken eyes stayed closed, but she stirred. She turned her head and grimaced for a moment.

"It's me, Josh Stoneburner. I … I came to see how you are doing," I said again, leaning carefully, closer to her ear.

Suddenly, with a shudder, her eyes opened and she tried to sit up. But she snapped back when she went against the cloth restraint bands that tied her down in her in bed. Startled, I hopped back away from her. She looked up and said, hoarsely, "Josh. It's you!" She reached with both arms for me, as much as the restraints would let her. "Hold me, Josh," she begged. I leaned down and hugged her. She couldn't hug back. She could only grip one of my wrists with her hand, and the grip was surprisingly strong. She sobbed as I stood back up, her hand still clasped on my wrist. "Josh, thank you, thank you."

Seedless let out a strange noise and rubbed his head with both hands and walked out of the room.

"I'm glad I got to see you, Emily."

"I'm glad I get to see you! Because I'm going to die soon," she said, looking at me intently. "I had a dream. Elder Brother came to me and said, 'Come with me to the mountain. It's time.' And he was dancing crazy and laughing. He kept saying, 'Hurry up! It's great, you'll love it at the mountain. Come on! I know the way.'"

"So did you go with him?"

"Then the dream was over," she said. "That was all. Any time now he'll come back and I'll go with him. It's okay. I hope he comes soon. I'm really tired. Oh God, I'm so tired." She closed her eyes and moaned lowly and slowly rocked her head back and forth.

"See you on the mountain someday, Emily," I said.

19. God's Hands and Feet

After filling tanks at half a dozen water stations on the reservation, we drove to the western outskirts of Tucson for a gathering at Cal Redfield's place. Several water station volunteer crews were gathering there to talk strategy and eat fresh tamales that were steaming in big *tamalera* pots under the porch. Rachel and Dad and Martha pulled a couple of longneck beers out of the cooler and found a shady spot to sit on a bench under a *palo verde* tree.

Cal warmly welcomed Seedless as a newcomer to the group and showed him around his property as I followed along. Seedless started waving his big arms with excitement upon seeing Cal's homemade methane collector. It was a tank into which Cal loaded all the manure from his goatherd. The methane from the manure decomposition filled a butyl-rubber bladder, which fed into a generator that enabled Cal to run his power meter backwards a lot of the time, so that his electric bill was almost nothing. He used the remaining manure sludge as fertilizer for his organic garden, where he grew native edible desert plants. Seedless wrote in a little notebook as he asked Cal one question after another, while they walked past the goats and the garden plots. Cal took Seedless inside the house and showed him a book on edible desert plants, and Seedless sat in Cal's old leather reading chair and lost himself in the pages. Cal and I sat at the heavy, dark wood table in the kitchen and talked, while the party continued outside.

"Father Crespi and Pastor Kate took me down to Naco not long ago, and I had a good look at that metal fence," I told him. "I don't know what happened to me, Cal, but when I looked at that fence, I got really upset. I think about it all the time now. It makes me so angry. I mean, I just want to go down there right now, and tear it down with my bare hands. But that would be violent, wouldn't it? And you are against violence, huh? 'Cause you're a Quaker."

Cal took off his cowboy hat, set it on the table, wiped his wrinkled, deeply tanned forehead with his handkerchief, and smiled. "Violence isn't just about not hurting people or destroying things. Tell me, when you think about the steel fence on the border, how does your body feel?"

"Tense. And I get, well, I get kinda hot inside."

"Is that doing your body any favor?" asked Cal.

"What do you mean?"

"Isn't that a violent thing to do to your own body? To let it get tense, to let it get too hot?" asked Cal.

"I guess so."

"So thoughts can be violent, and can hurt your mind and your body. And that is the wisdom of many great religions. That the way we think, the way we feel inside, is just as big a problem as what we do on the outside. In fact, what we do on the outside is very much shaped by what we do on the inside," said Cal. "Is there another way for you to feel about the wall?"

"I saw a spray-painted Virgin on the wall and when I looked at her, I got sad."

"Did she share your feelings, do you think?" asked Cal.

"Yeah. Yeah, she did. I felt close to her, even though it was sad. It was a good kind of sad."

"We call it compassion, that good kind of sadness that binds people together even in suffering," said Cal. "Which feeling do you think will help you join with other people who are working to get rid of that steel wall? Anger or compassion? That's what nonviolence is all about. It is about action, it's about doing something about injustice, doing what you can to relieve pain and suffering and lift oppression. We Quakers here in Tucson also call it 'civil initiative', actively living out the law of love that is written on our hearts, so that we can live our way into a new law of the land. But doing it through compassion rather than through the angry thoughts and actions that lead to violence.

"So you want to get rid of that wall?" continued Cal.

"Yeah, I do!" I said emphatically.

"How badly?'

"What do you mean?" I asked, startled.

"I think you know exactly what I mean." Cal smiled under his grizzled, drooping mustache.

I looked into Cal's eyes and saw compassion itself pouring out of them and flowing into my soul, like fresh water filling one of the tanks in the desert.

***

Father Crespi had come to the party late. Cal asked him and Rabbi Sy Saperstein to gather a prayer circle to end the party. The rabbi led the forty-odd people in chanting "Shalom" in beautiful harmony. Father Crespi led everyone in offering personal prayers.

Afterward, Martha took me over to the bench under the *palo verde* tree and asked me to sit down with her.

"This is who you are, isn't it?" she asked.

"What do you mean?"

"I mean, all of this. These people, this kind of work, this kind of commitment."

I sighed. "Yes, it is. More than ever. But I don't want it to get in the way of us."

"At first, I thought it might be in the way. But I don't think so anymore. This is your project, your work that you're supposed to do. I can tell that this is really important stuff that you are doing, even though I don't understand that much about the border problem."

"Neither do I. I feel like I understand it less than ever," I confessed.

"I want to be in it with you. I'm starting to see that it's a big part of the love we share," said Martha.

***

Rachel and Dad were in Phoenix that following weekend, staying in a hotel downtown and enjoying the art galleries and museums. I was left to take care of the horses at Rachel's place. After a day's work washing mobile homes, I picked up Martha at the café and we drove down to the ranch, unable to keep our hands off each other for even a moment in the truck.

We were mostly undressed before we even got through the front door of the house.

Three hours later, we lay in bed under an oil painting of a desert sundown. We breathed the sweet moisture of each other's after-glowing bodies.

"Martha, Dad says we can move into Grandma Greta's old house in Tucson. You and me and the kids. We can both go to school and work. It will be hard but it will be good. What do you say?"

"Josh, that's wonderful. But do me a favor and pretend you didn't ask that question before you graduated from high school, okay?"

***

There was a very good reason the graduation gowns were white. It had everything to do with the fact that at ten in the morning on Saturday, the day after the last class of my checkered high school career, the temperature was 105. The bleachers, where the spectators sat, were protected by a big awning, but its shadow didn't extend as far as the grandstand where the graduates faced the blazing sun. The seniors were sweating profusely, but at least the reflective gowns kept us from frying into *churros*.

After the principal, the head of the school board, and the superintendent of schools spoke, it was my turn. I mounted the podium and un-clipped the microphone from it and stepped back down to the stage. "Dana and Leon, come on up," I said.

In the stands, Martha was sitting with the kids, next to L. D. and Esther. On her other side was Rosa Beltran and little Ana.

The kids scampered down the bleachers and ran across the grass onto the stage. I sat down with them, took off my white mortarboard cap, and asked them, into the microphone, "Which graduation story do you want? See, the shelves are right there." I pointed to the side of the podium. "Which one?"

I held the mike in front of Dana, who said "That one."

"What is on the front of the book?" I asked. "What is in the picture?"

"A racecar." said Dana.

"No. A snake." said Leon. The crowd laughed a little.

"Of course. It's about a racecar that was driven by a snake. See the snake, smiling with his face over the steering wheel." I pointed at the imaginary cover. "Let's look inside. Once there was a snake who wanted to be a racecar driver. See? What's in the picture?"

"The snake is watching television," said Leon.

"And you know what he is watching?" I asked. "Look carefully. He's watching a race. He loved fast cars and all he ever wanted to do was be a racecar driver. Only there was one big problem. Let's turn the page.

"There was one big problem. The snake didn't have any arms or legs, didn't have any hands or feet, didn't have any fingers or toes, so it was going to be very, very hard for him to turn the steering wheel and push on the gas pedal or the brake pedal. So the snake was sad. Let's turn the page; see here? See how sad the snake is? What's he doing?"

"He is going into his hole in the ground all by himself," said Dana, sadly.

"He's crying in the hole," said Leon.

"Let's turn the page. See there; what animal is that?" I asked.

"A bird!" said Dana.

"That's right. It was the snake's friend, the quail. The quail poked her head into his hole and asked him, 'Are you okay down there?' I moved my head up and down like a quail. "And the snake said, 'I'm sad because I can't be a race car driver because I don't have any arms or legs.' Let's turn the page again.

"So the quail went to her friends, the coyote and the dragonfly and the two prairie dog sisters. She said, 'Let's get organized and help out our friend the snake.'" So they all went to the snake's hole and yelled, 'Come out! We have a plan.' Let's go to the next page.

"They took the snake to the race track and they found a race car that wasn't being driven. The dragonfly stuck his long, skinny tail into the door lock and he turned and unlocked it. The coyote bit on the door handle and opened the door. They all got in. The snake slithered up to the dashboard, see? There he is, sitting all happy, nice and warm in the sunshine, just like us graduates up here on the stage! The coyote looked out the back window, the prairie dog sisters hung on either side of the steering wheel. The dragonfly poked his long, skinny tail into the ignition switch. The quail perched on the gas pedal. When the snake said 'Let's go!' the dragonfly turned on the car, the quail fluttered and pushed on the gas pedal; the snake said 'Left!' and the prairie dog on the right let go of the wheel; and the snake said 'Right!' and the other prairie dog jumped off the left side of the wheel and the other one jumped back on the right side; and the coyote said 'Watch out!' and the snake told the prairie dogs to swerve ahead of the oncoming race car; and the snake said 'Slow down!' and the quail fluttered off the gas pedal and flew onto the brake. Okay, next page.

"And the snake kept saying, 'Left! Right! Faster! Slower!' and the animals were jumping and fluttering this way and that way and the crowd was roaring and the car was almost tipping over because it was going so fast . . ." I tipped over to one side, and then to the other, and the kids did it with me, giggling. ". . . And they were going faster and faster, and then they got to the finish line, and the announcer said, 'And the winner is . . . Snakey Diamondback!' Let's turn to the last page.

"And the snake slithered up onto the stage for the awards after the race, and he said to everybody, 'I have no arms or legs, no hands or feet, no fingers or toes. But I won the race because I have good friends. Please meet them all, the quail, come on, everyone, clap for the quail.'"

The stadium erupted in applause, Dana and Leon joining in.

"And the dragonfly. Give it up for the dragonfly."

More applause.

"And the coyote. And the prairie dog sisters."

As the applause continued, I closed the imaginary book and gave it to Leon. "Could you put it back on the shelf for us, please?"

"Sure," said Leon, and he carefully placed it back where it belonged on the imaginary bookshelf.

"Dana, Leon, everybody. Each of us got here to this stage because we had a team behind us. We had friends behind us, family behind us, and other people we didn't even know were behind us until now. My team is up in the stands right now. You know who you are! Come on, everybody, give it up for my team."

More applause, louder this time, and longer.

"Come on, give it up for the team that is behind every single person up here on this stage."

Everyone rose to their feet and roared and clapped.

"God has no arms or legs, no hands or feet, no fingers or toes, but ours, and those of all other creatures in the universe," I said, still sitting on the stage with Dana and Leon. "It's up to us to be God's friends, to call each other out of the hole. It's up to us to help, so that all of us, together, can cross over the line and win the race."

***

The rest of the ceremony was a blur. Somehow I got a diploma, and somehow my hand found Martha's in the crush of congratulation afterwards. I was surrounded by well-wishers who gushed about the speech. The editor of *The Pit* asked me for a copy.

"I don't have a copy," I answered.

"Do you have notes?" asked the editor.

"I'm sorry, but I read that story for the first time while I was on the stage," I said.

"You 'read' it?" the editor asked, looking puzzled.

***

My "team" gathered at Rachel's ranch for a graduation party. Martha and I wandered, people-watching. Esther, touring the house with L. D. at her side, loved the art on Rachel's walls and peppered Rachel with questions about them. Father Crespi and Paul Blewett were drinking beer and talking loud and louder. It turned out that Paul had grown up on a cattle ranch in Texas, and they were happily trying to outdo each other with cowboy tales. Alice Kahn was drinking a beer and laughing with them, too. Cal Redfield and Dad were drawing diagrams on pieces of paper, intently commenting on them, but I had no idea what they were designing. Pastor Kate and her husband Jeff were pitching horseshoes against Pastor Bob and his wife Margaret, who were way ahead in the match. Tekla Ballard was swatting flies away from her face as she lectured Ronnie and Mike about how it was time they shaped up and stopped smoking weed and got salvation. "Okay, okay," she snapped back at them as they laughed her off. She shrieked and giggled as the boys grabbed her, took ice out of their cokes, and slid the cubes down the back of her tight tee-shirt. Leonard Jose, Ajit Singh, and Siva Aggarwal listened intently as Tommy Keady, with a grave tone to his voice, extolled the virtues of ginseng tablets. He held out a bottle full of them and showed them the label. "You would not believe how helpful these have been in my body-building program," he muttered secretively.

On their way to look at the horses, Dana and Leon were dangling and swinging off Seedless' big hands. Rosa joined them, with Ana toddling beside her and excitedly pointing ahead.

And I noticed: Seedless Thompson was laughing.

About the Author

Jim Burklo is the Associate Dean of Religious Life at the University of Southern California. He is an ordained United Church of Christ minister and is the author of three previous books: *Open Christianity, Birdlike and Barnless,* and *Hitchhiking to Alaska: The Way of Soulful Service.* Find him online at www.patheos.com/blogs/souljourn.

Progressive Christianity
(practical)
To Be One - Supper table
all religions

Huffington Post Adam Smith
2nd Inagrual
Lincoln

Paul Woodruff - Greek
philosophy

Revive belief of compassionate
God.

earned benefit
social insurance
free market will not solve
problems

George Lakoff - linguist
reasoning is emotive
emotion moves people

Revelations 22nd

We are better than this.
See poutical.com - videos
Vtamation

CPSIA information can be obtained
at www.ICGtesting.com
Printed in the USA
FFOW02n0103200415
12741FF

9 781629 218359